ABOUT THE AUTHOR

Miller Caldwell is a Scotland-based writer of novels, biographies, self-help and children's books. He holds a post-graduate degree from the University of London. He has had articles published in health magazines and the *Scottish Review*.

During a life spent doing humanitarian work in Ghana, Pakistan and Scotland, he has gained remarkable insights into human nature through bringing an African president to tears in West Africa in 2002 and confronting Osama bin Laden near Abbottabad in 2006. He was the local chair of the Scottish Association for the Study of Offending for twelve years. He served on the committee of the Society of Authors in Scotland and was its events manager.

Miller plays a variety of brass, woodwind and keyboard instruments. They provide a break from writing. Married, he has two daughters, and he lives in Dumfries. As he has Parkinson's disease, the number of books he can write will be determined by his condition.

A RELUCTANT SPY

SPY

Miller H Caldwell

Troubador Publishing Ltd
Unit E2 Airfield Business Park,
Harrison Road, Market Harborough,
Leicestershire LE16 7UL
Tel: 0116 279 2299
Email: books@troubador.co.uk
Web: www.troubador.co.uk

ISBN 978 1 80514 337 6

British Library Cataloguing in Publication Data.
A catalogue record for this book is available from the British Library.

Printed and bound in Great Britain by 4edge Limited
Typeset in 12pt Adobe Jensen Pro by Troubador Publishing Ltd, Leicester, UK

This novel is dedicated to Larry, a friend for almost five decades. The former Dr. Larry Bart, a Clinical Psychologist in Vermont, continues to be a gifted musician, a raconteur and one of Alzheimer's victims.

Contents

Foreword

Just occasionally you find yourself in touch with history. Such opportunities often lurk in innocuous places. Yet if the interest is nurtured and explored at a steady pace, an intricate tale often emerges. For some it is mere history, a lesson to learn. For others, it is a lesson to celebrate.

Make no mistake; this is a work of fiction. It is however tentatively based around the remarkable life of my great Aunt, Frau Hilda Richter (née Campbell 1889-1956). Her niece Vera, my godmother, Vera Wild (née Caldwell 1900-1992) revealed to me the story of her life in her penultimate year. My uncle, Dr A. Stanley Caldwell (1920-2013), gave me personal communication and stamps from Hilda. The novel fills in the voids I have in Hilda's life while it concentrates on Vera's memories of a most unusual great aunt.

With the exception of identified historical personalities and events, this novel is the product of my imagination.

Netherholm
Dumfries
2024

Preface

Hilda Campbell was born in 1889 in Elgin. She studied modern languages at Aberdeen University and in 1911 went to Germany to further her knowledge of the German language and culture. At a concert at the Kunsthalle in Hamburg, Hilda met Dr Willy Richter, a local General Practitioner. They married in 1913 and spent their honeymoon in Scotland visiting relatives. They also met my godmother Vera Wild (née Caldwell) and invited her to come to stay with them in Hamburg the following summer.

Vera arrived in mid July with the promise of a two month visit before she returned for her final year at school. The First World War broke out on 4th August 1914 and found Vera trapped behind enemy lines in Germany. Through a network of friends Vera returned home via Harwich after an eventful trip. An account of her return home can be found in the Forres and Nairn Gazette of 2nd September 1914 by courtesy of the Elgin Library Educational Services.

Hilda taught English privately in Hamburg. Nothing else was known of her life until...

1

The Funeral

Branches of sycamore trees lovingly caressed each other as the funeral party gathered around the grave beneath. The Hamburg sky hung low. The light was grey and dull for mid morning. Clouds strained to retain their nourishment for leaves and roots at the Friedhof Ohlsdorf cemetery. The noise of the day could be heard faintly on the Fuhlsbüttler Strasse, beyond the civilian cemetery wall. It was 11.30 am on Friday 12th March 1938. A day all Austrians and Germans would remember. While in this city graveyard, the family congregated with their personal thoughts and memories as they buried Dr Willy Büttner Richter.

The graveside was surrounded by supportive patients, sad to see such a relatively young man deprive them of his caring attention at their popular medical surgery. There were many from the professional ranks of the city present retaining their solemnity. For the moment, they had to suppress the exciting news developing that morning of the Anschluss.

I, Hilda Richter, suddenly a widow in my late forties, took comfort holding the hand of my son Otto, smartly dressed in his Hitler Youth uniform.

'Dust to dust, ashes to ashes. In The Name of the Father, Son and Holy Spirit, Amen.'

The tall lean young Lutheran pastor, closing his prayer book of common order, invited me and Otto forward to sprinkle the sunken coffin with a dusting of earth. After I let the earth rest on the coffin I passed the trowel to my son. Then Otto stood back as I opened my handbag and from it, took a sprig of heather. I kissed it then dropped it onto the centre of the coffin. Unintentionally, it masked the brass nameplate. The sound of a breaking twig alerted me to the approaching hand which gently touched my shoulder.

'Willy would have liked that.'

I turned and smiled at my brother-in-law Karl, who had been as shocked as anyone on hearing of Willy's sudden fatal heart attack. They had been close brothers.

'We loved our holidays in Scotland.'

'I know you did, Hilda. These were happier days. The gathering clouds this morning... seem so menacing.'

'Karl... shhhhh.'

I looked over my shoulder. I saw pitiful eyes looking at me. I felt uncomfortable. Neither smiling nor looking sad I tried hard not to show any weak emotion.

An invitation by the pastor invited mourners to attend a reception at the nearby Vier Jahreszeiten Hotel. Shortly after noon, the mourners sauntered into the hotel's reception room garnered by a black paper table cloth with a central motif of the swastika. Sandwiches were offered from this table which had a coffee urn percolating happily at the far end. It was a table full with fruit, sandwiches and biscuits while the party emblem remained uncovered for all to see and appreciate.

'My condolences Frau Richter,' a man in a dark green suit, his lapel supporting the party emblem, approached me. He was overweight, exaggerated by a ruddy round face, a great lump of a loaf. He shook my hand, bowing his dark bushy eyebrows towards me.

'Thank you,' I replied with politeness unaware of who had addressed me. He noted my quizzical expression as I tried to place him. It was an awkward moment for both of us. Not knowing the man or how he knew my late husband left me void of any meaningful conversation.

'Do forgive me. Herr Gerhardt Eicke. I am one of your son's training officers,' he said, holding his head back like a proud peacock.

So this was the man who impressed Otto. I smiled weakly at him. He seemed embarrassed by my initial response for a brief moment. To compose himself he turned and lifted a cup of coffee from the table nearby.

'Otto is a fine young man, one of the best in the Hitler Youth, without doubt. He is a credit to you and of course, his late father.'

I noticed his cup-holding hand reveal a nugget of a ring that matched his lapel badge. It was on his marriage finger.

'I see. So Otto is doing well?'

He smiled with confidence in his wide-legged stance. 'These are exciting times. The Führer has taken Austria into greater Germany today. He has wedded us to the German speaking Austrians. It is a bitter sweet day for you, I am sure Frau Richter. Otto will be a great comfort to you, at present.'

'You must forgive me. I had not heard the news,' I said with concern etched on my brow.

He nodded understandingly. 'I appreciate your mind has been elsewhere. The 12th of March will go down in history. I can assure you of that,' he said with overt pomposity.

'It will be a day I shall have no difficulty in remembering, none at all,' I said, letting off a smile perfected in recent days.

'Indeed.' Eicke brought his heels together. 'If there is anything I can do for you now, or indeed any time, I hope you will not hesitate to get in touch with me. I have resources at my finger tips.' Herr Eicke's smile seemed artificially sincere as he made his offer. I suspected he used every trick in the book to gain an advantage.

'I will bear your kind offer in mind, Herr Eicke.' I said disguising my feeling that I could not warm to this self opinionated party man.

He gulped down his last mouthful of coffee and smacked his lips together. I was pleased to see him return his cup to the table. This was surely the end to a sticky conversation. He fumbled in his side pocket as he approached me once more. Then he held out his hand.

'Here, my card... again my condolences Frau Richter. I must leave now.'

I gave a weak smile. 'Certainly... you must have much to do,' I said feeling my shoulders relax.

I placed his card in my black bag as Herr Eicke

walked smartly to the hotel exit and turned to find my brother-in-law standing behind me. Karl was so different from my late husband. Perhaps because he was six years younger, he would have had a different set of friends. His outlook was sceptical though not off-putting. His sense of fun did not lie deep under the surface. I was fond of him.

'I hope you would come to family first.'

My mind wondered just how close he had been to our strained conversation. 'You heard what we were saying, Karl?'

He smiled supporting my left arm with his black-suited hand. 'No, not really. I saw he gave you his card. My advice, should you take it, would be to pay little attention to him.'

I had reached the same conclusion. That was reassuring.

'You know him personally?' I was both surprised and keen to hear more.

'We should not forget that in the present hysteria, I find Herr Eicke narrow-minded. He is a Gestapo officer when not training the Hitler Youth. He's a man on the up, from a very lowly base indeed.'

Karl's assessment did not surprise me. My wrinkled brow confronted him nevertheless as there was another factor to be considered.

'He is also Otto's training officer.'

'Yes, that's true. We can't change that. Caution is required Hilda. That's all I am saying.'

I nodded. Perhaps that was the sound advice I had to hear. A niggle nevertheless kept coming to the fore of my mind. 'I think you may have to speak to Otto from time to time, for me.'

Karl gave an avuncular nod. 'If you feel that would be appropriate?'

Without a father figure, I felt I would be leaning more and more on Karl. I thought he recognised the fact.

'Yes, Otto has loyalties beyond the family. It was something that troubled Willy, I know, but what could he do? He would stand out or worse still, be ostracized if he had not joined with all of his friends. He would have been fed to the wolves if he had stayed apart.' I found myself clutching my bag in both hands. My shoulders were still tense, and my breathing was intermittent.

'Yes, that's true. I may regret my current reservations, too. There is after all, my wish for Germany to regain its rightful place in the world.' Karl took out his handkerchief, to catch an advancing sneeze. 'Excuse me,' he said wiping his nose. 'It's the right policy I am sure, with the wrong leader.'

I was concerned who might be listening so moved a few paces from the table. Then for the first time at the hotel I noticed my son. With an egg sandwich in his hand, Otto looked lost amid the adults circulating and sharing their funereal and political conversations. He approached me.

'All these people, I don't know many of them.'

I placed my hand on his shoulder. 'I'm not surprised Otto. Many were your father's patients. You know how popular a man he was.'

He raised his arm to remove my hand. 'Yes, I know he

was.' He lifted his eyes to mine seeking my full attention.

'You saw Herr Eicke? I'm glad he came to show his respects.'

I seized the moment to gauge Otto's view of this enigmatic man. 'Did you know he was coming to the funeral?' I asked.

'No. But I hoped he would.'

'Your father did not know him.' My voice seemed to carry into the room. I walked over to the window to have the conversation in greater privacy.

'Herr Eicke is fun mummy. He is in the Gestapo, you know. That's his day job. We learn lots of skills with him and he gives us sweets. He is firm but good to us. He's a good leader, he really is.'

'Maybe so Otto, maybe so. Remember you are the man of the house now. You must study hard at school in your last year and make your father proud of you.'

That was enough Otto wished to hear or say at that moment. His nodded agreement ended our brief conversation and he left to find more juice. I returned to the centre of the room, where my family were in discussion in a loose ring. They parted sufficiently to accommodate me.

'Have you a headstone in mind, Hilda?' asked Karl's wife, Renate.

I was on comfortable ground with my dark haired sister-in-law. She and Karl was a perfect match. 'Yes, I have one in keeping with Willy's ideals. One without all the trappings of nationalism and banner waving.'

Karl turned towards me. 'Need any help with the wording? If you like, I could help you.'

Renate smiled at her husband's suggestion. 'That might be a good idea, Hilda,' she said.

I looked determined all of a sudden. 'I already know what it will say.'

'Really?' Karl's eyebrows raised a couple of inches. Renate's mouth opened wide enough to suggest I was ahead of the game.

I had the floor. 'It will read: "Precious in the sight of the Lord is the death of one of his Saints." Then his name, profession and dates of birth and death will appear leaving enough space for me and Otto, in due course.'

'I like that Hilda,' said Renate patting my arm.

'Yes, said Karl. 'Without any flag waving, as you said.'

I smiled at them. 'Yes, I'm pleased with what I have chosen, though these are hardly my own words.'

Then I saw both Karl and Renate perplexed as they tried to remember where such a quote may have come from.

'Then whose?' asked Renate as she was first to want to know.

'The Psalmist,' I said. 'As always, the Psalmist says it perfectly.'

2

The Letter

Widowhood had its freedom highs and its depressive lows. Kind words from my late husband's patients did increase my confidence. However I feared I could not depend on many patient friendships forever. In my memory lurked the pain and anguish of being an alien during the last world war. If a second world war broke out, as many considered inevitable, it would be a war to defeat Communism on Germany's eastern front door. There would be no Willy to support me now. As the weeks progressed these thoughts grew stronger in my mind. My blood was not German and never could be. Yet if it was Scottish, it was surely severely diluted.

One morning I rose early, even before my alarm clock sounded. When I parted the curtains the sun pierced my eyes and lit up the bedroom. From the trees outside, I detected the wind was negligible. I felt invigorated. I started the day by organising a thorough spring clean. I had slept on the dream of a tidy house the night before. I woke to make the dream come true. I dusted the high ceilings then folded rugs and hung them on the clothesline by the side of the house. I took my wicker cane beater to them, assaulting the rugs with a fury I did not know I possessed. Puffs of dust drifted skyward. Colour reappeared in the rugs through the haze. In my concentration I did not hear the postman approach.

'Post, Frau Richter.' He looked up and stopped in his tracks. 'I thought I heard some beating. Goodness me, I'm glad you were not my class teacher. You have a strong right hand,' he laughed loudly competing with the roof-top rooks nearby.

'You surprised me.'

'I could see that.' He sorted the letters with one hand flicking his fingers through them at a tremendous rate. Hans was in his late fifties. He had been my regular postman over the last decade or so and knew me well. He handed my letters over.

'There's one from abroad in this lot.'

My face lit up. 'Thank you... yes... from home... great.'

News from home was always welcomed. My parents' letters following Willy's death had been a great comfort for me. This letter would add to my growing satisfaction on this near perfect day. I wondered if they had received my last letter written a month ago. Would this letter just be a response to that or would there be fresh news from home? I gave the hanging rugs one final thrashing and looked upwards. A single spherical cloud made its way toward the sun. It would only interrupt its warmth for a brief moment, a superb day made even better by the letter in my hand. I left the rugs to hang and recover while I prepared my postal rituals, performed only with personal correspondence.

The whistling kettle bubbled on the stove as I washed my hands with vigour and excitement in warm carbolic soapy water. Prolonging the opening of the letter heightened my excitement. Clearing the kitchen table and setting a hot black coffee by my place, I took hold of a sharp knife to open my letter from Scotland. My eyes lingering on the Aberdonian franked envelope. The glue gave no resistance. I lifted the missive to my nose. There was a whiff of two glues keeping this letter closed. There could be only one explanation. The letter was brief. It contained news. That made me anxious from several different perspectives.

I sipped my coffee and held the cup with both hands as the letter lay flat before my tearful eyes. I read it twice then sat back to decide how I could respond to my parent's satisfaction, what would suit me and what would become of 17 year old Otto? The letter had perhaps come at an inconvenient time.

Nethybrig Hotel,
Elgin
23rd April 1938

Dear Hilda

I trust you and Otto are keeping well. We are too, although age is creeping up on us both, especially your father. He's really not too well. What worries us most is the developing situation in Germany and as a widow; you will be feeling the pain of loneliness during this time. We would love to see you of course but whenever that might be I hope it would be sooner than later. I am delighted to know the Hamburg to Aberdeen ship still sails regularly once a week. I hope Karl and Renate will understand and of course, Otto too. I suspect he will not be able to spend time in Scotland again for some time. He must finish his schooling and then head for university.

I seem to have left you with much to think about. But it is a letter I am sending with more love than enough to sink Hitler's latest battleship!

With our fondest love,
Mother and Father.

I cringed at my mother's last line. I hammered the table twice in disgust. Criticism of the State provoked dire consequences. What on earth was mother thinking about?

Perhaps the censor skimmed the letter in a way he might have read 'more love enough to launch Hitler's latest battleship'. My mind struggled to find another excuse which I might need to provide. I feared a knock on the door was not out of question later in the day. I shook my head in despair at my mother's casual caustic remark.

My parents' aging was a constant worry too.

I had not visited them for eight years and when leaving them on that occasion, as each time before, I wondered if I would ever see them again. Now it was more pressing, not just because of their age but also because of the tensions in my life at present in Germany.

Whenever I felt anxiety taking hold of me, I could rely on a personal solution contained in my black box. A box I had not opened much since Willy had died. I retired to my sitting room, unclipped the lid and assembled the double reed into my oboe. On this occasion I placed on my music stand Anton Bruckner's Symphony No 5 in B flat major and sat on a hard ladder-backed chair to play the Adagio: *Sehr Langsam*. While I played soulfully, I remembered Anton Bruckner was not German, he was Austrian. I dedicated my music that day in my mind to all who might suffer because of the recent forceful acquisition of Bruckner's land and people.

I had the rest of the day to dust and polish while reflecting on my options; one I had already taken. I had left my mother's letter on the dining room table for Otto to read when he returned home from school. At four I sat down and began to read a novel which I had started before Willy had died. I soon remembered what I had read and settled comfortably by the lounge fire somewhat tired after the day's hard work.

At 4:25pm on the dot, the key turned in the latch. A bag was thrown down on the hall floor. Otto was home.

'Hello darling. I'm through here,' I said marking my novel with mother's Scottish envelope. Then I rested the book on my lap.

Otto came into the lounge holding a glass of water. He raised it to his lips and drank it all in one gulp. A loud burping sound came from his larynx and beyond.

'Otto.'

'Sorry mother. I was thirsty.'

'Hmmm. Not what I expect you to do in public.'

He replaced the glass on the side table, with a solid thud. 'Of course not,' he replied feeling the reprimand was unnecessary.

I said no more and waited for Otto to find the letter. He sat down somewhat exhausted having run home from school. The letter remained untouched.

'Mum, I don't think I could be a doctor just yet.'

My heart sank. If not following in Willy's footsteps, then what? 'Why ever not?' I asked.

'Well, the Hitler Youth takes most of my time up in the evenings and in preparation for my joining the army. I can't see me studying medicine as well. By the way, I've just learned that when I turn eighteen on my birthday, I could be sent to the 7th Hamburg Motorised Unit. That should be good'

The thought of my son in army uniform and dispatched to far flung places gave me a shiver. To me he was still a young boy; to the State he was a combatant. 'Maybe so Otto, but even the army needs doctors.'

Otto felt somewhat outmanoeuvred. Of course his mother was right. 'True,' he said bending down to remove his school shoes.

'Give it some thought. Or perhaps you might like to be a dentist. The army needs them too and your Uncle Karl can advise you on that profession, not so?'

'Hmmm... maybe.'

He had not seen the letter and my impatience got the better of me. 'There's a letter from your grandparents on the table for you to read.'

Otto got up from his slouched position and gathered the letter. He read it as he returned to sit by me.

'You're not going are you?' he said staring at my eyes for an answer.

'I probably will.'

'What will I do?' he said in disbelief and anger at the same time.

I let his feelings subside for a moment. 'Karl and Renate would be pleased to have you stay with them, while I'm away.'

'So it's all agreed? You have made your mind up. You have decided to go to Scotland. For how long?'

'I'm not sure, Otto. Your grandparents are aging. I'm not sure if I'll see them again, especially if I don't go soon.'

I could see him adjusting his indignant outburst. He did have feelings for his grandparents and my home in Elgin. His tone was more muted. 'So when are you going?'

'September I think.'

'I have three months left at school. That means Christmas with Karl and Renate.'

'Yes, of course. That should be fun.' You are very much my young man now. You remember your father left a sum of Deutschmarks which you will receive on your twenty-first birthday.'

Otto looked thoughtful.

'I may need it then. If Communism is defeated, I can then start to study medicine.'

I smiled. His thought process may have irked me earlier but at heart he was true and I knew he wished to follow his father's profession in due course. 'Otto, you make me proud. Come here.' I lifted my book and placed it on the fireside table. I stood to receive him.

We lingered for a warm moment in a parental embrace, one which only a mother knows and cherishes.

Otto smiled at me knowing his perceived plan had met my approval. We came together again in a stronger clench. Otto's lips lay close to my ear. He whispered quietly like a wave sinking in the sand.

'Give my love to Grandmother and Grandfather. I miss them.'

'I will of course Otto. I will.'

3

The Gestapo Demands

The doorbell rang one afternoon as I was ironing one of Otto's brown shirts making sure his arm creases were pressed firmly and in the right place. I was pleased to open the door for Karl.

'Carry on Hilda. Don't let me stop you.' I gave him a kiss on his cheek as he entered throwing his hat on a hall chair.

'I'm ready for a break,' I said skipping through to the kitchen to fill the kettle.

'No second thoughts about us taking Otto on?' Karl inquired with a slightly raised voice.

'No, none. That matter's happily settled I think. Renate is comfortable with the arrangement, not so?'

Karl reached for the cups in their kitchen cupboard. He brought down the sugar bowl too.

'We'd both have Otto to stay anytime. That's not my worry,' he said placing the sugar and cups on the table.

'Something else on your mind?' I held on firmly to the kettle handle on the stove anticipating a concern.

'A couple of things have been bothering me.'

'Uh... huh?'

'Otto's lack of regular education, because of his

Hitler Youth meetings is one concern. It seems it's run on strict activity lines. No time for proper learning or education. It's certainly not like the Boy Scouts.'

'Scouts? They banned them a couple of years ago.'

'That's what I mean. Yes, they did. But I'm more concerned what happens after the Hitler Youth. He told me he'll be with the 17th Hamburg Motorised Unit.'

I stirred one teaspoonful of sugar into Karl's cup.

'It's almost certain they are drafted into the growing army at that age,' I said. I knew the direction was clear and unstoppable. 'Otto told me as much. He reckons he'll only be with you for a short while.'

'Hilda, it's not that he's naive or gullible. He's going with many other boys. They are all in the same circumstances. But I'll tell you one thing of which I am certain.'

I brought the coffee to Karl along with mine and sat at the table in the warm kitchen opposite each other.

'And that is?'

'Thank you. Hmmm... that's good. Yes, there can be little doubt we are heading for war. What allegiances are forming is concerning. Hitler sees Britain as Aryan and equally opposed to a Communist nation taking over Europe. He assumes Britain will not oppose him. I hope that's the case too. However it's an assumption. We cannot be sure.'

I found myself agreeing with Karl. I thought through his assessment and could not fault what he had said. The future looked bleak for me once more as the nations sharpened their swords.

'That is why I think you should consider staying in

Scotland until we see which way the wind is blowing. You follow me?'

'And how long might that be?' I asked.

'You could help run the family hotel for a while. I am sure your parents will appreciate that.'

That was a pleasing thought, for the moment anyway.

'How long do you think the authorities will let me stay?'

'Hilda, I think you've forgotten. You have an additional status, haven't you? Remember what troubles that caused last time there was war, when you didn't have dual nationality? I think you could put it to good use now.'

'Then a one way ticket for the time being?'

'Exactly, that's just what you need.' Karl seemed to be relieved at my decision, by his generous smile.

* * *

I booked my sailing from Hamburg for September 30th and began to get my luggage together. Bags and bundles sorted themselves out in my mind. But I had also made a seminal decision. The house should be placed in Otto's name when he turned twenty-one. Those years were not far off. I would take as much as I could to Scotland of my own belongings. I'd be travelling with two full suitcases and two large trunks for onward delivery.

I sorted out what I felt I could take and what I should leave. Then I started a notebook of instructions for Otto. It would be a book about cooking; washing and shopping. I covered the exercise book in a greaseproof paper first then in the excessive wall paper of the lounge which Willy had quite recently decorated. On the front cover I wrote in bold ink: *OTTO'S BUCH Kochen; Bugelservice; Waschen und Einkaufen.*

Satisfied with my afternoon's work, I opened my oboe case and began to play. As I came to the end of a sombre passage, I heard a knock on the door. I stopped playing immediately; perhaps it was Renate or a friend for Otto.

'Oh Herr Eicke. I was not expecting you.' My heart began to flutter.

'No Frau Richter. I have been standing outside your front door for the past few minutes. You play Mozart particularly well.'

'You know your music Herr Eicke,' I said, showing him an appreciative smile.

'Only that it is Mozart. You will have to enlighten me as to which piece you were playing.'

'The Hostias from Mozart's Requiem in D minor K626. Not usually played by the oboe of course. I was adapting from the choral part.'

'Ah... I see.' Herr Eicke entered the house uninvited. I stood aside to let him in. He stepped over one of the suitcases with an exaggerated high step.

'The sitting room is on the left, Herr Eicke.'

He opened the door and strode with purpose into the centre of the room. 'I intended to see you before you returned to Scotland. Sorry I was too busy to visit you sooner.' He held his hands behind his back. I heard him tapping one with the other, impatiently.

'You knew I was returning to visit my parents?' I asked with a throat as dry as the desert.

'If my wife and I go on holiday, as we did to Bad Liebensel last year, we each took one case. That was more than sufficient. I see you are packing two trunks,' remarked Herr Eicke pointing towards the hall.

'I am taking quite a lot as you can see to make the house less congested.'

His eyes lingered on the cases. 'I see. Yes, Otto told me. Well in fact he didn't. It was a change in his next of kin which alerted me to your intentions. Not just a short visit abroad, I suspect. He has named Karl and Renate Richter as his guardians.' He paused for a moment to let his disclosure sink in. 'A little unusual, perhaps?'

I was on edge. 'Otto is now the man of the house and I wish him to take greater responsibility. I cannot say how long I will be in Scotland of course. I have family and friends there as well as in Hamburg. So you can assume, correctly, that I shall return before too long.'

'I understand, Frau Richter. And I wish you a safe voyage.' He gave a generous smile as if approving my trip.

'Thank you.' It was a genuine response and I hoped it was a prelude to a valedictory remark.

'You will leave with fond memories of our land and of course, your much respected late husband.'

'Naturally.' I found myself defensively folding my arms to his obvious statement.

'And Karl and Renate and especially Otto, you will miss them?'

I felt like losing my patience with him. 'Herr Eicke, these are personal family matters. Of course I'd miss them but I am returning, I do assure you. I do not require such attention to my travel arrangements, surely?' I felt a brooding mist of anger cloud my arguments.

'You are quite right. Of course I would not interfere with domestic arrangements.'

Herr Eicke stood up and went to the window where he gazed up and down the street. I watched him feeling his pose was somewhat theatrical. It was a look-at-me-now; see how important I have become stance.

He turned round smartly. 'We are all insignificant as individuals. Together we realise Germany is on its way to recapture its prominent and rightful position in Europe once more and that England is, how shall I say, sympathetic to our cause, we hope.'

'It always amuses me to hear that Germany has so much in common with England, or to be more precise Britain.'

'Forgive me. Yes, Great Britain you are right of course. The British Royal Family has Hanoverian connections; the English are Saxons from central Europe and of course the Scots are pure Viking, Aryan stock, not so?'

'Well, some are, most are lowland Scots of Irish descent.' We were straying from our confrontations. It brought momentarily relief. I had to progress his agenda. 'Why should this interest you?'

Herr Eicke took a cigarette from a silver case emblazoned with a black swastika on a red background. He lit up and inhaled a second time before exhaling towards the ceiling then turned to look at me. His eyes seemed to be closer than ever, his eyebrows colliding. He was deciding how to answer my question.

'Since 1912 you have been a German wife. You will

be the mother of a brave German soldier soon and so I expect you will retain a firm loyalty to the ideals of our fatherland in all its aspects?'

'Yes, of course,' I replied with genuine conviction.

'It would be good if you would keep in touch with me, not on a personal basis of course, although I would always value your friendship, if it were granted.'

'I am confused Herr Eicke. I am going to be in Scotland for a while. I cannot see how I could be of interest or assistance to you when I am there.'

'Elgin is in the north of Scotland, isn't it?' he said in a pompous manner.

'How do you know that?' I felt my concentration sharpen.

'Otto has only told the truth. He told me you would be staying with your parents in Elgin at their hotel, not so?'

'Well of course, I have to go somewhere when I arrive and it is my parental home.'

'Of course.' Herr Eicke placed his cigarette in the ashtray and took off his spectacles. He wiped them with his handkerchief in an exaggerated slow manner. As the cleaning continued his expression grew more solemn. 'We have our contacts in that area.'

'I doubt that Herr Eicke. What a claim. It is in a remote part of Scotland. I tell you it is most unlikely that you have agents there. It would be a waste of their time.' I laughed at the thought of German men entering Mr David Harvie's bakers shop in Elgin without being noticed. The pomposity of Herr Eicke gave me a break. It was, so far, an interview with very little humour.

Herr Eicke seemed uncomfortable as he stubbed out his cigarette into the fireside ashtray.

'You know the airbase at Lossiemouth and the garrison fort at Fort George?'

I felt cold sweat drip down my back. I realised he was being serious and was playing his hand with caution and precision at the same time.

'If you know all these things then what use am I likely to be?' There was a moment's silence which seemed so much longer.

'Frau Richter, these are bases we would need if there was war against Russia and a naval attack on our country. We would rely on the British in such an event. If they refused, well... we would have to take the matter into our own hands, you understand?'

'I see. So that's why you need British assistance.'

'Exactly. Our agents may not have your ability to speak such fluent English. They may need some assistance, some reassurance perhaps. Or even just the opportunity to speak to someone who is familiar with both languages and cultures.'

I felt trapped. 'I would have no hesitation in helping any stranger if they needed assistance whether German or any other nationality.'

Eicke gave out a long full chest sigh. 'Yes, true, I am sure you would and if there should be a war, would you help our cause? In fact Frau Richter just where would your loyalties lie?'

I had avoided this question which had raised its prominence in my mind many times over the last few months. I turned my back on Herr Eicke to compose myself.

'Why would Germany be at war with Britain?'

'Of course not. We have no intention of being at war with our friends.' Herr Eicke began to walk up and down the room staring at his feet, awkward in getting his message over. Then he looked up at me. 'Should it come to war, you realise the Gestapo has to secure its borders.'

'Naturally. That makes sense. Herr Eicke, I think you have a lively mind. Britain has no land borders. You seem to enjoy playing mind games.'

He seemed annoyed at my response. 'Then let me make myself clearer Frau Richter. Your sister-in-law Renate and her husband Karl, Otto's guardians. We don't want any weakness there do we?'

I found my hands clasped together tightly. Beads of sweat broke out on my forehead. Soon they would descend. My eyes nipped. I awaited his next worrying remark.

'Most loyal Germans are keen to attend rallies when the opportunity arises. I think I can say quite confidently that neither Karl nor Renate Richter have attended such grand occasions. They may have to be given some... encouragement perhaps?'

'And just what do you mean by that?' I asked placing a fist on my hip in defiance.

'Times are changing. If Karl and Renate don't want to change, then I must see to it that they do. Everyone must adapt, with no exception. We must all support and serve the Führer.'

'Karl and Renate do too, as does Otto as you know. Karl is a busy dentist and his wife is his secretary. They work long hours.'

'It's my job to mend the cracks, Frau Richter. You don't see the cracks do you?'

'I only see what is right.'

'Then we agree.'

The barrage of conversation was leaning his way. I could not compete. I had to confront him eye on. 'What exactly are you expecting of me Herr Eicke?'

He responded with clarity. 'Troop movements in Scotland, Frau Richter. That would be interesting information for us. New and existing air bases in the north too, their exact location, please. Nothing else at present, I assure you. We will contact you when we need to. I am glad you see the need to remain loyal to the Fatherland. Rest assured that Renate and Karl will be treated fairly. As I said, you will hear from me or one of our agents abroad at the right time.'

4

The Voyage Home

A feeling of guilt filled my heart as I read the labels on my two trunks. They stared back at me. Was I making the right choice, the correct decision? Was I right to leave Otto at a crucial time in his life?

I decided I was past the point of no return. The mantelpiece was almost bare. Photos of Willy with Otto as a small child playing on the beach at Sassnitz on the Baltic shore reminded me of the happy family I once knew. Photos that brought back memories but they could not talk. I made them speak in my mind being unable to accept Willy's passing away from me. That feeling was still raw and of such a recent time. Time I could not turn back no matter how much I wished it would for so many reasons.

Yet I was convinced the right decision had been made. Only time would tell for I couldn't. The photos were neatly packed into my trunk all except two which I left on the mantelpiece for Otto to remind him of his disappearing mother and deceased father.

The Grampian Empress lay impressively in the Vopak Terminal Dock. I arranged for my two trunks to be transported to the ship and I accompanied them to ensure they were not inspected without my presence. I was aware I had developed a suspicious mind over recent months. This circumspection reinforced my anxious feelings.

Otto had said goodbye to me the night before I embarked and Karl and Renate spent the final afternoon with me, checking on my preparations. Herr Eicke's warning was taken seriously and Karl promised to attend rallies more frequently and close his surgery to show he was attending. That might make life bearable, even although it irked him to do so. When we parted, each knew our futures were uncertain. Our hugs were prolonged, tearful and loving.

* * *

I was escorted to my cabin by a crew member who was quick to pick up my accent.

'Thurs nae many Scottish women like you on board ye ken,' said Able Seaman Rory Tait.

'There are not many Scottish women in Germany at all,' I replied.

He looked at me as if I was an endangered species. 'There are only a few women on this trip. I guess families o' Jews. They Jews, they are nae welcomed here, are they?'

'You mean in Germany?'

'Aye.'

'They are victims of the State,' I told him.

'I ken. Worrying times.'

'These are the fortunate few. That's why they are on board this ship.'

'Aye... suppose so.'

He took my hand luggage and eased the cases through a compartment door leading to a carpeted aisle.

'Ladies always need their extra boxes o' perfume an' the like. Mind you, there will be nae ballroom dancing tonight, Miss,' said Tait.

I turned round to see he was looking at my black box. I laughed.

'That's not what you think it is. It's my oboe.'

'Oh I see. Well, ye'll hae nae use for that either. There's nae orchestra on board,' he said.

I chuckled a tuneful note. 'I am not travelling to play publically.'

Tait shook his head. 'If it has any sense, that oboe of yours should stay in its case on this voyage,' he said.

'Not keen on music are you?'

'Naw, not keen on rough seas. The barometer is low. It's gonna be a tricky crossing.' He laid my cases at my cabin door and I gave him a collection of coins. He looked at them.

'I'm sorry, I've no British change.'

He did not reply. It was not an unfamiliar happening on his sailings. He tapped his forelock and was gone.

True to able seaman Tait's word, even before the Grampian Empress left the embracing harbour, a swell was felt beneath my unsteady feet. After familiarising myself with my cosy cabin, I wrapped myself in the ship's liveried warm blanket and made my way to the deck. My hair caught the breeze leaving my forehead to face the salty air. I felt strands of hair entwine with the wind. Nevertheless I needed to see the land which meant so much to me, drift away. Where Germany was heading was uncertain and I wondered when it unleashed its ambition, would I be on its journey, or not? In fact would I be back in Hamburg or not?

Spires and cranes stood erect proud of their past accomplishments. Everywhere were the flags of the moment. The bright red gave warmth and delight to the nation. More sombre was the black swastika on the stark white background. Mixed feelings swept through my memories. They came to me in an ordered sequence, as order had become the feature of my recent life in Hamburg. Order was demanded.

I recalled that Germany had been my home since 1910 when, as a recent language graduate of Aberdeen University, I came to Germany to brush up my German. I met Willy by chance at a music concert. The memory gave me a warm feeling. I recalled with such clarity the Kunsthalle near the Binnenalster pond in Hamburg where the concert took place. We listened to Grieg's Piano Concerto and by the third movement, the Allegro Marcato, Willy was holding my hand.

Our honeymoon was remembered with equal pleasure in Scotland two years later. How proud I was to take my husband Dr Willy Richter around my relatives scattered around the country. Then the fateful visit of Vera Caldwell my cousin in the summer of 1914 and the trials and strains of getting her home after the first guns had been sounded in that devastating First World War. Perhaps I might visit Vera again on this trip, I thought. Could history repeat itself? Had we not learned the lessons of the Great War?

Then the ship's horn sounded and the thick restraining capstan rope harnesses were flung into the water and hauled on board. The Grampian Empress was at last set free. Set apart from a bellicose land heading towards a land of peace and harmony.

In the dying light of autumn, the golden trees and flags of Hamburg waved goodbye. I gave a lingering smile to the city which had brought me happiness, love, culture and family. Fear and foreboding now overcame the land but those happier memories could never be taken away from the treasures in my mind.

'Till the next time Hamburg. I will return, God Willing. *Deus Volente*, I will return,' I said to the breeze and it cast my words landward in the wind.

I made my way unsteadily towards my cabin as the ship lurched towards the open North Sea. As I passed cabin 227 I stopped. I listened. I made a note of the cabin number.

At the evening meal in the restaurant I ate alone, and noticed the dearth of single travellers aboard. I returned to my cabin and opened my black box. I dampened the double reed then left my room. My uneven steps retraced my previous sortie until I was at cabin 227. A family chattering in German could be heard from the room. I knocked. My knock silenced those internal voices. I waited for the door to open. I knocked again. This time the door opened slightly. Not more than an inch. I greeted my fellow passengers in German. More of the cabin came into view.

'Good evening. I hope you don't mind me calling.'

'What have you there?' I was asked by an inquisitive daughter.

'It's my oboe. I brought it to your door because I thought I heard music coming from this cabin earlier.'

'You are German?'

'Yes, I speak German. I am also Scottish. I am returning home.'

The door opened wider. I was ushered in. Three children sat on the top of the bunk bed with their legs dangling and swinging to and fro. Their mother was behind the door gripping a shawl tightly around her shoulders.

I could detect hesitancy from the parents. I understood how they must have felt. I had to show I was no authority figure plotting to have them returned to Germany. 'You are safe here. I mean you no harm.'

There was a pause. The father's instinct was to be cautious with me, this unannounced visitor. At the same time he knew I was someone who knew the land they were heading towards. The ship was also now underway and that was reassuring. I made a gesture with my oboe. It made up his mind.

'I am Hilda Richter. I am a widow returning to Scotland, my parents are there.'

The father of the family relaxed and gave a warm smile. It was a signal for all the family.

'My name is David Hortowski,' said the father sporting a triangular beard and a thin moustache. 'My wife Anna, my son Konrad and daughters Lilli and Petra.'

'You are right to leave Germany at this time,' I said.

'We had no choice. We prepared to leave Vienna

after the day of the Anschluss,' said Anna.

'12th of March,' said Hilda.

'You remember it well. I am not surprised. It pleased the German people,' said Anna. Her husband raised his hand indicating the remark was not called for.

'Yes, I can remember it very well indeed. In fact I can never forget that date. It was the date of my husband's funeral.'

Anna emitted a quiet apologetic gasp and Petra bit her lip.

'I am sorry about your loss,' David said.

'I am sorry for the treatment of your people,' I replied.

David nodded his head. 'These are difficult times.'

'We can make some moments happier. Who was playing the clarinet?'

Lilli raised her hand.

'My daughter Lilli was a pupil of the Mozarteum in Salzburg. It was her final year, she could not finish her studies, because she was Jewish,' said her father.

'Perhaps we can play together?' I suggested offering an encouraging smile.

Lilli's eyes shone brightly and a smile as wide as the Danube brought her clarinet to her lips. Her eyes were dark, playful and bright.

'Perhaps *Bist du Bei Mir?*' suggested Lilli.

'Johann Sebastian Bach?' I confirmed.

'Yes.'

Then there followed a performance of pitch perfect delight. The oboe, an octave higher, played in harmony with the gifted clarinet player. When we finished, a round of applause was received.

'We've not applauded for several months. That might have drawn attention to us,' said Anna.

'It must be a great relief to have left the German shore,' I said and saw their reactions in harmony.

'Yes but *Be With Me*' as Bach composed, surely gives hope for a brighter day in Germany, one day?' said Anna.

'Brighter yes, will it be without any Jews?' asked David leaving the question to swell in everyone's mind.

Petra asked her brother Konrad, to hold another piece of music. It was unfamiliar to me.

'*Zemir Atik* is one of my favourite Yiddish songs. I learned this tune when I was young. I used to play it when I was happy because it's a dance tune. I have not played it for several years. I feel free to play it now we are sailing away. Can you play it too?'

I was not familiar with Yiddish music other than knowing I would be playing in a minor key. 'I'll try,' I said feeling musically adventurous.

I soon got the timing as well as the melody of this tune and the family clapped in unison. I looked around the cabin at their smiling faces and saw a family tension dissipate after years and months of pent up anxiety and fear. I was happy for them.

The increasing swell of the seas made me and David unsteady on our feet and so the impromptu concert came to a sudden end, amid laughter.

'And what are your plans when you arrive, may I ask?'

'We will get a train to Manchester where we have relatives. We will stay with them a while before crossing the Atlantic to America.'

'What a grand venture,' I remarked showing my delight.

David opened his arms wide. 'It is our fate. We are a people constantly on the move.'

I agreed. 'And do any of you speak English?'

'I do,' said Petra, her legs still swinging in time from her position on the bunk bed. 'So does my father, but not the rest of the family, yet.'

'The voyage is not long enough for me to give classes in English,' I apologised.

'We will make do. We adapt easily,' said David with the palm of his hands facing upwards.

'Well if I can find my feet I think I should now return to my cabin and get ready for bed. Perhaps sleep is the best way to deal with a rough sea. Shall we have breakfast together tomorrow morning?'

Faces lit up. 'Yes please,' said Lilli and Petra together and Anna nodded in agreement.

'It would be our pleasure Frau Richter,' said David clearly pleased to have met a friendly compatriot.

I returned to my cabin, holding on to the sides of the aisle. On deck it was now ink-black dark. I had no intention of finding any coastal light for the last time. Instead I noticed a walnut cased radio by my bedside. I turned it on to hear Henry Hall play some popular dance music. To his music, I prepared for bed. I climbed into the fresh white sheets and lay my head on the marshmallow pillow and let my dreams be wafted to a warm clime by the tuneful and comforting dancehall music.

Moments later, before I was asleep, the music stopped abruptly for a special announcement. I was alerted by the sudden change of atmosphere coming from the radio. A solemn announcement followed. I sat up in bed.

'This is the BBC Home Service. The Prime Minister Mr. Neville Chamberlain landed at Heston Aerodrome earlier this evening, 30th September, after his meeting with the German Chancellor, Herr Adolf Hitler. The Prime Minister is preparing to address the crowds there. We go over now to hear what he had to say.'

I sat up clasping my bent knees wondering how the Prime Minister coped with Herr Hitler.

"The settlement of the Czechoslovakian problem, which has now been achieved, is, in my view, only the prelude to a larger settlement in which all Europe may find peace. This morning I had another talk with the German Chancellor, Herr Hitler, and here is the paper which bears his name upon it as well as mine. Some of you, perhaps, have already heard what it contains but I would just like to read it to you: ... We regard the agreement signed last night and the Anglo-German Naval Agreement as symbolic of the desire of our two peoples never to go to war with one another again."

'That recording was made two hours previously and now we go to the steps of 10 Downing Street where Mr. Chamberlain has a formal statement to give to the nation,' said the BBC Announcer.

"My good friends, for the second time in our

history, a British Prime Minister has returned from Germany bringing peace with honour. I believe it is peace for our time. We thank you from the bottom of our hearts. Go home and get a nice quiet sleep."

And in a timely response from President Franklin Roosevelt upon hearing of the Munich Settlement and the avoidance of a new world war, the nation heard his two word telegram to the Prime Minister: It was plain and simple. '*Good man*'.

I gave a large sigh of relief and ran my fingers through my hair over my head. There would be no war after all. It was now looking like a relaxed visit home. The thought that perhaps Otto could now concentrate on his medical studies at last, gave me the broadest of smiles of contentment. Sleep had never felt so rewarding even although there were moments when I felt queasy. I made sure I had access to a cardboard bowl, should the need arise.

The following morning after dressing in a warm knitted sea-green pullover, I went outside on deck. I breathed fresh clean and salty air. There was no land in sight. Instead, mesmerising waves with white flecks danced before my eyes. Seabirds perched on the taught wires from mast to bridge, taking advantage of a free trip. It felt good to be alive on the dawn of a new understanding between former hostile nations. A new start, a new month, a new anticipation.

Able seaman Tait passed by. He flicked his cigarette stub into the froth of the North Sea.

'Good morning Ma'am. Heard the news?' he asked.

'Yes, wonderful. I heard Mr. Chamberlain on the radio last night. It looks so promising. No war after all,' I replied, beaming with the air blowing my chestnut locks behind me.

'That wis yesterday's news, Ma'am. You hav'nae heard? Today Germany invaded Sudetenland.'

5

Confrontation

'*Baruch ata adonai eloheinu melech haolam …*' David got up from the table and pulled a seat out for Hilda.

'I'm sorry, I disturbed you,' she apologised.

'God knows we give thanks for our daily bread each day. He also expects us to show humility and service. And He lives and travels with us when we ask. No, you did not interrupt.'

His smile placated me. 'You have heard the news about Sudetenland?' I asked.

'Yes, it was no surprise. What will stop Hitler now?' asked Anna to no one in particular. The news made it a somber breakfast with the Jewish family.

'I'll never trust Hitler and I feel for all my brothers and sisters in the Sudetenland. The man must be mad. He is leading us into Armageddon,' said David

My lips tightened and my head shook. 'True. I believe you. Fortunately, like many others, you are being led away from the madness,' I said lifting my coffee cup from its saucer.

'Yes, we are fortunate ones. We leave so many behind. Lots are German Jews, they have no other nationality, and they fear for their lives from their fellow countrymen.'

'Yes, sadly true David. I distrust him more than ever now. He has lied to the Prime Minister and the British people as well.'

I retired to my cabin and focussed on arriving in Scotland again. Perhaps a day walking in the heather hills with old friends, a picnic by a quiet deep loch, back to a good traditional supper of peas brose, mealy and black puddings. Buchannan, the butcher's steak pies ahh... and Mother's cooking. There was still time in early October to sit with my parents in the garden of the hotel in sunshine until late afternoon seeing the chrysanthemums, dahlias, sprouts and kale that mum and dad planted each spring, come into season. Apples and pears too should be in abundance. I loved a Scottish autumn.

I let my thoughts slip for a moment into the sadness and awfulness that the news brought from Germany. What would be Europe's future? At that moment, I saw in life moments of sheer tranquillity, time to appreciate good fortune and days of sadness. Above all, there was time to remember that we are only a blink of nature's eye on this planet.

During my afternoon deck-stroll, I focussed on a grey-blue ship in the distance, and then another and another flanking the first. Moments later puffs of steam rose from their funnels. Not pure virginal white clouds of smoke, more a dirty grey bellowing trail from each ship. They grew larger as the moments passed. Behind the ships was an even larger ship, a battleship most surely, like the ones I had seen offshore at Cuxhaven.

They eventually passed by in their soundless and sinister gracefulness. Menace was in their wake, even although the red ensign was displayed at their stern.

On the other side of the ship... I could never remember which port was or which was starboard, I strained my eyes to detect any land on the horizon. I desperately wished land to appear. Some ribbon of raised interest. When it did appear, I was not so sure at first. It made me think how close Scotland was to Germany geographically. I rubbed my eyes and refocused. Land indeed it was. Given docking was in two and a half hours, it must have been somewhere on the east coast of Scotland, maybe off Arbroath or Montrose and that meant Aberdeen would soon appear. I returned to pack in my cabin. The chore did not take long. I returned to the deck in excited anticipation of seeing the growth of my beloved land and the Granite City.

When it came into unmistakable view, it shone like a palace of diamonds. The familiar spires of Marshall College seemed to recognise this graduate's return to her alma mater. I felt very much at home already and only the train journey to Elgin in the afternoon would bring me to my parental home and be back in the centre of a loving family.

The Grampian Empress docked and the gangways were lowered. I said my farewells to the Hortowski family and encouraged Lilli to play her clarinet every day to keep happy, now she was in Britain. I could sense that they were pleased to arrive on a welcoming shore and their relaxation was seen in their smiles and in agitated excitement gathering their cases.

I met with the liveried transport company which would deliver my larger trunks to the hotel.

Uniformed crew assisted in delivering passengers from the ship to the customs hall. I smiled when I heard the familiar cry from the street outside.

'Aberdeen Press and Journal, tuppence a copy. Get your Press and Journal. Only tuppence a copy,' shouted the young flat capped youth.

I wondered for a moment if he'd increase his sales if I played my oboe beside him. I kept the black box close by my side as I proceeded through the customs with the cheeriest of smiles. There were smiles all around as families greeted passengers and wives reunited with their oceangoing husbands, due a four day break. I enjoyed hearing once again the Aberdonian Doric tongue. It was so distinctive. I even recalled speaking that way not so long ago when I was as a student in this city.

Setting foot in Aberdeen again after all these years, I enjoyed the salty air and the freshness of the north-east cold winds. It was with me during my studies and at my graduation all those years ago. The German language tutorials had prepared me for the complexities I now faced. I wondered how different life would have been if I had taken French as my main foreign language. But I loved the guttural language of the German voice and it readily accepted my Aberdonian accent to its nuances.

Aberdeen was as ever the granite grey city and I loved it. I looked for a cab to take me to the train station. As I kept a lookout, two men approached. Both wore trilby hats and formal suits could be seen under their belt buckled trench coats. I noticed they also wore gloves, too premature surely in early autumn? I had no time to question further their attire. They stopped before me, like a brass band adhering to the drum major's raised mace.

'Frau Richter?'

'Yes, I am,' I responded with a degree of concern. Perhaps they had brought bad news from Elgin.

'Frau Hilda Richter?

'Indeed, I am.'

'My name is William Dynes, British security services. Mr Thornton accompanies me. Frau Richter we would like to ask you some questions. We believe, more than a suspicion, you may be an agent of the German government.'

'What? Good grief. This is nonsense, utter nonsense,' I protested feeling the colour in my cheeks fade to white and my mouth begin to dry up.

'Please come this way please,' said Mr. Dynes with Mr. Thornton leading the way.

In a state of shock I was led into a rather small room sparsely furnished. A lit gas fire faced the table at which I was asked to sit. It glowed with bright orange flames and gave off some welcomed warmth. Little else gave me comfort. Was I dreaming? Perhaps I was back in Germany. This seemed like a Teutonic confrontation I'd rather avoid.

'Were you expecting family to meet you?' asked Mr. Dynes, a man possibly contemporary with my age. His presence was overbearing.

'No. My parents are elderly. I was trying to find a cab to the railway station to get a train to Elgin.'

'You won't be going to Elgin tonight. That I can assure you,' said Mr Dynes, the younger of the two who wore a striped tie of some old boy educational network.

'I have been instructed by the security services, to detain you and to ascertain your real purpose of leaving Germany,' said Dynes.

'To think a homecoming would end like this,' I replied.

'A German surname, a son in the German army and as tensions arise, you suddenly come to Scotland. Well, these facts I cannot overlook, can I?' suggested Dynes.

I felt a shudder through my body. Such well informed interrogators. I hoped they did not see the tension gripping my body. I answered slowly, clearly and in my more Doric accent.

'That is one interpretation. I agree with you. However, I offer another. I am Scottish and I was under house arrest during the First World War in Hamburg. I have aging parents in Elgin and I am heading there to stay. I have no connections with political forces in Germany or Britain,' I said in defiance and added for good measure, 'I think your case must be weak.'

Both seemed to nod but smirked at my statement at the same time. 'We think we have a rather stronger case than you might think, Frau Richter. Your spirited defence has a crack. You cannot deny being under the instruction of one Gestapo Police chief in Hamburg. I refer to Herr Gerhardt Eicke.'

On conclusion of his coup de grace, Dynes sat back contented to study my face. I realised these men knew much more than I had given them credit. I would have to be as open as possible with them from now on.

'Yes, I do not deny I know of Herr Eicke. He is my son's Youth leader.'

'Come come Frau Richter, Herr Eicke is not a youth leader. He's a senior Gestapo man in Hamburg and you know that. He is also a schemer and deceitful man. Ideal for the German secret police, I would say,' said Dynes.

'Yes, I do not deny that I know him. I first met him when he came to my husband's funeral, but to say I work for him or that he sent me here is quite outrageous, in fact preposterous. I told you, my parents are aging. It was an appropriate time to travel here,' I said.

Mr Thornton took over the questioning. He had a Northern Irish lilt to his voice. It was tuneful but equally incisive.

'Your son, Otto. He must put you in a difficult position,' he said.

My head was now reeling. I could not fathom how they were so well-informed. It would be impertinent to ask how, but I did.

'You are extremely knowledgeable about my affairs.' My question sought to delve further into their secret working. It worked.

'Our Consul in Hamburg runs a very busy office.'

'The Hamburg British Consul offices, I see. I suggest that would be either Armstrong or Simpson perhaps?' He ignored me.

'And Otto, Frau Richter...?'

'If Otto had been much younger when my husband died, I would have returned to Scotland. Otto has visited

Elgin often. He would have settled. He has friends at school in Hamburg too and when the church groups and youth groups were banned, all children were enrolled in the Hitler Youth. I remind you, all children. What was Otto to do? Dropping out is not an option you realise? He'll be a man soon and he must make his way in life. He will always be my son.'

'Indeed as you say, making his own way in life, choosing to serve the German Army in Hamburg. Not the proud profession of your late husband,' said Dynes.

Tears welled up in my eyes. I took a handkerchief from my sleeve and dabbed them. My voice now had a pained tone to it as I realised I could not compete with their thorough knowledge of my family's background and movements. Herr Eicke appeared in my mind with his expectations being mouthed in silence in my head. To agree with him would save Otto, Karl and Renate. My allegiances were stretched and tearing apart. Two sides of the same coin. I was German in culture, language and family. I could state with confidence I was also a Scot. Why could I not be both? Yes, why indeed.

'And I thought this was a new start to my life. Perhaps I could teach in a local school, returning to my roots as it were. The only difficulty I foresaw was my German surname. Dr Willy Richter was a fine man, a peace loving man and a quiet opponent of Germany's military development.'

'So how did you really get mixed up with Herr Eicke?' asked Thornton in a less threatening tone.

Was this softening approach meant, I wondered? I should take it for what it may be worth. 'As I told you

I met him first on that black day for me. Perhaps that was when he realised my value to him was as an alien in his midst. I shunned him at first as did my brother and sister in law.'

'Karl and Renate?'

'You know them too?' I smiled at the thoroughness of the British Consul. 'My, you are very well informed indeed.'

Mr Dynes nodded as I looked up to him. He opened a pouch of rough tobacco and broke it down in the palm of his hand. He placed his pipe between his teeth. It was a pipe with character. Almost an S bend made it droop down his chin. I notice he smoked St Bruno tobacco. He opened his bluebird box of matches. The first match failed to light. He gave the sandpapered side of the box another strike. It failed to ignite too.

'Blasted dampness up here in the wilds.'

He took another match out. This time the phosphorus sparked and sweet smelling tobacco wafted clouds of pipe smoke into the room. Then I realised how I knew the tobacco. St Bruno's vapours were the tobacco my father smoked. I observed his ritual while thinking what more I could say to convince them that I had no malice in me to hurt our countrymen. I continued to show co-operation.

'I did not see much of him after the funeral. I heard about him of course through Otto. It was when I was preparing to return here that he took a greater interest in me.'

I raised my oboe case from the floor and placed it on the table. I laid my hands on top of the box and gently caressed it. I continued to feed information to the men in the hope they would see how I was a trapped fish and not a shark in their midst.

Dynes told me that there were German agents in Britain. Even up here in the north. That shook me, I can tell you. That's exactly what Eicke said too. He was taking his time to assess me. I felt his eyes penetrate mine. His glance to his colleague was deliberate but I could not think what he meant.

'Did Eicke mention the names of his agents?' asked Thornton as he poised his pen over his notebook.

'No, he said they would contact me.'

'So Eicke knows you will be staying in Elgin?' asked Dynes.

'Yes at the hotel, my parents home. Otto told him his next of kin were to be Karl and Renate on my departure. So that was how he found out I'd be returning home. That was my fault, my weakness, I suppose.'

'Why, in what way?' asked Thornton.

'Herr Eicke is using Karl and Renate's weakness in support of Hitler to frighten me. Eicke threatened me because he suspected I am not an enthusiastic German sympathiser and you interrogate me thinking I am Eicke's spy. I think you and Herr Eicke ought to sit round a table and sort the whole unsavoury mess out,' I said frustrated and not too far from tears.

Dynes sat on the edge of his seat to get nearer to me.

'I like your humour. Maybe I might meet Herr Eicke one day,' he said. I shook my head frustrated by their questioning. I feared what might happen to me next. Would this arrest lead to a court appearance, detention then imprisonment? I felt the stakes were very high indeed.

'Look, you can search my bags if you wish. I assure you won't find papers from Herr Eicke. I have no address for him other than Gestapo HQ in Hamburg. It is him who has promised to contact me. And if he does contact me, I can keep you informed. I'd also inform you of the agents in Britain who are acting for him as soon as I know who they are.'

Dynes sat back clasping his hands behind his head and crossing his legs. I was relieved that I had now shown my colours and they had been accepted. In Scotland, I knew where my loyalties were set, especially here in Aberdeen, in the great city of my education.

'You mentioned your two trunks. We have already checked your goods in the hold of the Grampian Empress...and found nothing incriminating,' said Thornton.

'You are thorough. I'm not surprised. You might as well investigate my suitcase here. Be as thorough as you like, I've nothing to hide.'

Mr Dynes opened my suitcase and placed his hands in my handbag. His hands fiddled about, and then he shook his head.

'Nothing sir.'

Hilda noted his deference. Thornton was the one controlling this interview.

Clearly I came with no spy paraphernalia. But they were on to me and they probably knew there was more information to be extracted. Honesty now dominated my thinking. Spying was not my forte.

'Eicke requested only two things.' They each looked up at me realising they had reached the crux of my case. I did not disappoint them.

'That I report on troop movements in the north of Scotland and also note how many existing or new air bases we have in the northern area.' I was relieved my orders from Germany were now out on the table, not under pressure but voluntary and freely stated. Dynes made a note of my declaration. Thornton smiled appreciatively at my admission and caught Dynes' smile. I found it awkward that neither responded immediately to this news.

Instead, Thornton pointed to the black box on the table. He opened it and saw the oboe resting in three pieces. The instrument's make was emblazoned in gold leaf beneath the case handle.

'Rudall Carte, German?' he asked.

'No English, makers of oboes and flutes since 1822. Very well established. Even German orchestras play them.'

In a compartment were the double reeds. Thornton carefully examined the instrument by looking down its barrel. He then felt the case's lining inch by inch and was satisfied there had been no tampering and the box was passed back to me.

'Over to you Mr Dynes. I believe it's your turn now.'

I made no sense of the interchange. Mr. Dynes left the room as if he had no more questions to ask. He returned a few minutes later with a tray of tea and some Glengarry biscuits. I was glad to accept some nourishment after the nerve wracking questions which showed no sign of diminishing. The tea refreshed me as it slid over a tightened throat, easing its passage. I was not prepared for the next round of questioning. This time Mr Anthony Thornton pulled up a chair, placing an elbow supporting his chin on the table.

'Frau Richter, we have to make sure who we are interviewing. That means uncovering any dark areas. Your background gave us some challenges. We are however satisfied with your explanation and your Scottish background.'

'Does that mean I am no longer arrested? Can I leave?'

'Wait a moment. Don't jump the gun. We understand your loyalty to Otto and your extended family in Germany too but we'd like you to work for us rather than against us. We need to track Eicke's demands. You are very well placed to do so. In a nutshell Hilda, you will have to act as a double agent. Do you understand?'

I took a deep audible breath. Was this a trick question? Had the volte-face always been on the cards? Mentioning my first name for the first time, was that to persuade me? It had certainly disarmed me. Would this lead to me getting home? The world of espionage terrified me. I was not suited to it. I felt trapped in its intricate web. My worry was that it was too late to break out.

'I'd not accept a posting back to Germany. I'd never survive. You cannot imagine how everyone is suspicious of everyone else. I'd make little progress and Eicke would be on my tail as soon as I returned. He might even send me back here, with more instructions.'

'That's very true. That's why I was thinking you should be sent back. However we're not ready for that,' said Dynes.

What I had let myself into was coming home to roost. A double spy, how complicated.

'So what happens now, may I ask?'

Dynes fumbled in his suit pocket. 'Here's my card. You can get me on that number at any time. Let me know if the German contacts get in touch with you and especially if Eicke makes contact. You understand?'

'Yes. I promise I will.'

'Just before you go, just out of interest. Does that oboe you have make a fine sound?'

I looked at my friend, the instrument, feeling sorry for its recent manhandling. 'It depends how you play it Mr. Dynes, doesn't it?'

6

Ereman Agents Provide a Delphin 7 Secret Radio

White steam followed the rail tracks like a bride's veil as the coast disappeared from view. I relaxed in my eight seat compartment and contemplated my unexpected encounter in Aberdeen. I could see why Messrs Dynes and Thornton had been interested in me but hopefully they were satisfied that Germany would not feature in my plans in the near future, apart from sharing any information I found out about the German agents. I knew it was therefore, important to co-operate fully with my British handlers.

I felt more relaxed than ever on that journey. Each coach was a self contained unit and as long as the wheels kept turning, no one would enter my world of espionage which I could not deny. I was both relaxed and anxious. How would I find my parents? Nevertheless I knew a warm welcome awaited.

One hour and twenty minutes later the Aberdeen - Inverness train pulled into Elgin. Sinister steam hissed along the side of the platform as I stepped down into very familiar territory with my suitcase and black box.

I proceeded through the station, crossed the road and walked down Hay Street and there before me was the welcome sight of the family hotel.

I climbed the steps to the reception desk and rang the bell of the Nethybrig Hotel. A door from the kitchen opened and my mother Madge, appeared.

'Darling, you're home,' she said fast approaching stuffing a dishtowel into her apron pocket then opening her arms wide. I placed my bags down. We hugged. We greeted each other saying things at the same muddled time but not answering the splattering of questions we had for each other. There would be time, of that there was no doubt.

'Welcome home,' said the bell boy. 'I'll take your luggage.'

'Thank you, Fergus. My, you have grown into a handsome young man now.'

'Thank you Mrs Richter, if you say so. Anyway, it's good to see you again. Is Otto here too?'

'No, Otto has just finished school and is kept very busy.' I replied.

'What's his work?'

'Fergus, in Germany we have national service, that's what Otto is doing. It's compulsory.'

'Wheesht Fergus, take Hilda's bag upstairs,' mother told him waving her arms to shush him on his way.

'It's wonderful to have you back home darling, wonderful. I have been so worried. But you are here. I almost can't believe it. Hmmm... you are looking so well.'

'I suspect it's the sea air you detect. I'm not getting any younger.'

'Well, neither am I.'

We both laughed at such an obvious thought.

'So now, you're in the attic if you don't mind. We've got a few guests this week, travelling salesmen. Your Father is in the back bedroom these days,' said Mother. 'He can't get upstairs now.'

'How is father?'

Madge's sad face said it all. She beat her chest. 'He's not well... not well at all. The doctor says his heart is weak and of course you know he had a stroke last year. He has little movement down his left side. That's why I hoped you would come. You had better go and see him while I'll organise a cup of tea for us, and some gingerbread I made yesterday.'

'Mmmm... Gingerbread. That's a treat.'

I went through the corridor to the back bedroom passing the wooden panelled walls with its pictures of the town in former days. They smiled at their long lost friend as I passed by. I opened the door but father seemed to be sleeping. I approached. I bent forward to kiss him. That woke him. A faint smile crossed his lips and his eyes shone a welcome as he recognised his daughter's return. His voice was weak but stronger than I had expected.

'Hilda... darling... my little girl. I'm so pleased to see you again.'

'You have been on my thoughts all the time, dad,' I replied with a lump in my throat.

'But... Herr Hitler... he worries me.' His effort to speak now seemed to exhaust him.

'He worries me too but not today. I'm home with you.'

Mother arrived with a tray and placed it on the dressing table. She poured out two tea cups and a mug for dad. It was the same friendly teapot which saw me grow in the family home. It had lost some of its shine but I knew one day, it would come into my possession for it was such sentimental things in the house that meant so much to me.

I settled back into a routine helping mother in the kitchen and staffing the reception desk. I brought father his meals and each course was met with a smile. In fact I picked up on the life of my youth very easily until a letter arrived.

I found it propped up on the reception desk held in position by the desk bell. The postman never left letters there. They were always placed in the middle of the reception desk, faced down. I was immediately suspicious. I lifted it up and saw distinctive German script in the address. The letter had no postmark. I suspected I knew who had been to drop off the letter.

I rushed to the front step of the hotel and looked both ways. Nothing was untoward. Those in the street seemed to be attending to their affairs. None was moving away in haste from where I stood. I waited in this position for a few more minutes.

Fergus approached.

'Can I get you anything Mrs Richter?'

I turned and smiled at him. 'No, I'm just getting some fresh air.'

'I see you have a letter. Is it from Otto?'

'No, not this one,' I replied holding the address close to my bosom.

I retired to my room and slid a sharp metal comb handle through the top of the letter. I immediately saw a handbook. It was a Morse code book. I flipped though it and read its instructions in German, of course. Was I to memorise all these codes? I unfolded the letter. Its message was brief.

That evening I telephoned Mr Dynes.

'I've heard from an agent.'

'What's his name?'

'I suspect a false name. I have been asked to go to the Bunchrew Country hotel near Inverness on Friday. I've to ask for Mr and Mrs Brown.'

'Then you must go. Have you been asked to stay overnight at the hotel?'

'No the meeting is at twelve noon.'

'I'll send a money order to cover your costs. I'll be waiting to hear from you on Friday night.'

'And if I'm not home at a reasonable hour?'

'Then Saturday morning, of course.'

I replaced the receiver having been reprimanded for not thinking the obvious response as mother entered the lounge where I had made the call.

'I have to visit a friend I've not seen for a while, Mother, in Inverness this Friday.'

'A school friend?'

'No, one I met when I was studying in Aberdeen.'

'I see. Why not bring her here?'

I hesitated. Lies did not come easily to me and yet I did not wish mother to know anything about my current secret affairs.

'Maybe some other time, mother.'

It was the first time, as an adult, I told a lie. Was this something I might have to do regularly to keep my life secret? Could I retain all the information I have gathered and keep my lies from tripping me up? Was espionage full of lies? I knew I was now at the start of my spying life and I had to protect my family in Germany without harming my native Scottish land. It was a very tight rope I was walking on and one which might not hold my weight, let alone my balance.

Never had four days dragged so much. On Thursday the postal order arrived from London. I somehow felt Dynes and Thornton lived nearer, perhaps in Edinburgh. I supposed they had superiors and they would be in London. That would have explained the postmark. I deposited it in the post office and pursed the money.

My mother Madge and I sat in the back garden on my return from the town. We sat and drank a lime cordial and gazed beyond the hotel grounds down the Lincoln green valley to Monaughty Forest and the pimple that is the affectionately known Heldon Hill. I gazed at it. Mother's eyes followed my stare.

'You remember climbing it?'

'That was some time ago. I am sure I can't do that any longer. I suppose I am just not fit,' I said. My mind unwound the years and my looks. It was all so peaceful then. I had no cares nor responsibilities.

'We are all getting older; no-one gets any younger. And then we die.'

'Don't talk like that mother. You have many years ahead of you.'

'Perhaps, but your father has not so many. In fact I see him fading almost every day. Do see him before you go to Inverness tomorrow, darling.'

On Friday I entered father's bedroom. My vital father seemed to be slipping away. I placed my hand on top if his and squeezed it lightly. His eyes opened and a wicked smile came my way. It was his way of acknowledging his daughter was with him. I could not stay long. I had a train to catch and I told him.

'You can take me to Inverness. I love that town on the river.'

I held his hand in both of mine. 'Not this time dad, make it next summer when it's much warmer.'

'That's a deal, darling.'

The train was on time and I saw the station master wave his green flag and simultaneously blow his whistle. That started the chug-chug-chugs and the train slowly took up speed. There was something about the greenness of the land which calmed me yet it was often the same dampened green I had been used to in northern Germany. Rural Scotland and rural Germany had its similarities; why couldn't its people be the same too? It was becoming far too late for compromise. I was aware that this was a seismic development in my affairs as a double agent. Could I retain all that I would hear later in the day and how soon could I safely communicate with Thornton or Dynes and then Eicke?

The train entered Inverness station one hour ten minutes later. No one explained nor apologised why it took ten minutes longer than stated. My watch showed it was 11.35 am. I took a cab to the hotel situated overlooking the Black Isle on the Beauly Firth. The taxi drove up to the stately home and I entered the hotel.

'Good morning. I have arrived to meet Mr and Mrs Brown.'

'Miss Richter?'

'Yes.'

'The gazebo in the garden is where they are having coffee. Perhaps you might like to join them there?'

'Rather,' I said as if I was pleased to know dear friends were waiting.

'Then let me show you where they are.'

The receptionist came from behind her desk and as a bell boy passed by, she instructed him to bring an extra coffee to the gazebo.

'How long have Mr and Mrs Brown been at the hotel?' I asked with a deeper curiosity than my question implied.

'They arrived yesterday. They are tourists, as you know. Heading up to Dornoch tomorrow, they said.'

I then saw the gazebo. It was south facing in the bright autumn sun. The door was closed, presumably trapping the heat. Then I saw a man rise from his chair and open the door as I approached. He wore a tweed suit; his shirt was green and his tie a mottled brown. He was not tall, his hairline receding, significantly overweight too. A Bavarian beer drinker was my first thought. His moustache followed his smile as I approached. He looked

60

the proverbial Scottish country gent. Seated behind him was a woman but the angle of the sun detracted from my total vision of her.

'Mrs Richter, delighted to meet you,' Mr Brown said extending his hand but I could already detect a Swabian accent. He was not from any of the hanseatic ports of the northern coast and far less from Bavaria. Instead he was a south-west German whose local characteristics were known to be humble. Perhaps he was an exception.

'Good afternoon.' I apologise for being a little late.'

'Not at all. I appreciate you have travelled quite a distance this morning,'

'Your coffee will be with you soon, madam,' informed the receptionist. She turned with a swivel, lifting her heels from the grass as she did to prevent them being sunk in the far from firm lawn.

Mr Brown's hand opened and invited me further into the summer house. I found it to be warm while cane blinds partly shaded the penetrating sun. Mrs Brown stood up to shake my hand. She was a much older woman which surprised me. I even wondered if she could almost be his mother. Her grey hair was tightly gathered in a knot at the back of her head. Her spectacles lay on the table beside her which also supported her coffee cup. She wore a dark, almost black suit with black shoes and a white ruff at her neck. A broach sat over her Adam's apple. There was a green stone in the centre. Jade perhaps but whether real or not might depend on how high a German she spoke. When she eventually did, I knew it must be a precious stone.

Mr Brown spoke in quiet German.

'Frau Richter. We resort to English as soon as we see your coffee arrive. You understand?'

'Of course,' I replied.

'Greetings from Herr Eicke,' he said.

'Ah, thank you. I wish I could return the compliment.'

'You will do that yourself before very long.'

I felt a tightening in my throat as I considered what he meant. An immediate return to Germany seemed my only interpretation. I was not ready for that.

'Here she comes with the coffee. Start talking in English, say anything other than in German or about Germany.'

I thought quickly. 'As I said I have a brother on the island of Bute and a sister, married down in London. I don't get a chance to see her very often. The distance, you see. But every second year...thank you,' I took the cup and poured some milk into it. 'I don't manage to get down often. I miss seeing my nieces and nephews, of course. You know what it's like?' She left closing the door behind her.'

'So you have a large family, Frau Richter?'

I made sure the receptionist was out of earshot. 'Quite the opposite. Just one son and he's in Hamburg.'

'Otto?'

Instinctively I raised my eyes. He could see me think through how he knew his name. 'Yes, that's right. He's leaving the Hitler Youth to go to a motorised company.'

'Yes, we know.'

'You are very well informed.'

'Of course.' He took off his jacket and placed it over the arms of his chair.

'This is a beautiful country, your country. You must be glad to be home with your parents.'

'Indeed I am. I had not seen them for a few years.'

'And how are they?' he asked.

'As well as can be expected.' Maybe, I was too quick in answering that. 'Actually, my father is poorly.'

'I'm sorry to hear that,' said Mrs Brown. 'Does this mean you intend to stay a long time in Scotland?'

'That is difficult to say.'

'What do you mean Frau Richter?' asked Mr Brown.

'I have loyalties to my parents of course but I also have loyalties to my son and my in-laws in Germany.'

'I understand. And your national loyalties?'

I knew there was a conflict coming and now it stared me straight in the face.

'I have lived in Germany since 1910. For twenty eight years I have been German in voice and culture and now the widow of a German medical doctor. I am a proud mother of a fine young man in the army bringing Germany back to its rightful place in Europe and standing up against aggressors.'

Mr Brown smiled then nodded. 'Just what Herr Eicke said you'd say.'

I found what he said slightly ambiguous. 'I am sorry, what did Herr Eicke say?'

'He said I'd find you loyal to Germany and I am of that impression too.'

'You say it's just an impression? I am stating facts,' I said with conviction.

'Indeed you are right,' Mrs Brown said. 'Remember sometimes our English is not up to a perfect standard.'

'I am glad you find no need to interrogate me. Herr Eicke did that before I left. I know his penalty if I let him down.'

'And that is?' asked Mr Brown.

'He'd make sure my brother and sister-in-law had a hard time.'

'And Otto?'

I thought through his question for a moment. 'No, my son has done well in the Hitler Youth and is keen to do well in the army. Eicke will have no concerns about Otto. As a mother of course I have my worries, but I know he is a good boy and one I love dearly. I can assure you I know where my interests and my heart lies, Mr Brown.'

'I mentioned earlier your need to be in touch with Herr Eicke. That is why I sent you the letter.'

'Yes, I did get it of course. I read it thoroughly too.'

'Did you understand it?'

'I saw it was a code and I have tried to learn it.'

'Good.' He stood up and from what I thought might have been and probably was a garden toy box of cricket wickets or a croquet set, he lifted out a square box from it. Mrs Brown took up a vantage point ensuring no one approaching would disturb us.

'This will be your equipment. A secret radio direct to Herr Eicke. This Delphin 7 has a range of just over 800 miles. It will operate at maximum distance for Hamburg. It is a crystal set with one valve. You insert the valve here,' he pointed to a socket. 'This is the Morse key. Try it.'

I tapped it a few times.

'With only 800 miles, will it give a good signal?'

'Ours works adequately with the occasional faint signal. I'm sure yours will work too.' This was the reality of espionage. I was now being fully immersed into the dark world of deceit. It was alien to me.

'This switch marks the transmit/receive position. These are the headphones. You can adjust them to make them comfortable. This is their socket. Now let me turn it around. This is the socket for the aerial. When you plug it in here, you will be ready to operate it. A 4 watt light will come on. You start with your call sign.'

'I see. And I have a call sign?'

'Yes, but you are impatient. I want you to go over what I have said. You must be familiar with its operation. You will be on your own.'

I spent the next ten minutes being examined about each button and switch's function. Mr Brown and Mrs Brown seemed satisfied with my progress.

'Now put the radio away back in the box.'

I did as I was told. I wondered if the radio stayed there but I was very wrong.

'Sit down. Now I want you to get the radio out, set it up. Wait two minutes as if you were sending a message and then unplug the sockets as quickly as you can and put the radio away.'

Naturally I obeyed, trying not to show any nervousness but I saw my fingers fidget as I inserted the aerial plug. I completed the task and returned the radio to the box after the required time had elapsed.

'That's good. Just under one minute, very good. You'll get quicker over time. That is important. You realise as soon as you transmit, there might be someone trying to locate your signals? Speed and accuracy, stealth and calmness, these are the qualities you must possess to be a good agent.'

My smile was one of total agreement. 'I will work hard on the codes.'

'Where will you operate?'

I had not given this matter any thought. I wondered what his perfect location might be.

'Late at night I could transmit from the attic in the hotel where I live. I'd not be disturbed.'

Mr Brown nodded. 'And in the open?'

'That would be if I could safely travel with the box. I know it's not large but it would be obvious. I'd have to think that question over in my mind. Transmitting is about secrecy and I can't sacrifice that.'

'Good, you understand.' Mr Brown took a deep breath. 'You asked me about your code. It is Avalon, you are Avalon. Memorise it.'

A violin came to mind. That could be one way to remember it. Just one letter different. A violin, music and me, seemed appropriate. 'I can make an association,' I told him.

'Good. Now for Eicke... he's Muskel.'

'Perhaps I can write them down and keep them in my purse till they have settled in my mind.'

'I'm not keen that you do that. If you must, destroy the note as soon as you can. Or a very able lad orders nine.'

I did not understand his meaning. Orders nine what?' I asked.

He smiled at me. 'Think,' he said. Then he stressed

every initial word. '**A** **V**ery **A**ble **L**ad **O**rders **N**ine. Avalon. Do you think you can work on the codes very soon?'

'Yes, I am sure I can. You mean er... **M**y Uncle... **s**ells **k**eys... **e**very **l**unchtime.' I laughed. So did the Browns.

'MUSKEL... very good. Then Herr Eicke can expect you to send him a message next Wednesday at 10pm 22:00hrs? Got that?'

'I look forward to that.'

We smiled as if we had reached total understanding of our roles.

'Perhaps we can have some lunch now.'

Lunch was a plate of soup and a salmon salad. We sat in the lounge to drink tea afterwards. The Browns felt drinking tea was so very British. They would have preferred coffee but that was one of the necessities of espionage, they told me. 'Be like the indigenous. Don't show your roots.'

I lowered my voice. 'I presume you are not really Mr and Mrs Brown. I also don't think somehow, you will be going to Dornoch tomorrow.'

Mr Brown smiled. 'Dornoch?' he said.

'Hmmm... you'll make a good spy. Germany will be proud of you,' said Mrs Brown folding her napkin.

7

A Dying Secret

I felt awkward carrying this wooden box. It was not particularly heavy. It was rather cumbersome. The Browns had given me a large shopping bag to carry it and to hide it, a winter scarf. By the time I reached the Nethybrig Hotel it was dusk and I had already prepared my explanation, should I be challenged.

'Good evening, Frau Richter.'

'Fergus, please call me Mrs Richter. I'm not in Germany now.'

'Can I take your bag?'

'No, it's all right, thank you. I'm just going to my room.'

'Wait, there's a letter from Otto for you.' Fergus lifted it from the desk and handed it to me. Sure enough, on the back of the envelope Otto had signed his name.

'You sit down and read it; I'll take your bag up to your room.'

'It's all right; I'd prefer to read it in my room.' I placed the letter on top of my bag and grabbed the handles before Fergus offered again.

In my bedroom I hid the radio under the bed making sure the pink seersucker bedcover draped down to the floor. I carefully opened the letter. I felt close to Otto as I followed his neat handwriting. It reminded me of Willy's script.

I heard footsteps approaching.

'You are back dear. How was your visit?' Mother came up and sat on the bed. I noticed the bag appear when she sat down. A swinging of her legs would attract her attention. I had to think how I could explain that predicament, should it happen.

'Very well, we had a delightful time. But look, a letter from Otto.'

His letter had come at the most opportune moment. Her attention now focussed exclusively on her grandchild, her only grandchild.

'He tells me he's at the Officer training school in Baden Baden.'

'Going to be an officer, that's good.'

'He says he's now an Untersturmführer.'

'Oh, I see... what's that?'

'A second lieutenant. The lowest of the officer ranks but he goes on to say that after a year or two, he will be an Oberstumführer, a lieutenant. They must have a high opinion of him.'

Madge placed her hands on her knees letting her fingers drum her kneecaps. 'So he's no longer staying with his uncle?'

'No, he's at a military college now.'

Madge's tongue travelled over her left inside cheek. 'He's not going to be a doctor then, like his father?'

'Not yet, mother. After his training they will need doctors too. He hasn't gone off the idea. It's more that the nation needs a strong army and he's following orders.'

'I see. Does he say anything else?'

'He sends his love to you and granddad. It's a short letter. I suspect they are told how many lines to write.'

'Uhha ... I never saw him as a soldier. Hilda, I hope he'll be well looked after, he's still a young man.'

'I'm sure he'll look after himself too.' My heartbeat fluttered. I wished mother to leave but any rebuke would be ill advised.

'When you reply, make sure you send our love.'

'Of course I will, from both of you.'

'Well, the meal will be another half hour. You have a wee rest.'

'Just what I need mother, a good suggestion.'

Mother left the attic and descended the floors to the kitchen. I pushed the radio further back under the bed and went down to the telephone in the ground floor lounge. I was alone.

'Mr Dynes?'

'Yes, what news?'

'I have the radio and codes,' I said in hushed tones.

'Whose codes?'

'Mine and Eicke's.'

'The radio, what make?' he inquired.

'Delphin 7. You know it? It has an 800 mile range.'

'Yes, you'll need that. Don't transmit yet please. I need to see you.'

'But Eicke's expecting me to contact him. Don't you trust me?'

A silence ensued. My challenge was being evaluated.

I listened intently. I found myself twiddling with the telephone cord.

'Hilda, then send a brief message and note his reply.'

'Of course I will.'

Fortunately no one questioned my use of the telephone, this time or the time before. I had to have a valid excuse for so many actions that I began to slow down. I became more deliberate in my actions as the potential for lies grew by the day.

That night shortly after midnight, I opened the radio. I had a sharp pencil and a sharpener if required, to hand. I had my bedside light on and the hotel was as quiet as the night itself. I opened the top of the window gingerly. It resisted momentarily. I tugged at it. It made a slight noise. Again I listened to hear if anyone had been disturbed.

Then I placed the box gently on my bed. I sat beside it and took off my shoes. In stocking soles I felt able to move around more freely. I turned the set on seeing the bulb illuminate, moments later. My code book was beside me on the bedside table. I then took the aerial and plugged it into the back. The cable led through the open window to the quiet darkness of the stone rear wall of the dormer window. I secured my headphones and then gave my call sign.

'Avalon to Muskel.'

I waited for a reply. I held one earpiece in place while the other focussed on any hotel noises. My stomach was in knots. I took a mouthful of water from the glass I had brought up with me for the night. How had I fallen into this espionage trap? Would I ever get out?

I dialled again.

Within twenty seconds the set came to life.

'Muskel to Avalon. Greetings. Hope all well. Advise of any troop movements and air fields in northern Scotland. In January report back to Hamburg in person. Over and out.'

Eicke seemed to be a man of few words but what he said was unambiguous. Had I disturbed him too late in the evening? Was he scared that any lengthy call might be detected in Elgin? I was not sure. I replied simply that I had understood. I took the aerial down and packed the set away.

Only two points kept me awake. How could I report troop movement or count air fields when I had been ordered to return in January? Before breakfast I telephoned Thornton with the message I had received.

The following day was as wet a day as I could imagine, wet and cold. Was Germany wetter than Scotland? Perhaps my happy memories of Scotland were clothed in days of sunshine. Germany was the place of my maturity, a practical life and the number of days I had used the washing line were less numerous I seemed to feel.

Hailstones fell on the roadside outside the hotel like a scurrying of marbles heading one way down hill. Winter assaults were not uncommon even after the daffodil season had died. Towards mid-day as I watched through the lounge window, a car slowly drove up. Its windscreen wipers flapped vigorously. It parked just out of sight of the hotel entrance. There were two occupants, but both were very hard to distinguish. I notified reception that we had guests and made them ready to receive the men. I made myself scare retiring to the kitchen and placed a water filled kettle on the stove.

From the corridor I heard their voices and realised the home truth that I knew who they were. I grabbed a towel to dry my damp hands and walked smartly through to greet Messrs Dynes and Thornton.

'Fergus, three lunches please, we shall dine in the library.'

I led the men through, along the corridor to the library situated on the east wing of the hotel.

'Stunning views,' said Dynes standing by the window with his hands on his hips.

'I wish my lawn was as well kept,' said Thornton

They looked around the room and Dynes closed the library door.

'You will stay for lunch, I presume?' I asked.

'Indeed, that will be much appreciated.'

'Well, you received my call. What do I do now?'

'I don't think Eicke will be looking for a quick response. After all, he has set you off on a wild goose chase looking for troop movements,' said Thornton fiddling with his pearl cufflinks.

'Do you think Eicke got any inkling of you being a double agent?'

'I doubt it, Mr Dynes. The communication was not long. But my fear is that the Browns might appear or become aware of us meeting.'

'Don't you worry about the Browns. Their natural home is in London. They are employees of the German Embassy. They got the early train from Inverness the morning after your meeting.'

'I see. So I need not over worry about them?'

'It only takes a day for them to return.'

Thornton was right. I must not let my guard down at any time.

During a lunch of the famed local steak pie, Mr Dynes asked to see the radio for himself.

'That might be awkward. I can't let you follow me up to my room in the attic. That would not be appropriate. It would arouse suspicions.'

'I see what you mean. Have you any other suggestion?'

I was not sure why, other than for nosiness, that they wanted to see the radio. But who was I, to question my masters?

'I can bring it down concealed in a bag. If you were to wait in the car, I could come out at an appropriate time. I'd have to make sure my mother was not aware or concerned.'

I saw the men contemplate the potential difficulty.

'What if we found you alternative accommodation? That would make it easier to send messages and avoid suspicion,' Thornton suggested.

'I can't see how that would work. My father is poorly and my mother enjoys the extra help I can give, here at the hotel. I'd have to stay nearby and that does not fit well as I have accommodation with my parents which is not in jeopardy.'

Dynes pursed his lips. 'Does your mother know about you returning to Hamburg?'

'No, I plan to tell her after Christmas.'

Footsteps could be heard running along the corridor.

'Schhhh, change the subject,' I instructed as Mother entered the library.

'Darling come quick, it's your father...'

Dynes and Thornton stood up.

'I think we should leave. There's nothing more I can add to our discussion today. But we will keep in touch,' said Dynes.

'Do stay for lunch. It will be with you soon. I may join you later. Please stay.'

'Thank you very much, then we will,' said Dynes.

I entered my father's bedroom where mother sat holding his hand. Father looked pale. The curtains were closed. His eyelids only a slit under which unfocussed eyes rested. His hands lay motionless on the bed. Mother wiped his brow with a damp cloth. It seemed to revive him momentarily. His head veered towards me.

'Hil...da,' he said making heavy his words. 'I'm sorr... sorry. For...gi...'

'Father you have nothing to be sorry for,' I said as his voice trailed away. It had been a real effort for him to speak.

Then it was as if he had fallen asleep but we noticed not a breath seemed to come from his lips. How glad I was able to be with him at this point in his life but how sad it was to lose such a wonderful father.

'Dr Graham should be here soon darling,' said mother recognising it may be too late.

I placed my hand on his brow and then lay a finger beneath his nose. I was right. I could detect no breath yet I was reluctant to cover his face with the bed sheet immediately.

'Mother, father has died. Let's wait for the doctor to come to confirm what we already know.'

I looked at my father at peace for several minutes, unable to take my eyes off his face. Only when I heard the hotel front door bell ring, did I wipe the tears from my eyes. I rose and left the room to answer. Dr Graham headed straight to the back bedroom. I followed close behind.

'Frau Richter, I'm pleased to see you. Are you home permanently now?'

'Yes, for the time being Dr Graham. May I ask you to refer to me as Mrs Richter? I am a widow living in Scotland. I do not want to complicate things. I am sure you will understand.'

'Indeed, now your father...'

'Yes, please this room. I fear it will be too late. We have come to our own conclusion.'

* * *

(Rtd) Major James Campbell had taken his final breath that Tuesday afternoon at 1:15pm. The atmosphere in the hotel was sober but not depressing. Madge found great strength and gratitude in that I had managed to see my father before he died.

The funeral followed exactly a week later. At the gathering after the funeral at the hotel, there were representatives of his former regiment and the town's bankers and clergy not to mention the regulars who frequented the hotel's public bar most nights and who would retire to their high bar stools before the sun would set. The Masonic brethren were very well represented too. Most of the townsfolk attended the funeral. Although I recognised some, many were nameless to me. Then my face lit up. Approaching me was a woman in the prime of life. I knew her but had not seen her for years. My steps quickened as I opened my arms to her.

'Vera, how kind of you to come to the funeral.'

'My condolences Hilda.'

'Thank you.'

'I'm a married woman now. No longer Vera Caldwell, I married Tim Wild.'

'Wild? That's a name to conjure with.' We both laughed.

'It's a Wiltshire name, Hilda.'

'Wiltshire? My, you have travelled far. Where are you living?' I asked still holding her arm.

'Tim is the manager of Randall's shoe shop in Sauchiehall Street in Glasgow. We live above the shop.'

'And you? Are you working?'

'Yes, as a pharmacist in the local chemists.'

'By local, you mean Sauchiehall Street?'

'Yes.'

'You must have been travelling all night.'

'It seems so.'

'Are you staying overnight here?'

'No, if you don't mind Hilda, not this time.'

I looked at my niece. She was beautiful. I gave her a hug. It was overdue as my last sight of her was almost hidden in a car heading for the Danish border in 1914.

'Ahhh... Vera. I suppose you still blame me for bringing you to Germany on the eve of the First World War?'

'Now I look back on it, it was the most exciting time of my life, Hilda. But I wouldn't do it again. I was petrified what might happen if I was detained as an alien in their midst.'

'No Vera, we knew we could get you out of Hamburg. Fortunately the war had not got properly underway.'

'Underway? We were treated like cattle until we got on that boat to Harwich.'

We laughed a nervous laugh for each of us knew how scared we both were in August 1914.

'When are you going back to Germany?' Vera asked.

'I'll stay a little longer.'

'Yes... yes that's a good idea.'

Just then mother passed by. I touched her arm.

'Mum, a moment, here's Vera.'

'Ahh Vera, thank you so much for coming,' mother said taking hold of Vera's arm and patting it unconsciously. I moved away to have a word with some other mourners.

The day passed quickly, too quickly. Family and friends drifted away with felicitations of good wishes for our futures and promises to keep in touch. I hoped they would for mother's sake.

In a quiet moment, I found mother sitting by the stove in the kitchen on her own. She looked up seeing I had an unresolved question.

'Before he died, Dad seemed to be asking for forgiveness. Do you understand what he was trying to say?'

'Forgiveness? No... I can't imagine. I suppose it might have been something about his childhood or his army days. He never spoke much of those times,' said Madge.

'I don't think it would have been his army days. Any forgiveness there would have been dealt with accordingly a long time ago. No, he seemed to be apologising to me. I can't see why,' I said with a puzzled expression.

'I would put it out of your mind. You won't find the answer to that question now that he's gone. Let him beg his forgiveness for whatever it was with the Good Lord, who will be with him now.'

I went to bed not long after it became dark. An early night was on my mind, to recall a time of happier years growing up in Elgin, with two parents who were my world.

As I entered my loft room I noticed a glow from the crystal on the radio which I had left on by mistake. I took it out from under the bed. I wished there was a key to the door, but there wasn't. I closed the door shut. I placed my headphones over my ears and trailed the aerial out of the window. My pencil and pad were by my side. I answered the call with my code. It was Eicke.

'Sorry to hear your father has died. Accept my condolences.'

My fingers quivered as I replied. 'Thank you for

your kind words, Avalon. Out.' I returned the radio to its secret location, opened the bedroom door and wrung my hands. How could Eicke have possibly known of father's death? Then I remembered I had phoned Karl to inform him. Yes, he would have contacted Otto and my son's shadow would have gathered the news. How else could he have known?

8

Handel.
Was he German or English?

If father's final words were of little concern to mother, it should have been of less concern to me. Yet the thought lingered and niggled. I could not put it out of my mind at all. Yet, Madge was right. There could be no answer.

Mother bucked the trend of 'time in black' and found my presence gave her enthusiasm for her work. In the evenings we would retire to the lounge with mugs of hot chocolate and I would speak of the situation developing in Germany and how Otto, his aunt and uncle were coping. Such information was eagerly listened to. The news I imparted was fresh too. I had received more letters from Germany that week.

They hinted at the hysteria gripping the nation. Those who fought against it were ruthlessly treated. Karl and Renate spoke of the wonder of the rallies but I noticed when he wrote the word 'rally' it was in smaller text. Otto had thrown himself into the army officer training and had many friends. His letters always ended with his flourishing Otto signature and heartfelt, undying love.

As light faded I asked mother to play the piano which stood in the corner of the room with its lid closed.

'Hadn't you noticed dear? These days are over.'

'You don't play anymore?'

Madge laid out her hands before me. Her fingers were more fused together with arthritis than I had acknowledged before. I held both of her hands for a brief moment, massaging her knuckles.

'Then let me have a go. It's been a while.'

Musicians who play by ear adapt well to music. Those who played by reading the music lacked that ability but often played with perfection, I recalled. I was certainly of the latter. The first book of music found in the piano stool was Burlington Bertie by Harry B Norris. Madge tapped her knees to the waltz.

I played a few more tunes before turning to see mother sitting back with her eyes closed. I walked over to sit beside her. My movement disturbed her.

'You have stopped? I was enjoying that.'

'You were dozing. I haven't played the piano for several months now. In fact I've only played my oboe a few times in my room since I've been in Elgin.'

'I know. I've heard you. Mind you, you have been somewhat pre-occupied with your family.'

I looked at mother with a generous smile. Widowhood had not taken her by surprise. Father's final years had required much nursing and that period of her life was over. Now she had her daughter by her side and she felt relaxed.

'These men that have visited, can I ask who they are?'

My heart missed a beat. But I was ready with an answer. 'You mean Messrs Dynes and Thornton?'

'I think that's them, yes.'

'Well, they are officials from the Home office. They want to learn about my time in Germany. How things are over there. That sort of thing.'

'Yes, I see,' she chuckled. 'You'll never guess.'

'About what?'

'I thought they were spies,' she said laughing till her eyes wept.

No they were not the spies. They controlled them. But mother was not to know. I joined her in the noisy mirth as I rubbed my bony shoulder to eradicate an itch.

Two days later, a woman, a decade older than myself, a woman who stood ram rod straight with a superior look on her face arrived at the hotel. She rang the bell and Fergus attended to her.

'Mrs Richter,' he shouted from the centre of the hall.

I heard his summons from my room. I opened the door and called down.

'I'm upstairs, Fergus.'

'A visitor to see you.'

'Coming,' I said taking a glance at my hair in the mirror before descending. I patted my head hiding a few grey hairs above my ears. With each step downstairs, I nervously patted my thighs to remove unwanted flecks of dust. I met the woman in the reception area.

'Good morning Frau Richter,' she said with a smile struggling through her nervousness. 'I am Miss Maureen Robertson. Can I have a few moments of your time?'

'Certainly. Would you like some tea?'

'Only if you are having a cuppa.'

'Two teas please, Fergus.'

'In the library?' he clarified.

'Yes, that's fine.'

It was the weather we talked about as we walked along the corridor. That subject took us to the door. I opened it. The fire had flame licking logs making them crumble. The heat was immediately noticed and gave an aura of comfort as we sat on either side of the fireplace.

'Forgive me taking this opportunity to meet you. I suppose I am acting on instinct.'

'Really?' I could not imagine what was on her mind. She seemed as nervous as I was. Perhaps she was a double agent too. I was keen to hear what she had to say.

'I conduct the local orchestra.'

'Ah, now I can place you. I knew I had seen you before.'

Fergus arrived with a trolley. Its wheels jittered as it rolled from the wooden floor onto the carpet.

'I always enjoy coming to the Nethybrig. It's such a pleasant setting and serves wonderful meals.'

'Thank you. Mother and her staff do try to please our customers.'

I let Fergus pour the tea. The first sip made me relax. My eyes returned to Miss Robertson. She too had had her first sip and it let her thoughts flow as if it had been a different product Fergus had brought from the bar.

'It was a conversation with your mother, which I had yesterday, which pleased me so much.'

'Goodness knows what mother has been saying,' I laughed quietly.

'She told me you played the oboe beautifully.'

My mind raced ahead. Why this conductor was enquiring about my oboe meant one thing only. An invitation to join the orchestra must be forthcoming. I would have to decline to prevent notice being made of my January disappearance.

'Our wind section is not as strong as our brass. The addition of an oboe would be a wonderful re-alignment. Would you be willing to join the orchestra, Frau Richter?'

'Please call me Mrs Richter, or Hilda. Not Frau as I am no longer in Germany.'

'My apologies, I should have been more circumspect. Er... but the orchestra?'

'My staying here in the hotel is a temporary situation. I will be moving early in the New Year. I'd rather not take up your kind invitation. I'd disappoint the orchestra if I joined and left immediately. I hope you will understand.'

'Of course, I had no idea about your intention to leave Elgin. I suppose the move will not be local?'

'No, I'm afraid it will be several miles away.'

'You say you will be away in January? I mean, you will be here over Christmas?'

'Yes, I'll be helping my mother. As you can imagine, it's a busy time for the hotel.'

'Then you could join us in the church for the Christmas day service? We will be playing Handel's Messiah.'

I had fallen into her trap. It would be churlish to refuse. Yet this was a cherished piece of music and what was more, I knew every part of the score.

'If it's made clear, I'm only joining while I am staying

85

with my mother then I could join you for the Handel performance,' I felt that would suit us both as I secretly wished to play this familiar piece. I tried not to show how thrilled I was just thinking about the music of the Messiah.

'We'd be delighted Mrs Richter. The wood section will be so pleased.'

In the first week of December I attended the first practice session of the orchestra. I was in a comfort zone which laid my worries at rest. I enjoyed the challenge. Elgin being the size it was, meant I was not entirely unknown. Too many chose to call me Frau but I left it to Miss Robertson to put that matter straight. The following week was our final rehearsal by which time we were all comfortable with our performances. Notices about the performance were all over the town shop windows, pinned to threes and a full page spread announced the event in the local paper. No-one in Elgin missed the announcement. Mother was pleased that I had integrated myself into the community so well, especially with the orchestral contingent. So too was Eicke, when I sent a message informing him that troop movements were minimal and insignificant especially around the festive period, at which I would be playing my oboe in an orchestra.

Mr Dynes was not pleased. He told me I should not have been entrenching myself in the community. I had to remain circumspect and, well, aloof and free from attachments. I assured him that I was not intending to find a new husband but he took the view that others might be interested in meeting an eligible and talented musical widow. That, he told me, would wreck my usefulness and place myself in danger. Spies had to be alert and anticipate situations. Not suppliant and distracted. I felt he softened somewhat when I told him Eicke seemed pleased. It gave him cold comfort. I felt Dynes was anxious for me to be returned to my German family. He had to maximise my worth while I was in Elgin.

On Christmas day the orchestra filled the chancel space. I could not see an empty pew anywhere and some extra seats appeared down the outer aisles. The Reverend James R. Haddow led the congregation in prayer then settled back in his pulpit to let Miss Robertson get the oratorio underway. I did not know that this had become a popular annual performance. It did explain why the orchestra was so familiar with the music as well as the four soloists. The women's dresses were seasonally red, while the baritone and bass singers wore traditional black dinner suits. It was for all to see, a very professional performance that day, on the happiest of Christian festivals.

The performance of the Messiah lasted two hours and for most of that time I was seated behind a music stand as well as behind the string section. There was also a line of spotlights on the orchestra to enhance the view shown to an appreciative audience in the dimly lit pews. It meant I could not see the congregation but merely sensed their presence.

My first solo was to play *O Comfort Ye My People*. I

played it from my seated position and as I thought about the words I was playing, I realised My People came from two lives. As a consequence I played it with such feeling asking my oboe to spread the word that peace surely was still possible.

When my solo performance was finished I received smiles of delight from the cellist and second violins. I knew my performance had gone down well.

There was a fifteen minute break at which we retired from the chancel abandoning our instruments. We headed to the vestry. We took turns queuing for the lavatory. In that line I was approached by Miss Robertson.

'Hilda, that was a wonderful performance,' she said tilting her head in delight.

'Thank you Miss Robertson. I did enjoy playing it.' That was most certainly true. My grin was self evident of my delight and unexpected praise from the conductor.

'The tone of your instrument pierced the Church's atmosphere. It was a wonderful moment. In fact, can I ask you to go to the front of the chancel, at the top of the stairs, when you play *I Know that My Redeemer Liveth*?

'Oh I am sure that is not necessary. We are all playing well.'

'Indeed we are. However you will be playing after the choir and full orchestra play the Hallelujah Chorus. The audience will be excited. The next piece is yours and we need to hold their attention. I would really like you to come forward to play it.'

I accepted Miss Robertson as a woman who knew

her music and how to get the best out of her orchestra and the audience. 'Then I will of course.'

No one else congratulated me or anyone else during that break, there was still much to do. Our minds were concentrating on the music of the second part of the performance. Refreshed by a cool orange juice, we filed back into the chancel to take our places and don our instruments while we awaited the audience to settle.

I gave no consideration of my next solo performance but let my feelings be washed along in a majestic wave with the Hallelujah chorus. I played with my eyes closed. I knew every note by heart. The final notes were sung by the choir. The choristers resumed their seats. I then made my way through the orchestra holding my oboe upright to prevent damage.

I paced myself to arrive not too early but in time to compose myself. First I had to get used to the fact I could see more of the appreciative audience. I dampened the instrument's double reed with my tongue discreetly and heard the opening bars of my solo. I took a deep breath and began to play *I Know that My Redeemer Liveth*. My first note trembled. Then I settled into playing this slower movement which required long breaths of air. On these long notes I could not stop myself giving a trembling effect. Then I realised why.

My eyes had strayed to the left transept. It was as full as anywhere else in the church that day but there was no doubt, two familiar faces. Mr and Mrs Brown were in attendance.

It was tradition for Mr Haddow and his wife to give the orchestra a glass of sherry and a hot Christmas pie after the performance ended. We retired to the church hall for this reception. There was much chatter but my thoughts were to wonder why the Browns had returned to the area. Perhaps they had never left. Perhaps they had seen or overheard somehow, my conversations with Dynes and Thornton. Perhaps they had seen the concert notification and their presence was not at all sinister.

'Hilda, there are a couple waiting to see you in the vestry,' said Miss Robertson.

'A London agent I suspect,' said the bassoonist standing beside me. I looked at him keenly. What did he know about London agents? Why, these words? He saw my stare.

'Only joking, Mrs Richter. Music agents can give you some tours,' he said.

I made my way to the vestry where Mr Haddow was entertaining the couple.

'Goodness, Mr Dynes and Mr Thornton. I was not expecting either of you here.'

'No, I reflected on what you said last time. I may have over reacted. I think we both enjoyed your performance this evening.' Mr Dynes nodded his agreement. Mr Haddow tried to make sense of what was being said.

'I did not see you in the church. But I did see Mr and Mrs Brown. I was not expecting them to come and I think I had better try to find them before they leave. Would you mind if I saw them before they go? I'll keep in touch, I assure you.'

'I fully understand Hilda. Off you go,' said Thornton.

Dynes looked at Thornton for a brief moment. They would have loved to have seen, but not meet the Browns. Their anxiety was whether the Browns had any knowledge of their presence. That could never be known. Staying lost in a crowd and not together was in order and the minister encouraged that too.

'A sherry gentlemen and a Christmas pie perhaps. Come through to the Church Hall. I am sure there are plenty left.'

I placed my oboe case under my arm and left with my scarf wound round my neck. My long coat gave me some warmth as did my gloves. If I met the Browns outside, I was sure to become cold. I continued to walk towards the hotel with my ears open for a German whisper. Its tone would determine the conversation. I noticed a few set off home from the church and some called across the street to thank me for my performance. I replied as normally as I could. The hotel was in view. They were sure to contact me tomorrow I thought, as I looked at my watch.

I climbed the steps to the vestibule of the hotel and took off my gloves. Fergus approached looking at me.

'Your mother is entertaining a couple in the sitting room. I've just served them tea. Would you care to join them?'

'Do you know who they are?'

'No, not really, not from round here. Oh yes, a Mr and Mrs Brown I now recall. Yes, that's who they are.'

'Fergus, please bring me a tea too. I'll be with them.'

My heart missed beat. I strode quickly towards the

room. I did not knock. I entered to find Mrs Brown in conversation with mother while Mr Brown listened on with interest.

'Ah here she comes, the accomplished oboist,' said Mr Brown.

'I had no idea that you'd be here. I was not expecting you,' I said wondering if mother would stay any longer now she knew that they were my acquaintances.

'We had business up this way and saw the advert for the Messiah's Hallelujah Chorus was to be performed. It was on the church notice board, the library and goodness knows where else. One of Germany's best musicians,' said Mrs Brown.

'Wasn't Handel English dear?'

'Both mother. Born in Germany and spent his first forty two years in Germany. Then he came to Britain and took out citizenship. He was British for the rest of his thirty two years,' I informed her.

'More German than English then,' mother concluded as Fergus brought my tea.

'I had forgotten you played the oboe. I had been told by our mutual friend,' said Mrs Brown lowering her head at the same time raising her eyebrows.

I took that to mean we should be in discussion without mother's presence.

'Mother, I wonder if I could ask you... er..to...

'I understand when it's time to leave. I'm sure you will want to talk longer. Can I take your cups?'

Mother took the Browns cups and placed them on the try which had brought them. I held on to my cup.

'Not finished, yet,' I said as she made her way out.

With her right foot she managed to close the door behind her just as I was preparing to close it after her.

'Well, as I said this is a surprise.'

'A pleasant surprise Hilda, I trust?' Mr Brown placed his left hand into his breast pocket and brought out an envelope.

'This is for you.'

'More instructions?' I responded with an air of professionalism.

'No, not instructions. Just a little gratitude and to see you through the next week or so.'

I felt the envelope. It seemed to contain a wodge of money.

'Twenty pounds, I hope you will find.'

'Pounds or Marks?'

'On this occasion pounds sterling. Your next payment you will receive in marks in Hamburg.'

'I see, I am grateful to you.'

'No, you are doing well. You are integrating into the community, gaining its support and getting to hear the concerns of the locals, keeping an eye on military movements too. That's the information we need to know. Are they up for a fight or just muttering?'

'You mean you came up from London just to give me this money?'

'Who told you we came from London?' asked Mr Brown looking at me with concentrated eyes. It dawned on me the answer to that question was Dynes.

'You have brought money for me. I have not seen you for several weeks. Perhaps you have had contact with your London Embassy. That was what I thought.

Of course I may be wide of the mark.'

Mr Brown's expression was relaxed. 'You have remarkable logic, just what we need in one of our promising agents. Well done.'

'You mean you came here on Christmas day only to hand over the money?' I asked.

'A Christmas present not so? Now, don't disappoint me so soon. Yes, that is true and to hear you play but one spy does not tell another what they are doing. There is much work up here for us to do in the north of Scotland, further north of here as well. It's a very useful part of Britain for us.'

9

Return to Germany

After breakfast, as the winds began to make the sycamore branches dance, I telephoned Dynes. It was not convenient for him. He asked to meet me at the entrance to the churchyard at 10:15 that morning.

I could not get over the near miss of the Browns with my British handlers at the performance the previous night. I played through the evening in my mind. Why could I see the Browns but not Dynes? At least I had some forewarning but it did upset me at the time and those whose musical knowledge was superior, would have noticed the unnecessary nervous trill I played on my second oboe solo.

I asked my mother for a shopping list and set off with my basket at ten exactly. It took only five or so minutes to get to the church and as I approached the open gate to the cemetery, I saw Dynes seated underneath an oak tree.

'Good morning.'

'Good morning. Shall we walk down this line of gravestones?'

'A solemn thought,' I replied

The ash walkway contrasted with the cut green grass

edge. A dusting of frost still remained on both in sporadic amounts. I read each stone as I passed by noting the era of the 1850s was well represented, punctuated by the sadness of children's premature deaths.

'Why were the Browns in town?'

I smiled. 'I'll tell you what I got out of meeting them, a packet of pounds sterling and some intelligence for you.'

Dynes laughed. 'This espionage pays well,' he said bringing a brown envelope from his jacket's breast pocket. 'Here, your earnings from us. I hope they are at least compatible.'

'What a coincidence. Perhaps you should stagger my next payment or better still, let my bank manager... there won't be another payment, will there?'

A sudden realisation of who my imminent masters would be once more, made me realise I had seemed greedy. Dynes chose to ignore the question.

'When are you going back to Germany?'

'In three weeks' time.'

'Hmm... three weeks. Have you told your mother?'

'Yes,' I replied.

'How did she take it?'

'I am not sure if she realises the gravity of the situation. She sees my return home as my need to be in touch with Otto, Karl, and Renate.'

'Your return home?'

'When you live in two places, both are home, surely?' I could see Dynes thinking through what seemed to me to be an obvious statement. As usual his looks never truly betrayed his thoughts.

'You mentioned some intelligence?'

'The Browns are heading north they said. I imagine they will be heading for Scapa Flow.'

'They won't leave it alone, will they? Homage to the last war. Perhaps they are going to resurrect the German Navy.' I gave Dynes a playful tap on his arm.

'Perhaps they have already. My understanding is that they are going to assess Orkney's use for their air force,' I said.

'Leave that one to me. We will be monitoring them closely.'

We proceeded down the second line of tombstones. Fallen leaves trembled in the breeze amid the erect stone monuments. The occasional posy of winter pansies and holly brightened up the graveyard. I stopped at one gravestone to pay my respects.

'Your family?' Dynes asked.

'No, a soldier friend of my father who was killed in the Asante wars of the West African Gold Coast.'

'Did you know him?'

'Just a little. I would have been about ten or eleven years of age when I last saw him. As you can see, he was killed in the Ashanti wars in 1901.'

'So National service is ingrained in your family,' suggested Dynes flapping his arms against his body to keep warm.

'Yes. So, it would seem,' I said throwing my scarf once more around my neck.

'That brings me to consider giving you some combat training. It has been on my mind. You may find yourself in some tricky positions when you return to Germany.'

'Can you arrange that, as soon as possible?' I asked feeling sure this was in my best interests but against time.

Eicke was pleased to learn I was keeping myself fit through long walks and swimming. Getting around was sure to produce facts. The facts I gave were of little consequence. He received some appropriate newspaper headlines I had read and that kept him satisfied. His demands were general. He permitted me an extra two weeks before I was due to return. The truth was the training was gruelling; exhausting and at times painful.

I was taken to the Cultybraggan camp near Comrie in Perthshire where I crawled through bogs; climbed ivy roots to gain entry into an empty house; learned how to use a handgun; route marched and orientated up hills and down glens. The ten days seemed so long, and I began to count down the last few days towards the end. I met several men and women who kept well to themselves and were probably trained not to ask questions. Nor did anyone ever ask why I was there, a woman of almost fifty-one years of age, hardly an active service woman. But I was much fitter after my training. I appreciated that.

Mother knew there was more to my life by the time I shared my last day with her. We played rummy and drank tea as my luggage was already packed and my one-way ticket secured in my purse.

'We may never see each other again,' she said.

'Let's not talk that way, mother. Life is stronger than you might imagine. There are good people around.'

'And there are some whose ambitions are out of control.'

I nodded and as I raised my head, I saw the winter sun was out, casting long tree shadows on the lawn.

'What about a walk in the garden?'

Mother donned a winter coat, gloves, and a scarf which did not match or contrast but performed its warming duties. I arrived with my Brownie box camera.

'Let me take a snap of you over here beside the plum red leafed berberis. Don't stand too near or it will prick you,' I warned then laughed. 'Now over here with the hotel as the backdrop.'

From the hotel back window, I saw Fergus looking at us. He must have seen what we were doing. I saw him run down the staircase at speed probably missing every second step and then sprint along the corridor to the back door. He arrived out of breath.

'Here... let me take a... picture of you both. How many pictures have you left... in the spool?'

'Catch your breath Fergus first. It's a twenty-four picture film and I've got ten left to take.'

Fergus got us shoulder to shoulder and again in the same picture close-up. He found angles and colour with us smiling at him till he announced there were only three photos left.

'Glad you told me. Otto must see one with you alone; one with mother and then with myself and you.'

Darkness fell soon after on this mid-winter day and I went outside once more after supper to gaze at the stars.

I wondered if Otto was seeing the same stars or if Karl and Renate would see them too. I pretended they did. Then I wondered when I would return to Elgin? Would mother still be here? If the hotel was sold, where would I find myself? It made me feel as if an embracing, protecting Scottish arm was slipping from my shoulders. Or was it that I was already adjusting to being back in sombre Germany?

Aberdeen harbour contained the ship which would take me back to Hamburg. It was the Columbus which had flying on its stern, the swastika. From the moment I stepped onboard I would be a German widow once again. I would resume my Frau Richter persona.

Out of the corner of my eye I saw Mr Thornton appear. He greeted me.

'A final farewell?' I asked.

'I hope not. I hope you will be back in a year if not before. We need to know what's happening in Germany. You are in a prime position. You must keep alert; note everything; every detail. Make room in your memory. Do you have your radio with you?'

'No, I deliberately left it hidden in the hotel. It is to tempt the German Abwehr to let me return to use it.'

'I see. You will be given a new radio in Hamburg one to contact German agents in Britain, I presume.'

'I presume so but if I do, I will stay loyal to Britain. I know it will not be easy, but I will do the best I can. I assure you.'

'Of course, I expect nothing else. It only leaves me to wish you well and be safe.'

I suddenly felt a shiver down my spine. I knew I had been very forgetful. I opened my bag and gave him the film. 'Can I ask you to have this spool developed? Send one copy of each of them to me and the other to my mother.'

'And not one to me or Mr Dynes?'

'Not unless you wish photos of the hotel grounds and its occupants,' I laughed, and the laughter eased the tension of this imminent departure. 'No, not clandestine secret filming. Just the family.'

I was just about to thank him when he lunged forward to give me a kiss. But it wasn't. It was a firm hug and from that awkward heels-in-the-air moment, I thanked him, then gathered my hand luggage and made my way to the gangway.

No sooner had we left the sanctuary of Aberdeen harbour than the waves took hold of the ship. Fortunately, my cabin was mid-ship which made its longitudinal axis bobbing minimal. My nerves got the better of me. Had I made the right decision? How would I find Germany now that its fervour knew no bounds? Would I be able to cope with remaining a foreigner in the minds of nationalism? Yet I should be part of that having spent most of my life in the country. Only thoughts of seeing Otto and my family again seemed to keep me comforted that night as my bed rolled while sleep did not wish to overcome me. I looked at my black box but knew it to be safer in its cocooned case. Nor could I think of playing it, though it would always be part of me and I hoped I could play it again soon.

I seemed to find sleep eventually and the nervous energy and anxiety, with which I had brought to my pillow that night, had gone. I looked at my watch. It was seven thirty in the morning. I covered myself and went on deck to see if any land was in sight. There was none and only one other man out of earshot had taken to the deck. A crew member approached. He stopped in front of me.

'Heil Hitler, Madam. Breakfast is now being served in the dining room.'

I raised my hand.'Heil Hitler, I'll be there in a minute. Thank you.' The salutation I had almost forgotten came back to me with fear. I'd soon get used to it of course and learn not to think about it, yet it symbolised the regime, and failure to salute had its consequences.

After breakfast, I retired to my room. I had only been there a few minutes when I heard a long blast of the ship's horn. It intrigued me. I went out on the deck once more and saw at close range the battleship Scharnhorst glide past at speed. Then like a school of porpoises, the Unterseeboot fleet followed in a regular pattern behind the Battleship's stern.

The Columbus dropped speed to permit the convoy to pass by. Each U-boot had a white ensign bearing the swastika. The power of the German navy was there to see, although that would only be a fraction of their naval force. Where could it be heading? To challenge the British Empire, straining as all its colonies fought to break free from colonialism perhaps? Would it be their ally and dissolve the decades of our Colonial history?

Or would it come to their aid with false promises? It seemed that the world order was being shaken up with no consideration for how it would eventually resolve and settle its anger.

Four hours later the Columbus slowed down and was taken under line by two port tugs. I returned on deck to see Hamburg reappear, that friendly city which had taken me to its heart all those years ago. On the quay, I saw official cars. Everywhere men were in military uniform or naval dress. Meanwhile, the women of the city carried on with their domestic duties. They did so in a spritely manner anticipating what I could not guess.

We tied up and with my money exchanged on board, I paid to return home by taxi. I opened the front door and felt fustiness, dryness too but also the familiar vague scent of the Richter household. I opened the shutters in the sitting room, then the kitchen and bathroom windows.

I looked in the kitchen cupboards. It seemed Otto had cleared out all the tinned fruit and most of the tinned fish and meat. I did discover one tin of corned beef but there were no vegetables and no milk. I needed a basic larder replenishment and went off to fill two shopping bags.

I was recognised at the butcher and the dairy shop. That made me feel welcome as they inquired about my family and that they were pleased to see me again. I was not far from Karl's dental practice so despite being laden down by two baskets, I made for his clinic.

I entered. Renate had her back to me writing notes and so I approached the desk and placed my bags on the floor.

'I have a dreadful toothache. I need to see the dentist,' I said in the best of Hanoverian accents with the broadest of smiles.

'I'll be with you in a ...Hilda!'

Renate came from behind the desk and gave me a hug but when we parted I saw her tear-filled eyes.

'What's the matter, Renate?'

'It's Karl.'

'Karl? What happened?'

'He has been ordered to report to the army and serve as a dentist to the troops. I have no idea where he is at present.'

'Oh dear, what is life coming to? But what's happening here?'

'You will remember Anton Huber?'

'Yes, the retired dentist. I remember him.'

'He was asked to take over here, against his better judgement I'd say. His eyesight is not as it once was, nor does he have a steady hand. But Hilda these are insignificant changes. It's happening to many others. Karl is, as you know, forty-eight. Had he been fifty he'd have been given lighter work but I fear when the war starts he'll be in the forefront of battle. It frightens me.'

Pins and needles ran through me. 'You said when the war starts. Will it and when?'

'It certainly will. No one can stop it, I am sure. But when? It depends. We are taking over countries that have German minorities. If any of these countries react it could be the flashpoint for war. Remember 1914?'

'I certainly do Renate. How could I forget?'

I could see the pain in her expressive eyes under her

black eyelashes. 'And Otto, have you seen him recently?'

'Yes, not so long ago. You won't recognise him. He's grown. All that food and exercise he's getting at Baden Baden. But tell me when you arrived?'

'This morning. I've been shopping and thought I'd come here to surprise you. But you have surprised, or I should say, shocked me. I hope you will see Karl again soon.'

Renate gave a sigh from the depths of her lungs. 'Why don't you come over to me this evening for a meal? You will not get settled in a day. Shall we say, 7pm?'

'That's very kind of you, Renate.'

I walked back home seeing the militarisation of the city now as permanent. It was like a boil expanding all the time. When would it burst and when it did, who would it affect?

I had no sooner opened the door when the telephone rang. I placed my shopping down in the hall and lifted the receiver.

'Hello.'

'Welcome home, Eicke here. I hope the crossing was not rough. I want you at my office at 10am tomorrow morning, Gestapo Headquarters. Come smartly dressed. I look forward to seeing you once more. I'm pleased you have returned promptly.'

'Thank you, Herr Eicke. I look forward to our meeting again too.'

I replaced the receiver but held on to the phone to steady my hand. It seemed I was with Thornton so recently. And I recalled my London error with the

Browns. Was I really cut out for espionage? Would I trip myself up with this professional interrogator? The one thing I must not forget was that I was to be seen and known as a German spy once more and I must not mix up my roles.

I chose to walk for my morning meeting. The streets had not changed. I knew every inch of the way. Only the veneer of politics over the city was different. Lampposts were draped in flags, even the square where I brought Otto in his pram on sunny afternoons many years ago, had been marked out for troops to drill in step with their military brass bands. The public had to support these highly trained men. There was no doubt that they were extremely smart in their military appearance. Their impact was appreciated by all.

10

Meeting Reinhart Heydrich

As instructed, my attire was more formal than usual. I chose to wear a navy-blue suit and a white blouse. I wore the necklace which Willy gave to me on the night we were engaged to be married. I had no idea why he had asked me to dress with greater attention. Perhaps I would be meeting officials, thankful about my efforts on their behalf, or perhaps they might find me out.

Outside the Gestapo headquarters in Hamburg, two armed guards stood at ease. Their outsized riding trousers were immaculately creased at the front and their stare was straight. Their helmets almost covered their eyes. Being on guard duty in a nation not at war seemed to be a menial position but they performed their duties with exemplary efficiency as they came to attention simultaneously as I approached.

I was about ten steps away from them when they withdrew their ceremonial swords from their sheaths and presented arms as I turned to walk between them. I did not look back but by the boot stamping that followed, I knew they were once again at ease, even though I wasn't.

I reported to the reception desk where a young woman greeted me.

'I have an appointment with Herr Eicke this morning at 10am. I appreciate I am a few minutes early.'

'Your name, please.'

'Frau Hilda Richter,' I said with a firm voice.

Without saying a word, the receptionist lifted her telephone and held it to her ear. I could see no one else around but heard boots and stiletto heels as their studs and solid leather heels drummed out their importance on the marbled floors above. I had known this building to have been the main bank in the city; one I had visited in the past. It had been commandeered by the state police but the marble floor and most of the banks' many paintings remained. On each floor level however, space had been made for a portrait of Adolf Hitler as I could see clearly on the floors above me.

'Frau Richer, SS-Gruppenfuhrer Eicke is ready for you now. Proceed to the third floor and you will be met by someone to take you to him,'

'Thank you,' I said realising either he had promoted himself or he had been seen to be a valued cog in the frenzied wheel. Major Eicke gave him authority, but would it be beyond his capabilities? I had my secret doubts. I made my way up the carpeted steps counting the floors. Not everyone was in uniform. Men dressed in double-breasted suits and often brown leather shoes walked purposefully with files under their arms. Everyone seemed to have files. Was I the subject of one?

As I cleared the last step, a man in a military uniform met me, his heels clicking as if to draw my attention to him.

'Frau Richter?'

'Indeed.'

'Follow me, please.'

He took me to the end of the floor then we turned left. The third door on the right caught my eye. I studied it carefully. SS-Gruppen Fuhrer Gerhardt Eicke, District Commander.

My escort knocked on the door and entered still holding the doorknob in his left hand. I was not yet invited in.

'Frau Richter, mein Gruppenfuhrer.'

'Bring her in please,' said Eicke rising from his chair. We greeted each other with formal handshakes and smiles in the middle of his office.

'I am very pleased to see you again, Frau Richter, especially this morning. But first tell me are you well?'

'I had a tiring voyage but I have recovered now. Good German air to breath and fresh vegetables and meats, how could I not be healthy?'

Eicke laughed at my response. He seemed a much friendlier, a less intimidating man from when I first met him, after Willy's funeral.

'Can you tell me more about how things are in the north of Scotland?'

'Certainly, I can, but today I am glad to be back home in Germany.'

'I'm pleased to hear that. There was not even the slightest doubt in my mind that you wouldn't return.'

'Of course,' I said to placate him. 'I have met the Browns a few times now. They are very well suited to be in Britain. Their accents are more than passable, they are really very good. Some even think they are South African, and I can see why they think that.'

'Excellent. The Browns are coming up to their fifth year in Britain.'

Eicke opened his silver cigarette case.

'You don't smoke do you?'

'No, I don't.'

'That's right, I had forgotten.'

He lit his cigarette from his lighter which he then pocketed. He drew in the smoke and exhaled as he turned towards me. It gave me time to question his new status.

'I could not help but notice. Your name on your door. Promotion I see.'

He smiled. 'I began in the police and then was moved to the state police, the Gestapo. Now I am in charge of the Hamburg question. The SS are driving it and I'm at the helm in this city.'

'The Hamburg question, you mean the Jews?'

'It's no secret Hamburg homes the largest Jewish population in the country. That will be addressed. It's going to take its time, as you can imagine.' He took another draw of his cigarette.

'Does this mean I won't be communicating with you again? Will I report to someone new?' I asked to clarify his information. I wondered if I should bring out my notebook and pencil to record this informative encounter.

'No, I need to know what information you will provide in the future. It will come in useful; I assure you. I have superiors too, you appreciate.'

'Then you have plans for me to return soon?'

'Plans for you to return, yes. But not yet.'

'What am I to do in the meantime?'

'You have done well when you were in Britain. I and my seniors am pleased with your work. Now we have a greater need for you. We'd like to improve your communication skills. We will give you a special state pass while you are in Germany and a cover British Identity card for when you return. You will need photographs taken and that is one reason why I asked you to dress smartly.'

'I see, but why did you seem so reserved to me when you telephoned? You could have told me that I was simply being asked to have photographs taken.'

'Yes, I know. That's true but I am meeting a senior officer at noon, here in my office. I could not tell you before. It was a secret. I hope you can attend. He wishes to meet you.'

'And who is he?'

'That remains, as I said, secret for the time being.'

I was taken to a photographer's room in a back room of the building. A light shone on a plain white wall with an umbrella directing the beam. There were two assistants: a man and a woman. The woman attended to my hair for the first picture. Then she placed a broach to hide the top button of my dress. I looked in the mirror to see it was a gemstone swastika. Flash. The first picture had been taken. Another flash before I got out of the seat. Then I was given a slightly different hairstyle, my hair almost falling over my left eye, and the broach was removed. Two photos were taken. The photographer retired to the dark room. The lady then brought me to a desk where my signature was required.

I was brought a coffee and asked to wait. Twenty minutes later the photographer returned with his pictures. He let me see them.

'Two different people,' I said looking at my two images.

'Two different lives perhaps,' he said. I looked at him. He was probably in his early twenties, young and impressionable. Was he that perceptive as well?

'I will post both completed passes to you tomorrow.' The telephone rang. The photographer took the call and as he held the receiver to his ear, he turned to look at me.

'You have to report to Gruppenfuhrer Eicke's room, now. Please knock first.'

I walked back along the corridor wondering who might want to meet me. It could be Karl as a good will gesture by Eicke perhaps, even Otto on leave from his training. I was excited to find out and hurried my pace. I stood in front of the door and knocked twice.

Eicke came to the door and smiled as he met my eyes. Beyond him I could see a tall, elegant, blond man. As I entered, he turned towards me with piercing blue eyes. I had seen this man in the papers, a cultured man from a family of distinguished musicians, I was about to meet one at the very heart of the State Police. "The man with an iron heart" as Hitler himself called him.

'Hilda, meet SS-Obergruppenführer Reinhart Heydrich.'

I held out my hand to shake his, but he took hold of it and turned it over, then kissed the back of my hand.

'It is a pleasure to meet you,' he said in a remarkably high voice which had been commented on in the papers during the very early 1930s but never since. He must surely carry a burden of embarrassment with his speech defect, but his actions were more profound. This man was a killing machine and proud to serve in that role. My knees were trembling. I was in a lion's den.

'Your late husband, Willy Richter, I think?' he said opening his hand to show me to a chair.

'Dr Willy Richter, yes, my deceased husband,' I confirmed wondering how he knew as I sat down.

'He began his medical career in Halle an der Saale, not so?'

'Yes, I believe so, but that was before I met him, here in Hamburg.'

'Of course. My parents were very fond of him.'

'Really?' I thought he must have noticed my incredulity in questioning any connection with this beast of a man whose flick of a hand sentenced a man, or woman, or child for that matter to death without a hint of a hesitation.

'Halle an der Saale is my hometown, where I was born. My mother had been very ill, devastating for a music teacher. Dr Richter was called to our house where he administered his medicine. Over the weeks mother's strength returned. They used to discuss their love of music too. But it was in an act of kindness, our family will never forget. The doctor asked for no payment for his services for my mother's condition and eventually, her full recovery was underway. We were very sad to hear he was leaving to go to Hamburg. That was of course your good fortune.'

My smile recollected Willy's warm nature. It did not surprise me he had not requested payment. His patient was always his priority. I smiled at the fact his departure from his hometown recognised my good fortune.

'I feel a debt is owed by my family to you, Dr Richter's widow.'

'That is very thoughtful, but I think not necessary.'

'Let me be the judge of that,' he said tapping the table twice. 'I hear you have been sending reports from Scotland, meeting our agents there and returning for more instructions. Espionage is a very courageous life, a lonely life too. I am not cut out for it myself. Spies do not always have the longest of lives and so we must be grateful for their information when it comes and I wish to show you how grateful I am, and to record my gratitude to your late husband.'

He lifted his brown leather case from the floor and opened it. He brought out a black box. Once more I was staring at a swastika.

'Frau Richter, please stand,' he ordered.

Eicke stood too. I was one of his own prodigies and his smile reflected that fact. I stood tall feeling he had a broach to give me in respect of Willy's appreciated healing powers. But I was wrong.

'Frau Richter, I hereby award you the German Eagle Civilian Medal in honour of your service to the Reich.'

He placed the red and silver ribbon around my neck and stood behind me to secure the eyes of the hooks. He then stood in front of me at attention and raised his arm in salute. 'Heil Hitler.'

I raised my arm even higher. 'Heil Hitler,' I said with gusto and false pride.

If only Dynes and Thornton knew how close I was to the centre of the Reich machine at this moment, they would have been proud of me. Receiving a German Eagle Medal however must have made them shake in their boots. Just whose side was I on?

We celebrated the moment with a glass of sherry. I discovered Heydrich was indeed a cultured man when the topic was music, but I would not be dancing to all his tunes. After fifteen minutes of social niceties, the meeting came to an end.

'We need detain you no longer, Frau Richter. Germany expects great results from you. You are a real credit to the Reich.' I had made Eicke's day. He walked with me to the door with the self-satisfied smug grin of a proud father.

My smile was neither strong nor weak. It was one designed to give him confidence in me and no more. I left their company and closed the wooden varnished door behind me.

I felt my shoelace had come undone. Indeed, it had. I kneeled to tie my wayward lace taking only one step forward. As I stooped, I heard faintly but clearly that Eicke had queried my award. I stayed frozen to the spot, slowly securing my lace. Heydrich's high pitched voice was bell clear. He responded that I needed an incentive to stay German. 'Once back in Britain, she must not lapse,' the Blond Beast said. They certainly valued my position. I could play that to my advantage if necessary. I moved away smartly quietly and better informed.

11

Otto Finds the Reward

Rain fell like a brooding spirit assaulting my lounge window with a lateral force that Tuesday morning. Outside, the traffic was scarce. Cyclists bent forward, pedalled hard but made little progress as the rain hindered. Pedestrians sought shop awnings and those crossing the road sprinted as quickly as their umbrellas would allow. I looked at the sky, heavy grey clouds lingering over Hamburg, arriving from the North Sea. It may have been spring, but the budding trees' branches hung low and the daffodils by the roadside were dejected and flattened.

It was a day to get small jobs done. I had a list to attend to. I sat down to darn a sock, my glasses slipping to the end of my nose to gain focus. Then the front doorbell rang. I was not expecting anyone. I put down my sewing carefully and stood up. I hesitated. Eicke may have brought some instructions worked on and approved over the weekend. He had arrived to deliver it. After all, I was not expecting anyone else. I made my way to the front door as the door was knocked once more. Taking a deep breath then relaxing, I fixed a welcoming smile on my face and turned the latch.

Standing before me was a uniformed soldier.

'Otto, my darling. Come in.'

Our embrace lasted the best part of a minute as I showed my delight in muffled comments, said as he spoke about his leave.

'Yes, two days only. But home cooking I hope.'

'Oh yes Otto. Now put your bag down and come through. Tea?'

'Er...coffee please.'

'So, still in Stuttgart?' I asked boiling the kettle on the gas stove.

'I'm not meant to tell you.'

'Oh, so not Stuttgart, you have finished there?'

Otto entered the kitchen and pondered the son and mother relationship for a moment. If he had secrets surely his mother, he could trust.

'Well, soon. My unit is still there for the time being. We train in other places though. But yes, Stuttgart that's the base and from there I've been allowed five days leave.'

I turned round in delight. 'Wonderful, five days, that's almost a week, darling.'

'Not really mother. Transport to Hamburg was not easy and I stopped in Andernach overnight, anyway. I've just got two days here, before I return.'

'Andernach? Between Frankfurt and Cologne?' I asked as he freely shared this new destination.

'Yes, visiting a friend,'

Thank goodness he had not lost his old friends. 'A friend from Hamburg? Would I know him?' I asked stirring his coffee. There was a delay in his response.

'It's a girl, Gisela,' Otto said almost as an admission.

'A girl? You must tell me about her. Where did you meet? What does she do?' I shouted through from the kitchen realising that my little boy had grown up and was becoming a confident young man. I brought the tray through with a broad smile on my face. The prospect of a larger family in due course came to my mind, a prospect I had hoped one day would come true. But with Gisela? How would I find her? I was keen to learn more.

'So, tell me how you met her?'

'You remember me telling you about my friend, Paul Hoffmann?'

'Yes, the red headed one?'

'Yes, a bunk mate. We're best of friends.'

'And Gisela?' I had to interject to keep my focus on his new friend.

'She's, his sister. She came to visit Paul and we went out to a few cafes together, all three of us. On the last day before she returned, I took her out alone.'

'So Gisela Hoffmann. How old is she?'

'She's eighteen, too.'

I recalled being a girl of eighteen myself. A student only just beginning to feel the first rushes of love.

'And what's her work?'

'She's a personal secretary.'

'I see, family business in Andernach?' I asked after sipping my cup a couple of times.

Otto stood by the window in a moment's silence. He was presumably contemplating how I might react; how I might take his news. I was right.

'She is Secretary to SS-Unterscharfuher Soren Böhm of the 9th SS Panzer Grenadier.'

119

That was not what I was expecting but on reflection, not an unsatisfactory relationship from my point of view. In due course it might be approved by Eike. 'So that's where his unit is, Andernach,' I concluded.

'If you promise on point of death, my death and yours, not to tell anyone, Andernach is where we have been training when we were not in Stuttgart.'

Dynes and Thornton would be pleased to have learned this information. Meantime I stored it in my mind, compartmentalised for security.

'It sounds so secretive. It's not really, is it?'

'Our training can be physical, manual, or cerebral. Andernach is our espionage centre. We learn how to recognise the enemy within.'

How funny. It seemed we had been recently pupils of the same dark arts. 'The enemy within?' I repeated.

'Yes, traitors, you know mother, Jews, homosexuals, vagrants, gypsies. All who do not support Germany's aspirations?'

'That's the work of the Gestapo surely?'

'Yes that's true but they need our information too,' said Otto.

I feared what my son had become. An agent of the State. An inevitable journey I supposed but one which frightened me.

'You realise, your aunt Renate... her grandmother, was a Jewess?'

There was a moment of complete silence broken only by the grandfather clock striking the half hour. It was a seminal moment for Otto to realise how complicated reporting people might become.

'But Renate, Aunty Renate, surely not, she's not a Jew?

'No, she is not Jewish?' Otto's eyebrows relaxed in relief.

'No, her mother married a gentile and Renate married your father's brother. So not all Jews are Jewish, are they? You must remember that.'

Otto seemed to contemplate the truth that there was non-Aryan blood in his close family, even if that was blood grouping through marriage.

'Then I will not divulge that. I promise not to inform about her... mother... I wish you had not told me.'

I internalised all Otto was saying. Indoctrinated by a system I had no control over or within. We finished our drinks contemplating what we had divulged.

We played chess after we had eaten that night. It brought back happy memories with our erstwhile family. Otto had not forgotten his moves, learnt from a loving father who had taught him so much. Willy was a keen board player and chess was his second love. Of course, he told me so often, that I was his first. I could never beat him at the game. My mind never stayed in concentration mode for long enough. That had now become a valuable ability as a spy as I had to always stay alert and adapt to the circumstances I faced.

It was almost midnight before we turned off the light in the lounge and we prepared for bed. I heard Otto in the hall but thought nothing of it. It was good to have a man around the house once more. Soon I heard his bedroom door close, the lights were out, and I entered sleep as content as could be with my indoctrinated son at home with me once more.

I made porridge the following morning and we sat in the dining room with our steaming hot bowls before us.

'Last night, before going to bed, I loitered in the hall.'

'Yes, I heard you. Admiring the paintings?'

Otto did not reply instantly to this simple question.

'No mother, I opened the sideboard drawer and found a German Civilian Eagle with its crease-less ribbon. Is it yours?'

My God, how silly of me. How foolish I had been. I should have hidden it in my bedroom but now it had been found. How much could I possibly tell him?

'If I were to tell you Otto, my life would be at risk...' I said looking at him for his response.

Otto smiled recognising his own statement of the day before being thrown back at him.

'Is it something to do with your joint nationality?' he surmised.

'Your training is good Otto. Let's leave it at that.' Had I placated him sufficiently?

'But it's an award. How did you earn it?'

I stood up and patted Otto on his back. I massaged his shoulders as I spoke.

'Too many questions my young man. I obviously pleased my superiors.' Then my finger was raised to my closed lips as I turned into his line of sight. He could be proud of me without obtaining the information I was keen to withhold, and he wanted to know. He relaxed and I knew he would find out one day how I had earned this medal. This was his last day with me, and I could see he did not want to spoil it, nor did I. But deep inside Otto must have been very proud of me. It showed in his youthful smile.

Otto left the following morning. I did not let him go without giving him a tight maternal hug in the hallway. He was once more in his smart army uniform but with my eyes closed, he was the schoolboy in his trench coat, heading for school.

'To Andernach then?'

'Yes, then back to base.'

'I'd like to meet Gisela one day,' I said.

He smiled a broad smile. 'You may. If all goes well, you will certainly get to know her.'

'Otto, I wish you much happiness.'

'Thanks, mother. You know you will always be my longest love.'

'I hope I'll be your second love one day, Otto. Now off you go and keep safe.'

I closed the door and went to the lounge window. Otto walked down the drive but never looked back. He was preoccupied with his youthful thoughts. I remembered that feeling so very well some thirty years ago. A first love was so precious. My eyes followed him until he was out of sight, and I wondered how, where and when we would next meet.

12

Baden-Baden: The Spy School

Otto's visit had pleased me immensely. He was after all, the only male in my immediate family, my only son. My only fear was that the war was inevitable, and I wanted to remain in close contact with him through this troubled time. I felt deep inside the war was soon to start. I hoped it might be over very quickly and that would be the best result for all.

The letters that dropped on the hall carpet that morning were my two passes. One to be kept safe in my home till I returned to Britain and the other to always carry. It was a guarantee that there would be no restriction on my travels. I wondered what the travels in Germany might entail. Then on closer inspection my British card showed my name as Mrs Hilda Campbell. I looked again at the German pass. Frau Hilda Richter. My split personality knew which pass was which. I telephoned Eicke.

'My passes have arrived today.'

'I had meant to tell you that when you are in Britain,

you must be called by your maiden name, Miss Campbell. It is a very Scottish name, I believe. Not so?'

'Oh yes, very much so,' I replied with an unseen gentle smile.

'You will soon get used to it once more. Your name Frau Richter must never exist in Britain.'

'I can't change my name in Elgin or when speaking to my mother. Rest assured not a word of German in Great Britain.'

'You will not be posted in Great Britain or Scotland.'

My mind was all over the globe. If not a return to home, just where might Eicke place me?

'Not home then?' I clarified what he had just said.

'No. Your next appointment, next month, I want you to go to a school. A school that will have spies like you. You have much to learn and time is of the essence.'

'Next month?'

'Yes 3rd July.'

'And where is this?'

'Bautzen.'

'Bauzen? Where's that?'

'Take the train to Berlin and then on to Dresden. We'll give you a rail pass. You will be collected from the station. Any questions?'

'How long will I be there? And can I tell my son?'

'You will be there for six weeks. At the end of that period, you return to Hamburg and I shall make arrangements for Otto to have some leave so he can visit you. I will also ensure his letters will be sent to you. But your movements are secret. It does not concern Otto. You understand?'

'Yes, of course. Of course, I realise I can't talk.'

'In difficult times, we have to make some sacrifices. Sometimes niceties can be fitted in to ease the mind. But there is a watershed. Woe betides those who cross it. If in doubt, don't talk at all.'

'So, I make my way on the third?'

'Yes. Your bank account has been funded for that duration, but you will be catered for and given the use of a launderer and cook.'

'Then I look forward to the training.'

I was awake at dawn. Trees were in full leaf. Swallows were soon in flight darting with style around the city and then lodging in gutters and I was ready to travel.

Hamburg Hauptbahnhof rail station was busy. Naval personnel were numerous making their way to submarines and battleships at ports along the north coast. Soldiers with different shoulder flashes consulted the overhead destination boards for forward postings and the debonair Air Force officers seemed aloof probably longing for the day when they could fly above the skies. Uniforms were many and comforting. I felt our troops confident and prepared for what would happen before long. Others in the station had a more sinister look about them and not before too long one of these officials approached me.

'Madam, your ticket please,' he said holding out his hand.

I showed him the voucher I had been given to travel. It bore Eicke's signature.

'Where are you travelling to?'

'Berlin.'

'What business do you have there?'

I took out my new pass and opened it. I turned it towards his eyes.

His hesitation was clear. His spot check was out of order. He climbed down. 'Very well madam, have a safe journey.'

I breathed a sigh of relief as I slalomed my way through other passengers to platform four.

Out of my eye I caught a commotion. I saw three men in trilby hats, with pistols to the fore, detain a family set to travel. The father protested in the loudest of voices, but no one came to his aid. Many just watched as the incident developed. Other plain clothed policemen came to assist in the family's detention and moments later they were dragged out of the station concourse, and all was in order again as if nothing had happened.

'They would have been caught at the port of embarkation, Cuxhaven probably,' a man said loudly, sneering his disdain of the Jewish family. I presumed they were Eicke's workers.

The change at Berlin went well with fewer in military attire but perhaps even more secret police eyeing every passenger's movement. Nervousness and tension attracted their interest as well as the age of the traveller. Perhaps I was already seen in a less-than-flattering age group. I was beginning to feel my age and that was no bad thing to realise in the present tensions. I felt perhaps if I let drop some longer pieces of grey hair from under my hat, I might just gain a little more deference.

My carriage seat was by the window. I pulled up the leather strap and lowered the window slightly. My compartment companions had no objection indicated by shakes of their heads. Everyone seemed suspicious of everyone else and conversation risked exposure to unwelcome comments. We set off to Dresden. I gazed out of the window. Soon industrial factories faded, and green fields dominated the land flying by at a good pace. How nonchalant were the cows ignorant at the pace the country was travelling with optimism. While hens and chicken scurried as the train approached their fences. Clothes lines had sheets dancing in the breeze and the occasional horse drawn milk carriage seemed to be stationary as we sped by. Such perfect silent calmness dominated my feelings. Being at one with my adopted home made me wonder if I would ever reach British shores again now that I had apparently tied my colours to the mast?

I knew what the next few weeks would bring. More training certainly, but it was crucial that I did not show any of my Scottish mannerisms. I was not concentrating when the man beside me spoke.

'I said are you visiting family?'

'No, on business.'

'I see.'

'And you?' I asked.

'I am visiting my grand-daughter, Elise. Her father is away in the army and her mother has her hands full. I thought I'd come and assist.'

I smiled realising domestic necessities remained in people's lives. I could see him reading to his grandchildren on his knees. 'I am sure you will be made very welcome.'

'And you have family?' he continued.

'Yes, a son. My husband died.'

'My condolences. He will avoid the troubles.'

'The troubles?'

'You don't think there will be a war?' he asked.

'It is looking like it will be soon,' I replied.

This man wanted to talk, I didn't. The strain of what I could say made me look out of the window. It was late afternoon, the sun still shone brightly and the air warm and clear. I closed my eyes but I did not sleep. I deprived my companion conversation and was left to contemplate my uncertain future.

I gathered my suitcase and belongings and left the train at Dresden. The car to Bautzen was comfortable until it drove through the town onto a minor road. Three miles or so later the car came to a halt and a series of huts came into view. I had arrived at my accommodation for the next few weeks. I was determined not to let it get me down.

The female quarters were at the end of the huts, and I was advised to go there where I'd be met. I made my way over and saw a woman at the window. She seemed to smile. I returned the gesture. She opened the cabin door.

'Hi, I guess you are Hilda?' she said in an American accent. I was very surprised.

'I'm Nancy Krause and you are?'

'Hilda Richter,' I said wondering if I had been led into a trap so soon.

'So we're here to learn the black crafts, yeah?'

'If you say so,' I said without too much enthusiasm or apparent knowledge.

'This is your room. Mine's at the other end. We've got a kitchen and bathroom. That's about it.'

'How long have you been here?' I asked.

'Sailed into Hamburg a week ago; got down here three days ago.'

'Sailed from where?'

'New York, of course.'

'So you are American?' I stated the obvious.

'Sure thing. Yes, naturalised in 1934, but a Nazi at heart.'

'So, you from England?'

I hesitated. 'No Hamburg.'

Nancy hesitated. 'Come on you can tell me. You're here to be sent home like me. So, where's home really?'

It became clear. We were all here to be trained as spies and sent to our homelands on espionage duties.

'Scotland. That's where I was brought up.'

'I guess we'll get on real fine. My German is rusty, and I guess yours is pretty good. You can help me if I'm not picking up the instructions.'

'When will they start?' I asked.

'Tomorrow at 8 am.'

13

A Pupil of the Dark Arts

The next day Nancy and I sat together as four men, probably in their late fifties, came into the room. They wore their hair very short, all rather well built, and had unmistakable American accents, hiding the occasional guttural German nuance.

'Hi, I'm Carl, with a C. Taxi driver from Baltimore. Carl Jaeger originally. Glad to meet you all.'

'Well, I see it's introductory time. I'm Max, originally Maximilian Becker, and since 1931, the naturalised American Max Baker. Ma Bakers' Diner. I'm the chef, cook and bottle washing manager. Breakfasts our speciality in Queens, New York.'

'And Carl, your surname Jaeger, that's a Hunter now, I presume. Carl Hunter?'

'Right first time,' he said.

'I'm Wilmer Lange. Willy Long now. Bus driver downtown in Boston. Naturalised American in1929. Pleased to meet ya.'

'That leaves me. I'm Arnie Koch. Naturalised in 1930. Arny Cook, post office worker New York.

'I'm Hilda Richter, widow of Hamburg doctor Karl Richter.'

'And your espionage identity?'

I hesitated. I was uncomfortable. It felt it was too soon to reveal the name I'd be using in Britain.

'Still to be confirmed,' I said and turned towards Nancy with eyelashes looking heavenward, as if in a tease.

'So I complete the happy spy ring. Nancy Kruse, airline office New York since 1935.'

The door opened and a man in military uniform entered. He epitomised the Aryan persona. Tall, blond, with immaculate trousers creased and a silver topped cane which he rested on the table. He spoke in a Prussian German to begin with, then in solid Home Counties English.

For the benefit of our American friends he began, he would speak English as a language we all understood.

'It is an honour to meet you all. My name is Sturmbannführer Konrad Glauber. I have detailed notes on all of your backgrounds and although most of you will be returning to America, except Miss Campbell of course, your training will be together.'

I felt eyes turning towards me questioning why I did not disclose my new personality.

'Did I say something...?' asked the Major noticing the eyes turned on me.

'I think they are questioning why you knew my overseas name was Campbell but it seemed I didn't. I can explain. I had just met everyone here and was initially reluctant to give anything away. I am Hilda Campbell, when I am in post,' I said hoping my explanation would not detract from our blossoming trainee friendships.

'Commendable, Miss Campbell. Our American friends are more open than we are. It is a difference we must make exceptions for. America is not at all like Germany. One day, however... well... let's leave it at that.'

There was a rumbling of approval from the wooden floor as feet stamped underneath desks.

The morning was spent outlining the programme planned. We would work in teams at times and as individuals in map reading, orienteering, and assault course muscle-building exercises. Muscles that I had put to rest over recent years apart from a brief outing at Cultybraggan not so long ago. There would be more specific espionage training in such areas as preparing coded messages and micro photography. Transmitting frequency apparatus was there to practice on and special codes were committed to memory. We were made privy to some Army briefings too.

After two weeks I was settled into the regime of instruction. I learned much about my American colleagues, who had left Europe to find a better life but had been disillusioned in the depression years of the early 30s in America. The rise of Hitler gave them that missing Messiah and their allegiances moved from the stars and stripes to the bold black swastika. They also told me of the network of fellow American spies already trained and in post along the eastern seaboard. There seemed to be dozens at work on the other side of the Atlantic. I wondered if Thornton or Dynes knew these details.

One night my sleep was disturbed. A distant rumble groaned as if an earthquake had hit a nearby town. The noise did not stop. It grew louder. I got out of bed, slipped on my nightgown, and walked into the corridor which faced the back of the compound. On the railway line some two miles away, it was plain to see carriage after carriage of tanks and military equipment thundering along the line at a moderate speed. I counted twenty-two carriages. Then a moment later, another train with another twenty-two carriages passed by, once again supporting tanks, cannon, light armoured vehicles, and some covered wagons, presumably keeping the ammunition dry.

Nancy appeared placing her hands on my shoulders.

'Disturbed you too?'

'Yes, shattered my sleep,' I replied.

'Exciting though.'

'But where can they be going?' I asked in bewilderment.

'North, in that direction. That's all I can say.'

Her hand lifted from my shoulders, and I turned towards her.

'War is getting nearer, isn't it?' I asked.

'With sights like this, it can't be denied. I'll soon be on my way home to New York, my calmer field of activity.'

'Yes, I'll miss you,' I said.

'Me too, honey.'

The newspaper, delivered each day, informed me that on August 19, the Soviet – German Economic Treaty had been signed after five months of negotiations. That was the best news I could have wanted. It meant Otto would not be heading into a war in Russia. With Russia in harmony with Germany economically, I had hoped in my heart that negotiation might be the way forward before military action would be unstoppable.

Some of my training was almost comical. We made chocolate bars with secret wires hidden inside the chocolate. Then they were wrapped in American Hershey chocolate bar paper. When the victim bit into the bar, the circuit wire would become exposed and would encounter a filling. An explosion would follow, enough to kill the subject. This was to be used to eliminate a difficult mature individual frustrating an agent's work. Methods of disposing of unwanted bodies were drilled into us and I engaged with enthusiasm, knowing I would be turning cloak as soon as I could, if only I could get back to Britain. That objective was now imperative. It was also proving difficult.

On completion of the many weeks of training, I was given five microphotographs containing instructions for preparing a code and detailing the type of information I was to transmit to Germany. I was also given a capsule which I must take if trapped and grilled by the enemy. A caught spy is a dead spy we were constantly reminded. It was left in our own hands, and not others, to take one's life.

On 1st September 1939, I heard on the radio, that Germany had invaded Poland. I cringed. Hitler had started his game of chess. It was also the day I received a package from Eicke. It contained my British identity pass.

I looked at it. It was not the one I had in the house. It was a different photo, it was me, nevertheless. At least I knew he had not broken into our home. His message was brief, simply wishing me luck and showing his total faith in me. Details of my assignment would follow, he mentioned. My present orders would come from Major Glauber. Tucked into the package I was delighted to find a letter from Otto. I put all my other thoughts out of my head and opened his letter. I was disappointed to read it was no more than a brief note. He wrote that he was heading north-west to Poland. He could say no more than he was in a motorized unit. Part of the blitzkrieg I knew. He did not speak of Gisela but spared me three kisses.

That morning I reiterated my news from Eicke to Major Glauber and took the opportunity to compliment him on his command of the English language.

'I studied English literature at Oxford. Brasenose College 1934-37. I stayed with my aunt in Reading.'

I felt a bolt of energy sparking my reply.

'We have much in common then.'

His smile was warm and charming. 'You married a German, and my father married an Englishwoman. Our cultures are very much entwined.'

'They are indeed. Our country at present has a future. That's the side I'm on,' I told him.

He placed his arm on my shoulder and patted it a couple of times.

'You will be a credit to the Reich.'

Three days later I had to pack my bags and await a driver. By then, Max, Carl, Arne, Wilmer, and Nancy were on their way back to America. Our farewells were real and touching. These agents had become friends over their short time together. I gave no hint of my intentions and wondered if our paths might ever cross again.

My driver was a young army escort. A boy trained to do his duty and ask no questions and no answers I got from him as we drove at speed along back roads till we got to Dresden. His hair was cropped, and his high hairy collar seemed to have rubbed an abrasive red mark on his neck. He touched it frequently to calm the irritation.

Everywhere in Dresden were flags flying. The news of the Gleiwitz incident, which provoked the war against Poland, had inflamed the population and they were in the streets of the city as if it was a national holiday. Trumpets were playing, dogs barking and children running along the pavements waving hand-held flags of support for National Socialism.

We crossed the city and once again passed through a flat area of countryside. This was the Germany I loved; virginal fresh and peaceful. Despite not knowing where we were going, I was resigned to one last effort to engage this youth.

'You know, my son Otto must be about your age, almost twenty. He's in the Army too.'

'I am not meant to talk to you. These are my orders.'

'But surely you can tell me where we are going? Is it far?'

'We'll soon be there.'

I gazed out at the greenness I was seeing. Mid-summer heat added to the pleasantness of a German afternoon. Above the hedgerow, I saw some camouflaged hangers. I was not surprised when the car slowed down at the airfield entrance. We were stopped. Inspection of the car and its occupants took place. The driver showed his pass and two armed guards peered into the car at me. They were satisfied I was alone. It was an awkward gawping moment for me. When we moved off past the guards, I enjoyed a sigh of relief.

'Essential I suppose but scary,' I said to no response. At last, I'd be heading home to report all I could to Thornton. Just in time too. With the invasion of Poland, we would soon be at war with many more countries. The sooner I got back home the better.

The car drew up to the administrative building while I gazed out at a variety of different-sized aircraft. All bore the swastika on their tail fins.

When I alighted, I was greeted by my handler. He had come down from Hamburg. I disguised my surprise as much as I could in a warm lip-sealed smile.

'Good morning, Frau Richter.'

'Good morning, Herr Eicke. I am surprised to see you here this morning.'

'I wished to, no, I needed to see you off to a good start, but first, a coffee. We have some business to attend to. Follow me.'

I followed him to the building as my departing driver engaged first gear. I waved to him. He responded with a raised arm and a genuine youthful smile. I turned and gave him the Hitler salute making sure Eicke noticed as I did so.

'A fine young man. He'll make a good soldier,' I said.

Eicke turned round to face me. 'Did you have conversation with him during your journey?'

I shook my head. 'He was as silent as the night. I tell you he'll make a good soldier.'

The room had been converted recently. While there were two offices at the end of the building, the rows of tables and chairs looked like a school dining room. The erstwhile rooms had gone to make this large space. On the wall were faded markings, showing the former room partitions of which there seemed to have been four, all equally sized. I was led to the office on the left where Eicke had arranged the meeting. From the coffee pot on a stove, he poured two mugs and offered a plate of Schwartzwalder roulade.

'Ahh, my favourite cake. A real treat. Don't tell me you baked it?' I asked knowing that this would be beyond his capabilities.

'I'd be proud if I could. No my wife Martha is from the Black Forest and makes it for special occasions.'

'And today is special?'

Eicke turned to me as if surprised I was not privy to dramatic developments. 'Third September 1939 and you ask me, is it special? Have you not heard the news?'

'The news? I don't think so.'

'Britain has declared war against Germany.'

My worst fears had been realised on hearing this reality. The maternal pull towards my son pulled against the maternal love I had of my mother. This was at the heart of my dilemma. It was a dilemma that would never be satisfactorily resolved now. It was not a topic for the moment.

'Then this is might be tricky for me to return to Britain,' I suggested.

'It will be arranged, but not yet.'

Not for some considerable time I thought. A German aeroplane crossing the English Channel would hardly survive a landing. Getting back to Scotland was simply impossible now.

We supped our coffee in harmony. The cake was rich and spicy; warm and satisfying.

'Your wife is a fine baker.'

Eicke nodded and lit a cigarette.

'You will be flying in less than an hour. I need to explain. You will not be returning to Britain. The flight will take you to Lisbon this evening. You will be at the German Ambassador's house tonight.'

'Portugal?'

'Yes, this is where we will receive messages from America. The air is clear and so the transatlantic messages are too. I think you met some of the American agents?'

'Yes, of course. I got on well with them, particularly Nancy.'

'Yes, I know. I received a very good report about your enthusiasm and ability to undergo the rigorous training, from Major Glauber. He was impressed with you. I have every confidence in you too.'

I was pleased to hear Eicke say this. I seemed to be eating out of his hand without him knowing. I also felt I had the power to strike back at him, but not just yet.

'But what will I do in Portugal?'

The cigarette's blue smoky flame drifted upwards and

mixed with the atmosphere. I took another mouthful of cake and waited to hear my job specification.

'You will receive the messages sent in English from America. They must be in English so as not to arouse any suspicion from the Yanks or Britain, should they intercept them. You will pass them on to the German High Command, in Berlin translated into German, of course. Here, this is their code and number.'

'And is America in the war yet?'

'No. This is why this link is so useful. We do not have a foe in the USA... makes it a little easier. You will have a small house at Peniche on the coast at Cape Carvoeiro. You will broadcast from there.'

'I see. And what is my cover?'

'You will tell them you inherited from your late father and decided to come to enjoy the better weather Portugal has to offer. Tell them you have decided to write a novel. It must be in English of course. That will mean many hours in your cottage. Late nights with the cottage lights on but you won't be writing novels. It's the best time to transmit. Get to know some of the locals eat their food and drink their wine. Try to learn some of their language. Make them feel you are becoming part of their small community. They will all want to get to know you. Attract no attention to your real purpose, or your radio activities.'

'So I am to be Hilda Campbell from today?'

'Yes, Miss Campbell, you have your British pass?'

'Yes.'

'Then give me your German pass.'

I opened my handbag. But his request had confused

me. I was perplexed. I took a sip of the cooling coffee first. I brushed some cake crumbs from my skirt. I clarified his demand.

'When in Portugal, at the German High Commission, surely I should have a German pass for them?'

'No need. They know your work and that you are expected. They will support you as much as they can.'

'Then won't I need it when I return to Germany? Won't I?'

'When you return to Germany, we will arrange that.'

'And how can I return, now war has been declared? Return to see Otto and my family?'

'A U-boat will be provided, perhaps a light plane from Portugal... maybe we next meet in Britain?' he said with a leering dreamy-eyed smile. 'The options are numerous. It depends on which suits us better at the time.'

I could not bring myself to acknowledge this thought. My stare made him somewhat embarrassed. An impulsive thought it was and a further example of his maverick mind, set loose within the regime. Nevertheless, I handed over my German passport at his request.

'Meanwhile, Karl and Renate will not be troubled?' I asked for my satisfaction.

'These are matters we need not concern ourselves about at present. You have a job to do. And I know you will do it well. Your wireless skills are good. And now you have met the team providing the information. Are you clear about what we expect?'

'Very clear. I shall provide the information promptly. But to Berlin, and not yourself?' I clarified.

Eicke reflected on my question, tapping yet another

cigarette against his silver case. It seemed I had discovered his Achilles heel.

'For the time being, our paths will separate. I am very busy cleansing Hanover. Incidentally, I have made quite an impact in the moving of Hamburg's Jews. Heydrich is very pleased with what I have achieved so far. But your work will be known to me as we make greater strides against our enemies.'

I looked out of the window. I heard an aeroplane approach the landing strip. It was not a large craft.

Eicke offered his hand. 'I do not believe in luck. I believe in hard work which provides results. You can do that, Hilda.'

We shook hands and I held his hand as firmly as I could. He had placed his faith in me. My faith was elsewhere but he must not think that. I gathered my luggage. The heavier bag sat on the floor erect, the base being my oboe case. Eicke lifted it and we made for the plane. Before us was a Heinkel He 70 Mail plane. We approached it as the propellers kept rotating. The pilot jumped down from his cockpit. We all raised our arms and hailed in unison. But no German insignia was emblazoned on the tail or fuselage. That satisfied me.

'A moment please,' the pilot said running off to the hanger and its facilities.

'We are at war in Europe, but Europe is not at war. Portugal and Spain will remain neutral. Spain has had its struggles and it is a broken country. The Portuguese people should welcome you in their midst after you have endeared yourself to them. Take your time, be seen, and be liked.'

'I ought to be grateful to be sent to Portugal in September. It will make you jealous, all that sun and sea,' I said smiling at him but his face did not respond to acknowledge my apparent delight.

'It is because of the weather; we will get good signals from America. The quality of air is good as I said. Don't forget your duties.'

'I won't,' I said. I turned towards the aircraft and lugged my bags on board.

'Careful, don't break the radio.'

I turned round. 'German fabricated. Solid as a rock. I'd be more concerned for my oboe.'

Eicke supported my arm as I mounted the eight metal steps into the craft.

'Get that oboe of yours to play Beethoven, Bach and Schubert, none of that Mendelssohn nonsense. You hear?'

I put my thumb up towards him. The pilot arrived.

'Welcome on board. I'm Werner Metzger. Your seat is behind me. Wear the cap that's on the seat. We can communicate through that.'

I made myself comfortable despite the gradient which gave me sight of blue sky only. Werner closed the fuselage door. I waved to Eicke who raised his arm and then waved. I wondered when I'd see him again. I wondered if I'd ever see him again. I made no plans for either scenario.

Werner explained that the route would be due south over northern Italy then over the Mediterranean Sea, along the North African coast then north to Lisbon where I'd be met. I looked behind my seat and saw several mailbags.

'Are you still able to provide a postal service now the war has begun?'

'Diplomatic bags. Maybe some addressed to you?'

'I doubt it,' I said thinking they would have to get my name right, for a start. I'd also just been given all the instructions I needed from Eicke.

'So you are staying at the Embassy?'

'Perhaps for just one night.'

That was a moment for Werner to reflect on.

'Perhaps you are on a government mission?' he asked.

'That would be more accurate,' I said and the conversation died.

I wrapped a provided blanket over my lap with my hands clasped under its warm cover. The altitude brought me nearer the sun but I was not warmer in the aircraft. Before long a regular rhythm of the vibrating propellers relaxed me. It made me drowsy. We had not spoken for some time.

'You all right?'

'Yes, lulled almost to sleep.'

'Good idea. Not for me though.'

I smiled at his humour. I placed my life in his hands and soon the dozing became pure nirvana.

The flight gave me time to get over the disappointment of not being flown home. But Portugal was a new country for me. A new land to discover and explore at a steady rate. There were, I thought some strange benefits in being a spy no matter how reluctant that role had come my way.

14

Cape Carvoeiro

Werner informed me we had flown down the shin of Italy. We had reached the toe and were now flying west along the north coast of Sicily. How different the coastal sights seemed from class textbooks. The flecks of white waves and the cries of far-off birds thrilled my eyes and ears. We'd drop altitude soon and pass between Tunisia and Sardinia. Even the words of these land masses had a certain Mediterranean mystique.

The sun-washed bays and sun-flecked waves were only familiar to me in adventure books I had treasured in my childhood. Now they shone brightly oblivious to the state of war. I wondered if the conflagration would ever reach the colonies of France in North Africa, or the multitude of countries tied to the British Empire. I had a dreadful thought that the war would come to Africa for Germany to return to its former territories in Trans Togoland, Mozambique, and South West Africa. I realised it would not be the most welcome of times to arrive because the Commonwealth's many countries were beginning to strain and stretch for their independence as were the French colonies. I wondered if India would supply men and materials as they had done in the Great

War. Would Australia see it as a European war? How lonely we might be, I thought as the afternoon turned to evening.

The remainder of the flight was uneventful and when I reached Lisbon airport, I was pleased to be on firm ground again. The warmth of the air surprised me at the hour of eight at night when I was driven into the German embassy grounds in the city of Lisbon. Crickets clicked and frogs sounded their bass notes from the borders of the garden. At first, I thought there had been a party that evening. All the lights of the Embassy were on, and Portuguese staff were being directed to take boxes of various sizes to different locations. It was a hive of activity. I was not sure what was happening.

The car drove up to the steps of the Embassy and I alighted. The driver took my cases to the hallway and Ambassador Wilhelm Klee welcomed me to Portugal.

'Frau Richter, I am delighted to see you have arrived safely. You must be tired, no, hungry. Let me take you through to see what we can find to feed you. It must have been a long flight.'

'Your Excellency, you are well informed. Do you know why I am here? Do you know my real name?'

The Ambassador stopped in his tracks.

'Forgive me, Miss Campbell. Knowing you were the widow of Dr. Willy Richter, and I being a Hamburg-born man myself, my memory slipped into the past. Dr Richter was a fine doctor and a wonderful man.'

I smiled as he brought back thoughts of Willy.

'I see. Then we have much in common.'

'Yes, we have indeed. But I must send you on your

way tomorrow. There are eyes and ears around. Lisbon has a nest of spies. A viper's nest I might add. First, some nourishment, then you will be shown to your room. With the war underway, we have been planning here. Do excuse the noisy confusion. We expect our numbers to increase soon.'

'Numbers?'

'More like you I suspect. We have a greater need for ears than ever before.'

I slept in comfort despite the movements around the house and a full stomach. I was asleep well before midnight. The feathered mattress welcomed me enveloping me in thoughts of excitement for the new day and horror as I was being sucked into the emerging Nazi war machine outside Germany.

After black bread and scrambled eggs, I left the Embassy without any farewells the following morning. A local taxi took my bags and we set off north along the coast. Waves dashed against stout Atlantic boulders as gulls shrieked their calls and dived low out of sight, then reappeared in their soaring maneuvers. The sky had a few playful puffed-up clouds, but the warm sun burned through their vapours. Donkeys pulled boxes of fish along the side of the roads. The smell caught my nostrils.

Eventually, we came to the fishing port of Peniche. It lay at the bottom of a high basalt cliff. The road bent and twisted down to the harbour which harboured several red and green fishing boats in the Portuguese national colours. It was not a large harbour. A simple fishing village port but numerous nets lay drying on the key and some women were mending the nets and throwing out any trapped seaweed. In the distance, I could see small fishing boats fighting the waves to get home in time for lunch. I saw also that there were some shops selling bread and other provisions. There was a clothes shop too. Perhaps I needed a wardrobe change. I'd certainly try to look more local, and the shop would be interesting to see.

'You should go to the port to meet the people. They will be very interested in you,' said my driver. 'Not far now,' he said as we climbed up out of the port.

We drove on another mile or so and then turned off the road. The car slowed down on the uneven ground then I saw my house. A stone cottage, dressed in a bright white coat of whitewash. Perched almost on the top of the cliff, it had a spectacular view over the sea. I got out of the car and found a pathway leading from the house towards the cliff. It veered to the right and descended. I peered over the end to see the most wonderful sandy golden beach below. I noticed a steep path that would take me there. Not a soul was on the sand. The only movement I could see was gigantic waves pounding the foreshore and running up the beach, nibbling the sand. I took a deep breath of maritime vapour, then another. It was so refreshing. War seemed so far away.

My driver deposited my cases in the house and I paid him from the allowance the Ambassador had arranged for me to have. Inside, was a loaf of bread, tins of sardines in tomato and sardines in salt water, and the same fish in a light garlic oil too. My bedroom was at the side of the house. From the window, I could see my nearest neighbour's cottage, some four hundred yards away. I wondered how long it would be before I met their acquaintance.

There was a radio on the sideboard. I tuned in searching for a British frequency. Eventually, I got London's Home Service and learned of the country getting ready for war. I had missed most of the broadcast so found Henry Hall's music play for me. Much as I enjoyed his music, I had to lower the volume. Not that it would cause difficulty but if I played it too loud, any visitor might catch me unaware. And unaware I was for my very first Portuguese visitor a moment later. It was a plaintive meow.

'Come here, come here to Hilda,' I said wondering from where it had come. The dark glossy black cat with white socks slowly walked towards me and circled my legs.

'Well, have you come to visit me or are you staying? Will you be a mouser perhaps?'

I opened a tin of sardines without knowing this stray cat had already found a home that welcomed him. He was not going to leave now that he was seated before a bowl of fish.

It took almost the rest of the day to unpack and get a feel for my lodgings and their surroundings. The cat followed my every movement as if trying to trip me up. For its duration with me, I had to give the cat a name. It was a name to describe its dark coat rather than its white socks I thought and so, Inka became part of my new life in Portugal.

As the sun was sinking into the azure sea before me,

I heard a bicycle's bell approach as it bounced over the rough ground. I looked out of the window to see the local priest arrive.

'Good evening,' he said in Portuguese.

I hesitated. 'Pardon me, I don't speak Portuguese yet. Come in, please,' I said ushering him in with an extensive gesture of my arm.

'So, you are English. You are very welcome here.'

I smiled at the constant correction I could not help myself make. 'I'm Scottish actually, but you were not to know.'

'Ah, then we speak English too. There are not many British people living here on the coast. Not as many as those of you who have made their homes further south.'

'I am not sure how long I'll be here. I plan to stay for at least a year, maybe two. You see it will take that time for me to write a novel.'

'Ah, so you are an author?'

'No, this is my first book. I thought I'd write it in the sun, by the sea, away from the rush of the town. That's why I chose to come here to Peniche.'

The priest cast his eyes around the room.

'You have chosen well. You could have gone to France or Spain, but we are delighted to have you with us.' He held on to his wooden cross necklace as he spoke.

'Then perhaps you will be able to tell your parishioners why I have come to live with them?'

'My parishioners? I was hoping you might join them. You might even pick up the language. Of course, the Eucharist is in Latin. You'd be familiar with the hymns, I am sure.'

I wondered if he realised I was not Catholic and how I should inform him. I think he saw my unease when my folded arms began to scratch each elbow.

'I come from a different Christian tradition.'

'Yes, I would have thought so. The Tridentate Mass might even surprise you, however.'

'Do all your worshippers understand Latin?'

'No, very few. It's the tradition they like.'

'I see,' I said understanding how the church played a significant part in dominating native life. Just then Inka jumped up on my lap. I stroked him. The priest smiled.

'I see you have a friend already.'

'Yes, a stray who has settled with me. At least I think it's a stray.'

'It will be. There are many stray cats. They find their homes, the homes that suit them. Perhaps you'll find a home in St Peter's.'

It would not endear me to the people if I stayed aloof, not speaking their language. Although I thought I might consider his offer should the need arise.

'You can come to join us especially if you find yourself lonely. You would be made most welcome.'

'That is very thoughtful of you. Let me think about it. I don't want to make a rash or a rush decision.'

'Certainly. There will always be a welcome,' he said standing up. I settled Inka on the floor.

'Thank you for visiting. You were my very first human visitor.'

The priest smiled, pleased that the church had been quick off the mark, being the first to call.

'I hope I won't be the last,' he said leaving the door.

My weak smile probably gave him enough information. I was unlikely to attend so soon after arriving.

That night I walked around the house. Cottages were lit as the light faded. The occasional dog barked then a voice shouted at it and a front door closed. The moon cast an eerie light over the sea and then to the shore where it lost its way among the rocks. I stood for a moment mesmerised by the travelling waves. Waves from the west may have started out near New York. Waves, New York, it was time to make contact.

I returned to the cottage and lodged a stone to keep the front door open, facing the sea. I unpacked my radio. I looked around outside again. No one was about. I took a blanket and placed it by my feet. If someone approached unexpectedly, then I'd cover the radio immediately. This would be my first transmission and my stomach knew fear. It rumbled like crashing waves.

I secured the aerial, placed earphones in position, and dialled my code. I sent my message to Nancy. Mixed feelings of success and doubt accompanied my transmission. I kept the message brief. I simply told her I was now in position on the Portuguese coast and was ready to receive.

Her response came three minutes later. 'Great. Also in post... no news today... will keep you informed...'

I tried to work out whether America's east coast may have been five or four or even six hours behind. I closed the radio box. I took down the aerial, packed away the earphones and hid the radio under my bed behind a pottery bed pan. I chuckled for a moment recalling how we called it a gazunder in my youth. I brought the reciprocal container to the edge of the bed for visitors to notice briefly before them diverting their eyes. I checked all angles. The radio was hidden well back, out of sight.

I sat down. I had made my first contact in post. I took a long sigh causing Inka to look towards me. So far so good. Yet my hand still shook. How many more times would I have to bring out the radio and transmit? Would frequency increase slackness? Inka's eyes reflected my unease.

15

Meeting Villagers and Sending Co-ordinates

I did not sleep well. I tossed and turned in my bed causing Inka to jump off and seek a more stable position for the night. I was recalling Nancy's mundane message. What should I be doing with it? It was not news. That might not be welcomed by Berlin, but it would give them reassurance that we were in position and communication across the Atlantic was clear. What niggled me was the fact I would not be sure who was getting the message in the German capital.

I decided to get up and put on my dressing gown. The moon gave enough light with the curtains closed to enable me to crawl under the bed and bring out the radio. I opened the door, and a draught of cool air surrounded my legs. I saw Inka stretch in the room. The day had not yet been announced outside.

I set up the equipment. I entered the code for Berlin. *"Made contact with New York. Good line. No current news."*

The reply was almost instant. I realised I was contacting a twenty-four hours available ear.

"Glad to hear positions intact. Await developments if and when they occur," came back the message in German of course.

I was relieved that the message had been received with a degree of gratitude and understanding. They were not to know I had delayed several hours before sending the message. They might have been impressed however that it was sent at two thirty in the morning.

Sleep then was satisfactory and even Inka realised that the disturbances were over. She had taken to sleeping on the bed by my feet, as there were fewer disturbances at the end of the bed. As I lay down again, I could hear faintly the rush of dying waves on the shore below. Perhaps I'd go there tomorrow.

When I woke a little after eight in the morning, the sun had resumed its climbing position to shed its warmth. I wished to go and make my presence known to the port by buying some provisions and be seen. I wondered if Inka would be there on my return as I locked her out when I set off. Fortunately, she did not follow.

I needed paper. After all that's what an author would need. Pens and pencils too as well as a rubber. Provisions would see me through the weekend, and I'd keep an eye out for any non-German food.

It was a pleasant mile walk along the top of the cliff and the descent provided different angles of the village and its port. Already I could see activity at the harbour. Haggling for fish prices seemed to be their focus. The local women were lifting fish, inspecting them and then discarding or placing them in their baskets. The earlier the fresher, seemed to be their byword. I proceeded along the front to see the collection of shops. There was a provisions shop, a cobbler, an undertaker sign at a joiner's shop and a garage.

I returned to the first shop and entered. I was greeted with a silent gentle smile. I gathered a selection of vegetables and a pineapple. I purchased a sizeable notebook and some pens and pencils. I brought them to the shop assistant's counter. She walked around the wooden table and went to the newspaper section. She selected a small book and placed it in my basket. It was a Learn Portuguese booklet. I took the hint and nodded my approval. Whether the booklet was a gift or not, I could not be sure. I paid what she asked. Then I opened the book.

'*Adeus e obrigado,*' I read to her. She seemed to appreciate my first Portuguese words. I'd soon get used to saying goodbye and thank you at every opportunity.

I left the shop and looked in its window before departing. I saw a notice which needed no interpretation. A drawing of the church and an orchestra of violins woodwind and brass implied a concert would take place. Indeed, I read of the *Concerto de Advento 5 de dezembro*. I made a mental note of the Advent concert. It was something I'd really enjoy. As I smiled at the prospect of attending a concert after so many years, I heard a man arrive behind me. I turned to see him with his sleeves rolled up, showing a smearing of oil on his forearm. A thatch of black hair had avoided a brush and his razor must have been missing for a day or two. His eyes were an expressive and gentle dark green and his arms muscular.

He pointed up to my cottage on the hill. I nodded that I lived there. He nodded his knowledge of that fact. Then he pointed along the street and encouraged me to follow him with a curling index finger.

It was daytime. I felt him honest if perhaps down on hard times. However, when he stopped it all fell into place. He encouraged me to enter his garage. Lying against the side wall by a truck was a bicycle. It was a women's bike. He brought it to me. I held on to it, placing my provisions in the pannier in front. He gestured that I should ride it and I got on. I had not ridden a bike for years. Not since the days I'd go off in the Moray countryside passing the distilleries of the glens. But once learnt, cycling skills came back as I circled around the garage with a wobble or two then onto the street where my confidence grew. I felt comfortable making sure my skirt did not reveal more leg than it should and returned to the garage. I placed the bike on its stand which I had found by the chain. I took out my purse but he placed his hand over it. He shook his head. I did not understand. I could see a tear develop in his eye and for a moment, he could neither speak nor gesture. This strapping mechanic had had his emotions laid bare. It was then his fellow workman came out from under the car from a ramp. He gestured with both hands and nodded his head to show it was a good offer. He then pointed to his marriage finger and then his ring. Then he pointed to his colleague and shook his head. He then lowered his head and leant it over towards his shoulder with his hands beneath representing sleep. It was then I realised the bike had belonged to his wife who had passed away. Again, the man held the bike out for me. My head dipped in sorrow for him and I extended my hand to shake his. He made a show of wiping his hands on his trousers then our hands clasped. He smiled. The deal was done. I had a bicycle.

I set off in gratitude. I stopped once more at the first shop and bought some lard and treacle. I found some course oatmeal and that I paid for too. I now had transport which might be useful on the flat road above the port. I set off with a heavily laden basket to see how far I could climb but had to stop before the first bend. The heat had sapped most of my energy. The bike would not be coming down this hill nor up again. It was far too steep. When I was on the level, I got on once more and made use of all three gears speeding me along the road. My hair flowed behind me, the sun on my forehead and the sea air making my cheeks blush. I felt a freedom I had not experienced for some time. The peddling made my heart pump louder and faster and my breathing was hard. I was enjoying my new transport, but I was so dreadfully unfit.

That afternoon, I took a towel with me and descended to the beach. It was late afternoon approaching four thirty. I counted down the steps as they winded down the precipice. One hundred and eighty eight steps I counted and then I was on the burning sand. I lay my towel down and sat at almost eye level to the sea. I looked both ways and found myself totally alone. It was as if September had announced the end of the season of relaxation on the beach. After a while I stood up and went to immerse my bare feet in the gentle curtain of the arriving waves. The water was warm, deliciously warm. My feet sank into the sand, so I moved a step at a time from each stance. The water was so inviting. I longed for a swim, but I had no costume. Again, I looked along the cliff and the beach. I was alone. I decided to risk the moment. I took my dress and bra off and lay them on the towel then ran ahead into the water.

No need to splash around fearing the cold sea water as I had done on the beach at Nairn and at Cuxhaven but here in Portugal, I had discovered the unknown warmth of the sea. I swam for about twenty minutes. I let out a squeal when some seaweed wound round my toes, then I came out dripping, leaving footsteps of a moment of time in the sand. I gathered my clothes and dried myself with the towel.

I did not count the steps up to the cottage again. I breathed heavily with each step. I stopped for more breath many times. It was the result of the gradient and not the swim I told myself. That had invigorated me. But I really had to buy a swimsuit.

Inka met me on my return. She was a welcome sight, and I now knew she had settled to be my partner in the cottage. But I had to test her in one more way. I made a cup of tea and while I waited for it to cool, I took out my oboe and began to play *Santa Lucia*. Inka looked up unsure where the noise was coming from, for she would not interpret my sound as music. I was sure she could not differentiate noise from music, but I hoped the sound would not make her scarper. I placed the oboe down on my bed and came through to drink the cool tea. Inka jumped onto the bed and sniffed around the instrument.

I poured a fresh cup before I went to the kitchen and began to gather ingredients. I had to remember not to bake anything German. I relied on one of my mother's specialities. I mixed the ingredients into a bowl and stirred it to the right consistency. An oven tray accepted the contents, and a traditional Lancashire Parkin was placed in the oven to bake. That would take one hour ten minutes. That left sufficient time to check any messages from the States.

I set up the radio with the usual precautions and sent Nancy a call sign. *"All well here...no news to give... any to receive?"*

Nancy was ready to transmit. *"70... 40 then 60 and 42... x 50... 9.15.39 out.*

Brevity was the name of this game. I made little sense of the numbers, other than the date. I only hoped they would satisfy Berlin. I repeated the message to them. I felt I had to clarify the date, which might confuse. It was the American way of placing the month before the day, I told Berlin. The response from the Capital was pleasing.

"Excellent work... more when you can. Heil Hitler."

I took out the Parkin and let it cool on a wire tray. It stayed there overnight. Perhaps it was the swim, or the hill climb, or the cycle's appearance or the success in transmitting data, but I was tired and elated at the same time. I retired to bed at 10pm. I played the radio quietly. A book at bedtime was being read but I had not heard the start of the story and by the time it ended I had lost the story and felt sleepy. I never found out who wrote the book.

Inka was pleased I had settled down for the night once more. She was not a night-time prowler. I had found myself a contented lap cat and that was just what I needed. Before she slept, she stretched her hind legs back and her front paws forward making her the longest cat in the world I thought. Whatever she was doing, she showed she was content living with me on the edge of a cliff.

16

Death in the Atlantic

I woke up cold, goose-pimple freezing. Was I really in Portugal? Rain was battering my window as the howling wind raced over the open sea. The cottage windows rattled like castanets while my cottage was receiving the full force of an Atlantic storm. This home had been purchased by the German Ambassador's staff. I should not regard it as permanent. But I felt it was home to me. The inclement weather was a minor irritation, more like home. No more than that. Yet I was beginning to love the setting and the friendly Portuguese people.

The war really did seem so far away. It had not touched me yet and I was satisfied I had not betrayed my country by merely sharing a set of numbers. As the storm continued unabated, I ate my breakfast and then studied my Portuguese language book. I had to get the basic phrases learned by heart and said with conviction. That would not be as easy as it seemed. I was more a numbers individual. I wondered why they thought writing would be my cover. I concluded that perhaps we all have a balance of mathematics and language. Mine was leaning more towards mathematics despite teaching English when I was in Hanover. That memory came to mind as I finished my second cup of tea. To think I had eight private pupils all wishing to perfect their English, sent by loving German parents wishing to educate the next generation. I wondered what they would be thinking of the language now they were at war with its people.

By mid-day the storm had abated. The air was mountaintop fresh. The breeze was cool and more autumnal than I had experienced before at my idyllic head point. Inka was reluctant to get her feet wet and cried a plaintive meow somehow expecting me to dry the outside land for her.

I placed my bag over my shoulder and set off on my bike to the port. People were beginning to emerge from their homes and I waved to them as I passed by. The word must have got out by now that a middle-aged English woman, probably eccentric, had settled in their community. Either that or they had recognised the bike. There was no hint of a hesitation in greeting me.

I lay the bike down on the verge at the top of the hill and proceeded down to the port. In my mind I was rehearsing the Portuguese I had learnt. The language would be on my terms. I could make myself understood, but I'd not be able to understand what they might say in response.

I arrived at the garage. It was quiet. No-one was at work it seemed till I saw a light in an office at the back of the workspace. I slipped by, past a car requiring attention and saw my benefactor's back at his desk. I called out to him.

He seemed a different man. He had recently shaved, and it gave his smile a youthfulness I had not seen before. He came out to greet me. I attentively used a couple of phrases which he listened to with patience. Then he said the words back to me in the proper accent. We laughed.

'I have a present for you,' I said handing him the Parkin. He uncovered the cake. He looked at it. He lifted it to his nose.

'*Hmmmmm... Bonito, eu gosto muito disso*,' he said his face lighting up with the brightness of the appearing sun. There was no doubt what he had said to me as he then took me off my feet and planted a kiss on each of my cheeks. I was taken aback but tried not to show it. It had been an unexpected act of gratitude, but I felt and enjoyed his manly force. It was a real culture clash. One of which I could hardly disapprove and enjoyed even more as it was so unexpected and so intense.

To emphasise why I had brought the Parkin, I pretended to be pedalling. I held the imaginary handlebars apart, moved in a circle then rang an invisible bell. I then placed my hands in a cross over my chest. My acting was understood. Perhaps I even over acted. He knew I appreciated his kind gift.

At the store, my Portuguese was again increased as the shopkeeper costed each item and told me the total. I was getting used to monetary transactions. Indeed, to all intents, I was being absorbed into the local community. I'd never be one of them, of course, but I was certainly seen as one of their fold.

I cycled back to the cottage. I parked the bike by the side of the dwelling. Inka was pleased to see me, or perhaps was appreciative of my return so that her meal could be prepared. I opened a tin or sardines and spooned the contents into her saucer. I had hardly withdrawn the spoon before Inka was sitting, her neck stretching over the plate and eating.

As she lapped up her lunch, I heard a car slow down. I looked outside and saw a rather superior car stop. A driver stayed in the car as a man in a suit descended and looked at the cottage. I instinctively checked that the radio was out of sight. I was satisfied. I moved Inka's dish away from the door and opened it. The man spoke in cultured High German. I welcomed him in.

'Good morning, Miss Campbell. I am Herr Kurt Maurer, second in command at the Embassy.'

'Good morning, sir,' I said not showing any anxiety at his sudden arrival.

He looked around the room with a smile on his face.

'You like your accommodation?'

'I could not have asked for anything better,' I replied with an open smile.

'Even a cat, I see. You have settled in well.'

'Yes, an arrival I had not expected. It is a very bracing spot. I love it.'

'Good. I knew you would. I chose it.'

'Ah, ha ... so you know the house well.'

'Indeed, I do. With no barrier to the Atlantic Ocean, it is clear you will be getting good results. One of the reasons I have come to see you is to congratulate you on your work.'

It seemed clear he knew exactly what I was doing. Yet I still waited for him to convince me completely. I could not jump to any premature conclusion. I tilted my head enticing him to tell me more.

'Your communication with Berlin went down well. You cannot imagine how well your work is being received.'

'Thank you, Herr Maurer,' I said now relaxed to see what else might transpire.

'Can you show me how it is done?'

I hesitated. It was mid-day here, very early in New York, and told him so. I stood up and looked out of the window.

'Don't worry my driver will alert me if there is anyone approaching.'

I lifted the chair and placed it by the open door.

'Excuse me, if I could ask you to sit over here. I need space and room to hide the radio at a moment's notice. I moved the gazunder to the top end of the floor under the bed. Herr Maurer laughed when he saw its function. I placed my pencil and writing pad by the right of the radio. I opened the set, switched it on, donned the headphones, and erected the aerial.

I gave my call sign. I waited... and waited. Then a signal was received.

'38... 47... and... 41... 50... 9.20.39 X 55.'

Herr Maurer saw me draw a line under the message. Again, these random numbers played on my mind. This was not the time to question them.

'Finished?'

'No, I must send the message to Berlin now.'

I sent the code immediately, followed by the numbers from America.'

I took off the headphones and coiled the wire. I switched off the radio and closed the case. I took it to the bed and slipped it under. I brought forward the gazunder with its China lip showing enough to be recognised. Such pottery was never the subject of polite conversation.

'Very professional. You are a credit to the Reich.'

'I thank you.'

Maurer's eyes wandered behind me, as Inka came forward to rub her scent on his trousers.

'That black box. It intrigues me. What is it?'

'You mean my oboe?'

'I see... you play it well?'

'That's not for me to say but I have played in public many times.'

'Then perhaps your musical services would be appropriate at an Embassy function?'

'Maybe.'

Maurer smiled in a self-satisfied grin. He gathered his gloves and stood up.

'Keep up the good work, Miss Campbell.'

'I will.'

Without a further word he left a brown envelope on the table. I thanked him assuming it was either further instructions or my pay.

'Goodbye. We will meet again before long,' he said as he turned towards the door.

'Goodbye,' I said remembering not to raise my right arm in Portugal. His wave was equally insignificant. Moments later the car drove off. Inside the brown envelope was local currency, just what I needed for my daily journeys to the port.

Two days later as I lay down on my bed and tried to figure out the numbers. I got nowhere and wondered what I'd do that afternoon. As I prepared a sandwich for a beach and rock exploration, I turned on the radio and tuned into London. I learned that the SS Athenia had been sunk by U-boat U-30. The Deutschland pocket battleship and the Admiral Graf Spee had both been at sea when the war was declared and now they were attacking British and French ships. Meanwhile Britain's blockade of Germany had begun, the newscaster reported.

He continued. On 14th September HMS Ark Royal had survived three faulty torpedo attacks which exploded prematurely forcing U-39 to surface then scuttle, becoming the first U-boat loss of the war. Three days later HMS Courageous was sunk by U-29. The programme then changed to some poetry readings, and I switched it off.

The war seemed to have started in the Atlantic, I realised. That same Atlantic I woke up to each morning. How close was I to the nearest U-boat I wondered as I looked out into the bay? I set off to have a shore walk, possibly a swim too.

This time I had a costume. Not a Berlin fashion costume but a simple seersucker patterned costume I had bought in the clothes shop on the seafront. I put it on before I set off. As usual, going down the zigzag path made me concentrate on each step. The thought of a trip and a loss of balance would undoubtedly have been fatal.

Soon I was on the deserted shore once more. I lay

out my towel and sat on it with my hands clasped over my knees and my head nestled upon them. My hair was let loose and flew behind me giving my forehead a dose of sunshine's vitamin D. I was alone, appreciated by the Axis powers but not fully understanding what I was accomplishing. I let my mind wander in the silence of unheard human voices while in the volume of breaking waves, my thought process led me on an unknown path.

Suddenly I felt a chill spread through my body, then a pounding in my heart. 'My God,' I gasped holding my head in my hands. I felt my body shake. The sinking of the SS Athenia. Had I passed the message to Berlin for the U-boats to home in on a supply ship? Am I a murderess? I tried hard to remember the numbers.

70 and 40 then 60 and 55. I divided them, subtracted each then I realised. 'Oh God,' I begged, how obvious it became in the light of the sinking. 70-degree longitude; 40 latitude. 60 degrees longitude and 42 latitude. I knew Britain lay between zero- and 10 degrees longitude and 50 and 60 degrees latitude. I had been given the coordinates to sink our cargo ships coming with supplies from the Americas. The multiplication by 55 would be the number in the convoy and the date would be when the ships would be at these points. I had become far too identified with the Nazi war machine. It was time to cross over as soon as possible. But how? How could I possibly undo my life now and pretend all I had done in the world of espionage was a dream?

17

Hilda Drowns

I returned to the cottage feeling very low with a determination never to relay another message to Berlin again. How could I ever face the widows of the men drowned on the SS Athenia? How could I ever imagine the horror of drowning, caused by me? I had to blame no one else but myself for those losses. How long would it be before the German coders might suspect my reticence?

I had to make thorough plans and make them quick. If I were to hide my tracks, I'd have to travel light. The nearest safe house would be the British Embassy in Lisbon, but I'd have to pass a seething contingent of spies who had gathered in Lisbon. Surely some of them would be German, assessing who was coming and who was going from the British Embassy. To that end, I thought I'd arrive before the Embassy opened. I consulted a map of Lisbon which I had noticed in the bookcase. The British Embassy was located in the *Rua de São Francisco Borja*. It was in the centre of the city near the sea.

I prepared a bag which I could leave as a decoy. My oboe case filled the bottom of my other bag. I would wear as many clothes as I could. Then a trickle of fear ran down my body. I was meant to be an author for goodness's sake. There was clearly no time to write a book. I made myself a cup of coffee and sat down to write a potential plotline. I made notes. I added words and crossed them out. On the folder I wrote First Draft and filled it with several blank pages but my outline was in Venn diagram form with shoots of ideas spreading to the corners of the sheet. I tentatively called the novel "My Destiny in the Highlands." I wondered if it really was my future. My coffee finished, I had enough to show I had been working on some thoughts of my book. I would have surely taken it with me if I was simply moving on. Nothing must show I had planned my disappearance.

I looked at Inka and she came to me. I stroked her and told her I was going away. Somehow, I believed she understood me as she went towards the door. She had come into my life at the right time, a mature cat who thought she'd have me for some time, if not a lifetime. It was not going to be forever. I let her out of the cottage. I hoped she would not betray me. I'd leave the door open for her to return, after I had gone. Indeed, that would be part of the plan I was devising but first I had to contact Berlin with the latest readings, my latest death invoking readings.

I opened the radio. I knew what I had to do. There was a clear line from the States, and I placed my headphones on.

'50... and... 34. 65... and 32 x 22 10/3/39.'

I replied, received, over and out. Then I sent the message to Berlin, changed as my final message.

'43... and... 31 62... and 31 x 22 10/4/39.'

The clock was now ticking. That message would be sent promptly to the pack of submarine wolves. They would be on a wild good chase. They would question their information. They might look to me first or to Nancy in New York to see where the fault lay. I had better not be around when they discovered the discrepancy.

That night, an hour after midnight, I went to the beach. Moonlight fortunately was sufficient for me to make my way safely. I took my towel, a jersey I'd never see again and an extra pair of shoes. The tide was out. I lay down the towel in a position that it could be seen from the road. My shoes I laid on a corner of the towel to prevent it from blowing away. I lay a book down with a bookmark in it. There was no point leading my steps to the water as the tracks would have to come back. I left my watch in my shoes. I had to make the scenario convincing.

I observed the setting with the pride of a movie director. It may well become a murder scene or a missing person's inquiry by daylight. I had to move on, with haste.

It was a quarter to three when I set off, leaving the bike resting on the side wall. It was still dark. I walked swiftly and quietly. I did not attract any canine interest. I had a nibble of cheese to keep me going. I reached the village of Sintra at five and made for the bus park. The first bus to Lisbon set off at five thirty. I was in good time.

It was an hour's bus ride. For most of the journey I was the sole passenger. That pleased me. Every hamlet seemed to have been served by the slow-moving bus.

As dawn broke, I saw many farmsteads with crops of barley and wheat and vineyards galore to support the Porto wine industry. Lisbon was much larger than I had imagined. That gave me some reassurance. I could be lost in the city. The day had started. I wanted an earlier arrival at the British Embassy. If I went there now, I would have been spotted. I could not take any risks. I had to make other plans.

I entered Hotel *Duas Nacoes* on the *Rua da Vitania*, a family run hotel and asked for a room for the day. I signed the guest book with a name which came into my head. I don't know how it arrived, but it would do during my stay in the hotel.

I was delightfully taken aback when they produced a breakfast. Deputada Theresa Soares had made a tomato omelette which had never tasted so good. I devoured it as if breakfast had been the main course of the day. I explained that I would be leaving very early the following morning and hoped a taxi could take me at 6am. That seemed to be no problem. They understood my broken Portuguese.

I was taken to a room overlooking a park beyond which was a row of tenement buildings, housing the poor of Lisbon. Far from salubrious this was an ideal place to hide for the best part of the day. I lay down on the bed still wearing my clothes and rested two tired feet. Soon I was sound asleep. I slept with the window open. It warmed the room and kept me sleeping.

I woke to a knock on the door. It was my landlady announcing an evening meal was ready. I came down the stairs pleased to see I'd be dining alone. I sat with my back towards the main window and found a plate of lobster with melted cheese on the white meat. Small tomatoes and roasted potatoes with a few runner beans lay on the plate and a carafe of red wine was provided with a glass for me to fill.

The lady's husband arrived and came into the dining room. He spoke broken English.

'English lady welcome. We welcome all spies,' he laughed loudly. His comment put me on edge. How could he have come to that conclusion I wondered.

'You think I am a spy?' I laughed to seem less worried.

'In Lisbon you are either a spy or Portuguese.'

I joined him in his laughter, taking a drink of the wine while I assessed this maverick host.

He opened the reception book.

'I apologise. Spies are usually men anyway, so you can not be a spy, er... Miss Brackenridge.

'You must be a spy detector to come to that conclusion,' I said to please him.

'No, but you are not far wrong. I am Chefe de Policia Edmundo Soares in charge of the south of the city.'

I finished my meal and asked to pay my expenses. The landlady said she'd have a taxi waiting at six the next morning.

I hardly slept all night, not because I had slept most of the day but because the fear of being discovered by the German Embassy kept prompting me to be alert. In darkness I saw Lisbon come to life. Street music and dancing went on till after 10.30pm and I watched every movement from my bedroom vantage point. My body was still not ready for sleep. That left worry on my mind and my thoughts returned to abandoning Inka at first then the sending one of our ships to the bottom of the Atlantic. I would never ever come to terms with this crime. I stifled some crying to prevent detection, but my heart was heavy.

It was nearer one o'clock in the morning before I lay down and took a few naps.

The morning was another rotten day with squalls of rain shining on the cobbled streets. For me that would be a good omen. I could move swiftly and more covered under rainy conditions. I had been awake since four. My excessive afternoon sleep was coming back to haunt me. No wonder my stomach was in knots. My future was in the balance and my eggs all in one basket to be smashed or served at the British Embassy if I got there. And when I did, would they believe me?

At 6.12am the car arrived. Twenty minutes later I had paid him and walked smartly towards the side of the Embassy. A few people were on their way to set up their market stalls and many rode on bicycles. But men in suits were not around nor cigarette smoking characters on street corners, taking in the vista. I saw the front door of the Embassy had not been opened. The smell of wet vegetation caught my senses as I passed by some garden-growing vegetation at the side of the property. I continued round the building and was surprised to see a lawn with beautiful flowering autumn colours of chrysanthemums and creeping juniper with a common walnut tree at the end of the walled garden. Then I heard some noise. A voice or two speaking, coming from the Embassy. I approached the open window. It was the kitchen. I peered into the room and caught the eye of a cook. She was startled. I smiled to show I harboured no harm.

'I have travelled, I have come to the Embassy too soon,' I said.

'Who are you to see?'

'The Ambassador himself,' I said.

'That will not be possible. He's in London.'

My heart sank like a lead weight. 'Then I must see his deputy. I have important information to give the Embassy.'

'Wait... I am coming.'

I looked both ways. I saw no eyes looking at me. Then a woman in white trousers and a checked apron arrived. She was small and round. Her hair was black tied up in a bun and her skin olive. Her eyes danced in their sockets.

'Come, this way,' she motioned by her hand.

I was taken into the kitchen and my overcoat was opened out beside the roaring fire to dry. A hot cup of tea arrived, and I relished it. I felt safe around me, yet it was not guaranteed. I watched the cooks prepare breakfast for the staff. I kept out of their way.

Eventually I heard English voices in the dining room and that pleased me no end. I felt I should be there with them, but I had to bide my time. They had to find out who I really was.

I was informed that the Embassy opened at 8am. I kept my eye on the kitchen clock.

The cook returned from the dining room and told me she had mentioned I was here, in the kitchen. She asked of my name, and I told her. She returned to the dining room.

At ten minutes to 8am as I was looking out at the wet garden through the kitchen window, a man entered.

'Miss Campbell?'

I turned round to see a man at least ten years younger than myself. He wore a dark blue suit with a white shirt. He sported a darker blue tie and his shoes shined as if ready for a Guardsman's parade. His accent was midland I thought but I was wrong. I was to learn it was a cultured northeast accent, from Sunderland.

'Yes, I am Hilda Campbell. I arrived very early. I hope you didn't mind.'

'Not at all, I'm glad the cooks looked after you. I am third in command here, Gavin Stevens.'

'They certainly did refresh me,' I said lifting my overcoat from its warm surroundings.

'Please come with me to my office.'

I thanked the kitchen staff in my best Portuguese which brought smiles to their faces revealing bright white teeth and they seemed to bow as I left in appreciation.

We walked along a corridor with picturesque Portuguese art on their walls. Then we climbed the staircase. Before we reached the top, Gavin Stevens had a question.

'A stranded lady wishing to return home before the war gathers pace or needs to renew a passport. Am I right?'

I shook my head from side to side, 'Mr Stevens, the war is underway, and I have much to report.'

'I see. Then I think you are not one of our usual visitors.'

I was pleased to hear he had come to that conclusion. 'No, I think you will find me most unusual,' I said to him. 'I may have to make some important requests to you.'

I could see he was assessing me. The war had not come to the fore of his mind as keenly in a neutral country. He seemed a little out of his depth. To ask him to make requests of him was crossing a line. He must have realised he had a formidable woman before him.

'MI6 must know I am here. They are my handlers.' The words took him to a different level of expertise.

His expression was serious. He lifted the phone. It seemed to me as though he was securing a more senior member of Embassy staff to attend. I was right.

'Nigel, can you come to my room. I have a lady I'd like you to meet.' He replaced the handset.

I was seated in front of Mr Stevens's oak desk. A portrait of King George VI hung from the wall which made me feel very much at home. The older man arrived closing the door behind him.

'Mr Sloan, this is Miss Hilda Campbell,' said Mr Stevens.

'Good morning,' I said bringing my hand forward to shake his.

'Now Miss Campbell, what are you wishing to tell us?'

'I am a spy, a somewhat reluctant double agent whose activities before the war were in Germany but now MI6 directs me. They need to know where I am, and I need to inform them about the loss of shipping in the Atlantic.'

'I see,' said Mr Stevens.

There was a pause. I did not wish to say more than I needed at this stage, but one question was at the tip of my tongue.

'Can you get a telephone line through to Mr Thornton or Mr Dynes at MI6?'

Mr Sloan looked at Mr Stevens and nodded to him. Rank seemed to have been pulled and Mr Stevens left the room.

'So, what are your German connections?' asked Mr Sloan.

'Herr Eicke in Hamburg was my first handler but when I arrived in Britain, I was quick to show where my allegiances were. I was sent back to Germany by MI6 but then the war began, and I was sent to Portugal to receive messages from America and send them to Berlin. That put me back in the German camp.'

'So, you are a counter spy. Of course, I need to know which side you are really on, you understand.'

'If we get through to either Dynes or Thornton, then I'll be pleased.'

He drummed his fingers on the desk. I tried to ignore the resultant threatening beat.

'And if not?' he asked stroking his chin.

I hesitated. I had to think what the consequences could result if my story faltered against someone else's version. Then I remembered what might be happening at the cottage.

'I need to stay here. I will have been reported as a missing woman, probably drowned at sea two days ago.'

I saw Mr Sloan crease his eyes and pout his lips. I

suspected he might be thinking I was deranged with feelings of grandeur.

The telephone rang. Mr Sloan lifted the handset. He listened. Then he looked up at me.

'It's for you,' he said.

'Really?'

He handed me the telephone. 'A Mr Thornton,' he said. I smiled and was ecstatic. I took the phone with indecent haste.

'It's wonderful to hear your voice again... yes... I'm fine. I need to return to London... I am in Lisbon... Lisbon Portugal. Can I... what?... yes. From America. Yes I can name them... understood... certainly. So good to hear you again.'

I handed the telephone back with my heart beating in triumph. Mr Sloan took over.

'Hello again. Yes, so that's who she is. Definitely one of ours? Okay, it's just past 8 am now. Yes... okay. When? Let me see... ah... the flight will leave at er... at 2pm. Yes... we will. Easily arranged, it is no problem. Can I pass you back?'

He held the phone to me once again.

'Hilda, it's looking like you won't be going back to Germany now,' said Thornton.

'I certainly won't. I decided to drown yesterday...so locals will come to terms with my disappearance and when the German Embassy follows that up, they should swallow the hook. That gives me some time. Looks like I could be Stateless today.'

'No not Stateless. We'll see to that. You will be flying back today. We'll pick you up when you land.'

'Wonderful, I look forward to that very much indeed. Goodbye.' I said replacing the telephone. I was beside myself with happiness. I could not help but show the broadest of smiles. I had achieved my disappearance perfectly and was now in safe British hands.

Mr Sloan took off his jacket and placed it behind a chair. He stood before me and scratched his head. 'I guess you are a bit of a celebrity,' he said straightening his tie.

'What me a celebrity? Far from it.'

'We don't get cases like yours in the normal course of events.'

'Maybe not. I have not finished my work. In fact it has hardly started. A spy's work is never ended.'

18

The Flight to Northolt

I was driven to an airfield outside Lisbon that afternoon. It was a beautiful day and I should have been relaxed however I had to sit well down in the car in case I was recognised. Perhaps posters of the missing English woman were beginning to be circulated. I felt like a mouse smelling a cat.

I felt the breaking of this umbilical cord would start a new life, as I rode in the Embassy car. Perhaps I would return to help mother run the hotel. That would undoubtedly be delayed while I was debriefed. Was I thinking ahead of myself, I wondered, as the car approached a fixed wing propeller-driven Breda Ba.65 sitting in the sunshine of the forecourt. The only doubt I could contemplate was if the flight might not fly safely through a war zone.

Then pilot, Marco Matti, descended from his plane and approached me. He was dressed in flying gear with his loose helmet chin strap swinging in time with his swaggering steps. An escaped curl of brown hair was all I could see, the rest hidden to reveal a broad tanned forehead and in his smile two rows of brilliant white teeth.

'Good morning, I am Marco, your pilot. I'm pleased to meet you.'

'I am Hilda Campbell,' I said shaking his hand.

'My orders are to take you to England. I have the right passenger?'

My grin put him at ease. 'You have indeed but, your accent seems more German than Portuguese, not so?' I asked with more than a degree of concern.

His response was to laugh. I thought it odd, very odd indeed.

'Yes, my German is very good as is my French but my first language is Italian.'

'So you are from Italy,' I deduced.

'No, let me settle your nerves. I am Swiss, as Swiss as a Swiss army knife, as pure as the water falling from the Matterhorn and prepared for our flight with our famous Emmental cheese. I have some on board. You will enjoy it.'

His response put my nerves at ease. His rotund body shape gave him a slightly comical look. I imagined him to be the soul of any party.

'I'm more than glad to be your passenger.'

He pointed a finger at my bag. 'Is that all your luggage?'

For a moment I thought of my abandoned shoes, clothes and possessions. 'Yes, not much, just the essentials to travel home.'

He lifted it and walked me towards the plane.

'A definite solid bottom to the bag, a picnic box perhaps?'

I smiled and shared my joy.

'It's my oboe. I'd never part with it.'

'If music be the food of love, play on. Give me excess of it,' we both laughed.

'Twelfth Night?' I suggested.

'Lovesick Orsino, yes in Twelfth Night.

'Lovesick?'

'Not I. I just love my flying,' he said in a slightly effeminate manner.

I eased myself into the plane sitting behind Marco. He placed the flying cap on my head with the microphone securely held in front of my lips. I was strapped into the seat.

'Testing 1, 2, 3. Over.'

'Receiving loud and clear, 3, 2, 1,' I replied.

He turned round with his thumb up and offered a generous smile. I interpreted that digit appropriately and reciprocated with my thumb sideways on in error. His thinking must have been that I was a rookie at telecommunications. I wonder what he'd think if I told him I was German trained.

Then I saw my driver run towards the plane. His hands were waving. He frantically sought Marco's attention. He drew back the hooded cover and peered down at him.

'I have just heard, Miss Campbell. Police are making enquiries in Peniche that the English woman has drowned. Nobody yet found her body but they have definite circumstantial evidence. They have much to go on. They are searching the coastline and her cottage. The whole town are involved. They are very concerned. They say she was a lovely woman. English they said.'

For a moment, Marco tried to assess the information.

'Then it's a ghost I have in the rear, behind me?' teased Marco.

'That's right. I've never really existed,' I said with smug satisfaction.

There would be pressure on the German Embassy to recover the radio. They had to make their own enquiry and be satisfied with an explanation why their valued trained spy was no longer receiving messages.

The driver continued with his messages. 'The police have been asked to trace another English woman as she may have known the missing woman.'

'Really,' I asked in disbelief.

'Yes, a Miss Brackenridge they said. But she had been staying in Lisbon. Perhaps they never knew each other. There are only a few English women around the city.'

'Anyway if you haven't noticed, just for the record, I'm not English.'

'No? Then I'm just telling you the talk of the town,' said the driver.

'Thanks,' I replied realising that if they linked the two women they may resolve that I have not drowned after all. 'I think it's time to take off. Pronto, I think they say in this country.' God, perhaps I should have gone directly to the Embassy. Had I been too cautious in trying to avoid the spying community? That had led to the creation of Miss Brackenridge who nobody would be able to identify. Two missing English women? Very suspicious. I had made a mistake there. I really hoped the German staff would not detect a ruse. Time might tell if they have.

The hood was closed and we taxied to the end of the runway. I saw Marco give a final check of his instruments to ensure the plane was ready to fly. We set off. Then a force pinned me to my seat and moments later the nose of the plane rose and we were flying. I saw Lisbon's red pan tiled roofs shine in the afternoon sun. The contrast with the white speckled azure blue of the Atlantic was an artist's dream. I raised my arm and waved to Portugal, to Inka and to the many friends searching in vain for this speck in the sky.

I held the microphone close to my mouth. 'Marco, so why is a Swiss pilot in Lisbon flying me to Britain?'

'Hilda, I used to fly with light cargo all over Europe. When war was declared, I hesitated about how I could find work. I had lost my freedom. I had delivered cosmetics to Lisbon, down there. At the airport I was approached by one of your Embassy staff. He told me they had a very secret mission which demanded a woman to be flown to Britain. I guess that's you. So why did I do it? They paid me well. You seem to be a very precious cargo.'

His answer satisfied me but I had one more question.

'How long will the flight be?'

'We head straight north to the coast of southern Ireland then sharp right to England. We don't want to get too near the English Channel or the French coast. I make it a three and a half hour flight, if the wind is in our favour.'

'And if it's not?'

'It could delay us by as much as three quarters of an hour on this flight. That is of course... if... we are not shot down.'

The sobering thought found the hair on the back of my head startle. 'And the likelihood of that?'

'I'm not a betting man. But won't fly if I didn't think I'd make it.'

'Even for the money?' I asked but there was no mirror. He'd not see the mischief in my eyes.

'I have a wife and two daughters at home in Cevio. After this flight I'll fly in Switzerland. I'll work there till the war is over. We will not be partisan. It would tear our country apart. We will not fight.'

'Cevio, near Lake Como isn't it?' I asked from a school geography lesson, of many years ago.

'No, Cevio is north of Lake Lugano.'

I did not know my Italy as well as my Germany.

The Swiss cheese sandwich was enough to satisfy me. Its nutty flavour lingered in my palate. A bottle of water was passed to me over Marco's shoulder.

'That should keep us going.'

I agreed. Then he passed a brown paper bag over. Inside were three chocolate bars.

'Three? I doubt if I could eat even one of these bars. They are huge.'

'Then keep them in your bag. A present from Switzerland,' he said.

I caught a glimpse of what must have been the south coast of Ireland. It vanished quickly under increasing cloud. By the time we crossed over the Irish Sea it was dark. Land was difficult to see. There seemed to be a night black out in force as not a light gave any direction.

'How long now?' I asked feeling my return home

was almost immanent. Where would I spend this night, I wondered?

'Not long now. We're over friendly land at last. You can relax. We'll be at Northolt in less than an hour.'

'Northolt? Where's that?'

'Not far from London, on the north side.' he replied.

That hour passed by ever so slowly as I thought through the repercussions of a year under the control of the German Nazi secret services. What if I wasn't believed, when I landed? What if I was imprisoned? Was I already starting to wish I had never boarded this flight? I could have lived happily in Portugal on the cliff with Inka, sending the occasional wrong coordinates claiming a faulty line? Then I'd be acting in no-one's interest.

'Ready for landing in two minutes,' Marco announced.

I looked out of the side window. All I could see was darkness. I felt the descent, glad that there had been no flak or attack on our journey. The mother country like a magnet seemed to pull me back home. I felt a relief about that and I was ready to face the music in whichever key it came.

Landing was jumpy. I felt we bounced a couple of times before the brakes were applied. I was pulled forward, restrained by my strapping, digging in to my shoulders.

'Well done, a safe landing,' I said.

'Not one of my finest. But we made it.'

A surge of relief shot through my skeleton bones.

'So where will you go now?' I inquired. 'Back home to Switzerland?'

'To Switzerland, as I said.'

'Ah yes, but flying across Europe might be dangerous.'

'I would think so too. I'll fly to Portugal, then east along the Mediterranean, and then north to Switzerland tomorrow. That should be safe,' he said turning around to see me. 'I'll refuel in Lisbon and see if I can find some more deliveries. None as animated as you I imagine,' he laughed. 'You have been the perfect passenger.'

I had much to thank him. 'I'll be thinking of you, when you fly tomorrow,' I said. He heard my sincerity and acknowledged my remark with a nod and a thumb-up sign.

The plane came to a halt. I unclipped my leather helmet and my strapping. The hood drew back and I breathed a cool breath of British air. It felt wonderful. The stress left my shoulders and I felt something satisfying come over me. Perhaps it was a familiarity. I could see a car approach. Marco got out and came to assist me. I gathered my bags and came down the improvised stair backwards.

'Hilda, welcome home.'

I turned round to see Messrs Dynes and Thornton. In turn they came forward to shake my hand. Their smile was one confirming in my mind to which side they saw me. To them I was really loyal to the King. That was all that mattered.

'It's getting late. You will be staying here for the time being. We'll return tomorrow at 9am and we can debrief then. Is that understood?'

'Perfect. I think after a good night's sleep, I'll unload.'

'I've left a wee dram as you might see by your bedtable. You'll sleep soundly tonight,' said Dynes.

19

Forgiveness

I was the only woman in the dining room, apart from those working as kitchen staff. The eyes of the sky blue airmen sat at tables looking in my direction from time to time. I tried to ignore them. It wasn't easy. Perhaps I reminded them of their mothers? I looked at some of them and thought they were probably contemporary combatants like Otto.

I had had a restless night despite the tot of whisky I was given. A night in which I held back sleep as I tried to place in order what I had observed in Germany and Portugal. I'd be sure to be asked about all I could remember. I knew I was not at my best when I sat with cupped hands over a cup of tea the following morning. Nor was I refreshed. I had not discovered a wash room other than the one used by shaving airmen. How long might I be here? What would happen next? Surely they would not send me back to Germany now, even if I longed to see Otto again?

I made myself ready for my interrogation. I kept an eye out of the window to the forecourt where cars would arrive. It was some twenty minutes after nine that they appeared. We greeted each other and asked the usual pleasantries. We then walked over to a hut in the grounds, booked in advance for our deliberations.

It was a carpeted hut. A functional multipurpose facility. When I entered I saw the toilet door markings on the right and through a door I saw the room where I would share my knowledge. A table stood in the centre and a coal fire had been lit an hour or so ago. The smoky yellow flames were diminishing and red glowing coals were now appearing. A full coal bucket lay beside the fireguard for us to use.

We sat down at the table. It was rectangular. I sat on one side and Dynes and Thornton sat at the other. The ends were left clear.

'I must say finding you in Portugal was a surprise. I look forward to you telling us about that. But first, when you left to return to Germany, that should be a good start,' said Dynes.

Recalling the early days was a little unclear. It was the atmosphere I recalled first. It gave them an indication of how National Socialism had grabbed the nation's attention and Hitler seemed to have the answers. His annexation of the Sudetenland was popular and the invasion of Poland was too. Many Germanic peoples were in both countries and it was their excuse to invade. But at that time they felt Britain was all bluff, more interested in protecting its own commonwealth countries. I opened my handbag and took out my handkerchief.

I decided to tell them about my Eagle Civilian Cross. I saw the expression of utter astonishment in their faces.

'Presented by Reinhardt Heydrich himself, I might add.'

'By God, Heydrich... do you know about Operation Anthropoid?'

'Anthropoid? No can't say I've heard of it.'

'Last month, Heydrich was assassinated on the instruction of the exiled Czech government,' Thornton advised me.

'Marvellous, I detested that man for his thoroughness in rounding up the Hamburg Jewish population and elsewhere.'

'It was not a wholehearted success. The reprisals have been brutal. Anyway, tell me, you seem to have been appreciated by the Reich. How the hell did that come about?' asked Dynes.

Of course I told how my late husband had served the Heydrich family well. 'He also wished to honour me to ensure I stayed loyal to them.'

'Think twice about who you show this to, won't you?' requested Dynes.

I nodded. Only for your eyes, one day. Just imagine if I had it with me, and I had not shown it to you and it fell out of my bag. Or was discovered? I would be in hot water then. In fact to this day, the medal has remained in the hall cupboard in Hamburg,' I informed them.

'As ever, you are covering your tracks well,' smiled Thornton.

I told them about the training camp where I had met Nancy Krause, the New York airline office official, Carl Jaeger the Baltimore taxi driver, Wilmer Lange, Arnie Koch and Max Becker, the Bronx cafe owner.

'It was from them I was receiving signals to relay to Berlin,' I said my voice cracking towards the end of the sentence.

I could fight it off no longer. My shoulders began to quake and soon the tears filled my eyes and sobs were heard. For the first time in a stressful year, I had no energy left to fight the truth as it emerged.

'Are you all right?' asked Thornton while Dynes offered his white pressed handkerchief.

'I'm a murderer,' I sobbed shaking my head. I had embarrassed my interrogators. They were unsure how to react. I could not stop the flow of tears. 'A murderer. I murdered so many people. I sank the S S Athenia...the Athenia... I murdered the crew.'

My eyes were red. All the pent up anxiety of keeping my identity secure had come undone. Yet this was the right place for it to be offloaded They should see the strains I had been under playing for each side. I hoped their interpretation would be favourable.

'I think we should have a break,' said Dynes. I thanked him as I wiped tears from my face.

Half an hour later, Dynes brought a tray bearing three cups of coffee. I had composed myself and welcomed the beverage. It felt good to hold a warm cup in my hands again and sniff the aroma.

'The sinking of SS Athenia was not your fault, Hilda.'

'But I was not diligent. I did not interpret the numbers in time,' I said still showing the guilt in my forehead's creased rows.

'Yes, but when you did discover what they meant,

you said you gave a false reading next time to save others. Think of those you saved.'

'I had to cut short my time or I'd be sending many more ships to the bottom of the Atlantic Ocean.'

Both men nodded their agreement. 'You left at the right time,' said Dynes.

'It was a good ruse to leave suspicion that you drowned. That was quick thinking,' said Thornton.

I was glad to be appreciated as I had accomplished my disappearance without a trace. I informed them about the information I had right up to the time I left the airport in Lisbon.

'I have left behind a confused cat, a bicycle and a radio, all of which I had become very fond,' I said.

'I imagine the radio is back in German hands by now.'

I gave an encouraging smile. 'That would have been the first priority of the German High Commission. They knew where it was hidden. They would have undoubtedly been first to seize it.'

Thornton turned the page of his wire spine notebook. 'Tell me about Eicke again,' he asked, making me concentrate my thoughts once again.

'Eicke won't leave Hamburg. He's now in charge of cleaning the city. I suspect you know what that means?'

'Deporting Jews?' clarified Dynes.

'Exactly. That must have been the subject of his meeting with Heydrich. He was the director of cleansing Germany of Jews. That means also, he has less control over where Otto might be.'

'No bad thing perhaps,' said Dynes.

'By now Eicke may have been told I drowned in

the Atlantic waves. That would suit me fine.' Then I wondered if he had informed Otto of my demise.

'It suits us even better,' said Dynes.

I was not following what he meant. I asked for clarification.

'We have no intention of sending you back to Germany,' said Thornton.

I gave a voluble sigh of relief. 'Then it seems my work with you is over?'

'Almost, I'd say. Hilda... I have... some bad news for you.'

I could not think what the source of this could be, my mind focussing on Germany.

'I feel now is the right time to inform you. Your mother... died six weeks ago.'

The news had a strange effect on me. Thoughts spun round in my head. In a way it meant she would not have the anxiety of the war anymore. Her fears for me and her grandson were no longer playing on her mind. That was a small compensation. Her death however might make me the resident hotel owner. Then the reality hit me.

'Oh dear, you said six weeks ago? She will have been buried by now.'

'Yes, she was buried next to your father in the Elgin graveyard. Hilda, go up there. Sort things out. I suppose you can either sell the hotel, or let someone else take it over.'

Perhaps they were right. 'I'm not really a hotelier. Perhaps when the war is over, I may return to Germany to live. First, I suppose I'll have to sort this out with the family lawyer in Elgin.'

'When you have made you decision Hilda, and been up in Elgin to sort things out, please get in touch. I have some work which I think would suit you. You could make a substantial impact,' said Thornton.

'And what would that be?' I asked in anticipation.

'Not today. That's for later. Highly secret work is all I can say.'

'In Britain?' I had to ask.

'That's for later,' he said.'

The following day, with back pay in my handbag, I took the overnight train to Inverness. In the morning I went to the Nethybrig hotel. It had not changed and its vestibule seemed to welcome me home as ever. Fergus was not around. A hotel cleaner informed me that he had joined the Highland Light Infantry and left more than four months ago, at the call to arms.

I called a meeting of the hotel staff. I told them I had decided to put the hotel up for sale with a provision that the present staff remain in post. I gave the long standing Mrs. Creanor the responsibility of keeping the hotel running meantime. She received the news in a fluster. I reassured her that she had costing abilities and a most pleasant nature. She was well suited to follow Mum's role.

The next day, I made an appointment with Mr Adam Gates, mother's solicitor. His oak panelled office had stained tobacco walls with his family of lawyers long since gone kept in perpetuity, overlooking the present generation's professional services, strung up on picture rails. It wasn't the friendliest of greetings he offered.

'It was disappointing that you could not attend your mother's funeral,' he began.

'I was out of the country. I did not hear of her death until a couple of days ago, Mr Gates.'

I thought his comment was less than civil, rather harsh.

'I tried to contact you of course, but out of the country... Germany you mean?'

'No, not Germany I assure you but my business here today is not about me. I have come to give instruction not seek an enquiry,' I said with my pulse rate rising. 'The hotel, it is my wish to sell it as a hotel and retain the current staff. Can that be arranged?'

'It can be sold of course, but the buyer could employ whomsoever he wishes, even knocking it down and building for himself or make it land for a chicken run or pig sty.'

'Even so, my request is for it to be sold as a commercial property and that the same staff remains in post, is made in good faith. I trust these employees who have been with us for some years to run this hotel.'

'Very well Frau Richter, I shall make a note of that.'

'May I say I call myself Hilda Campbell, my maiden name, for obvious reasons? I urge you to inform your acquaintances, I wish that to be my name.'

Mr Gates twiddled his pen between his fingers as if a magician. 'Very well, as you wish, Mrs Campbell. After the funeral I attended to your late mother's wishes as follows. Her estate is divided 75% to you and 25% to... Otto Richter. That will have to be held back of course for the time being. I can provide you with a cheque for

£7,000 pounds sterling. I suggest you bank the cheque as soon as possible, it is a princely amount and so that it earns interest too. The sale of the hotel will be notified to you in due course unless you wish to personally conduct the sale.'

'Thank you Mr Gates. I shall leave that in the good hands of your office and be glad to pay the due fee, in the fullness of time.'

The lawyer nodded his approval. Then he stood up to put away a file into a wire tray on a nearby table. I thought it rather rude. Was this a signal that I should leave? I was not ready to do so.

'So you attended the funeral,' I asked to break the growing silence.

'Did I attend? Who didn't? The whole town came to pay its respects. The hotel is at the centre of our community, not only was your mother well known she was very well respected.'

'I am pleased to hear that.'

There was a moment's silence as we each recalled my mother. I felt he was also using the time to show a more friendly face.

'Will you be staying long?'

'No, I will be heading south soon.'

'And you will give me a forwarding address?'

'I will, of course, as soon as I have a forwarding address.'

That should satisfy him that I intended to remain in the country, I thought. Although that address was still to be found, somewhere.

'Your mother's grave. It is beside your late father's grave.'

'Thank you, that is my next obligation.'

He opened his desk drawer and sat back to let the drawer open.

'Before you go, this is your inheritance.'

He handed me the cheque which he had prepared in advance. I placed it in my handbag.

'Thank you. Now I must not interrupt your work. I should take my leave,' I said rising up from the seat.

'Will you be... seeing Otto in the near future?' he asked out of curiosity.

'That depends doesn't it Mr Gates, doesn't it?'

He nodded also wondering how long the war would last.

'I can assure you I will not be returning to Germany in the near future.'

'Of course not,' he replied.

That afternoon I set off to the churchyard. I knew exactly where I would find their graves. Chrysanthemums lay withered by Mother's grave. I placed them in a nearby bin and returned to stand between the graves. Together again I thought, at rest and oblivious to the unfolding war. This had been their community. It was no longer theirs and certainly no longer mine.

My thoughts recalled my childhood with loving parents and how I asked questions and sought answers of my father's time in Africa, during the Gold Coast wars at the turn of the century. That inspired my spirit of adventure I suppose. So Germany had chosen me as much as I had chosen it. I loved their language, wholehearted food, song and dance. The dance was now macabre and I no longer wished to be associated with it. Perhaps one day Otto might find a way to reappear but now I had no way of communicating with him. Tears filled my eyes. Tears of sorrow, now that I no longer had parents. Tears, for the tender moments with mother, which brought security and peace when we talked. Tears, wondering if I would ever see Otto, Karl and Renate ever again. I knew my parents were there in their graves physically but their spirits were loose, who knew where? Perhaps they were following me, perhaps guiding me? It was a thought I valued and took from that moment of reflection. As clear as a mountain stream I knew now, that after I had cleared out their possessions, I could no longer live in Elgin.

I lay out mother's better clothes and the Hotel staff ladies took what they wished. The auctioneer came to take away surplus heavy wooden furniture from my parents' bedrooms and some small artefacts. I wondered about taking the family teapot but it was an awkward shape. For one memento, I chose a pot Pori china pot. It rarely contained any scent but might one day. It had always been on display in the lounge and that was why I chose to take it with me.

My father's roll top desk was dismantled to be sold and as I helped to do that, I came across a letter. It seemed to have got wedged under the front drawer. I tore part of the envelope as I eased it out. I opened it and read it.

The note, for it was not addressed to anyone, had been written by my father. It was dated 3rd January 1901. The paper was brittle and thin with stained water marks, which I presumed may have been dried tears. I opened the sheet carefully and read.

As I did so, a realisation came to the fore. Was this the substance which father had begged forgiveness on his dying bed? I thought it must have been, for it spoke of an incident in the Ashanti village of Bekwai, in the Gold Coast. Father had been part of a detachment seeking out Ashanti warriors bent on saving their Golden Stool. They had come to a village and saw guns resting against a mud house. Father gave the command to shoot at the house supporting the most rifles. No sooner had the shots been fired when a young female child came out of the house screaming. She held her younger brother in her arms. He had been shot, murdered. It was a death which would haunt my father all his life. He had never told me about this sad incident. Yet it seemed clear that this forgiveness he sought stemmed from that moment. My mind was put at rest. His guilt was gone now and I forgave him as one who also had death on my hands. The nature of war was largely responsible for our actions of regret. It was all I could accept while sharing in the grief of those families in the Gold Coast and in the homes of those lost in the Atlantic, through our interventions. It gave me no comfort to know that maybe these deadly decisions were made with good intentions. But good intentions could never equate with murder.

I would be leaving the town, my people, the hotel and the churchyard soon without looking back. I took with me their memories. I had a future to face, elsewhere.

I had been in Elgin for eleven days. I was anxious to leave. I telephoned London.

'Hello, Mr Dynes?'

'Yes Hilda. I hope you are well.'

'Yes, and you?'

'Busy, but well. So what news have you?

'Only that I want to leave Elgin,'

'Well, we've much better news for you. I can't tell you on the phone. Can you come to London?'

'Tomorrow?'

'Excellent. Come to our office.'

I took the overnight Inverness – London sleeper train. It was a journey of eleven hours, most of which I missed being asleep with the soothing rattle of the rails for most of the journey. There was some deviation inland we were told. It was strictly confidential too. But I wondered. The driver, the signalman, the guard and the station masters would have known too. I was not aware of the detour but welcomed the early morning cup of tea which arrived at 6.30 am.

20

London and a Celebration

I was pleased to be in a city again. Maybe I was more of a
city person after all. There was urban activity in which to
hide and be absorbed. My rural years were in childhood
and adolescence. London to me, even in its darkest hour,
was where I felt safe this morning. War however had
created a visible intensity in the population. It seemed
people walked around half expecting something evil to
happen. That it hadn't, for some time, surprised me even
more as I knew how effective and eager the blitzkrieg
over Warsaw, Paris and Oslo had been. How soon would
London experience this new and terrifying, incisive and
destructive German airpower again?

I reached the offices, surrounded by sandbags at its
entrance. I was led to a room where I saw Messrs Dynes
and Thornton had been joined by a colonel. They smiled
and gave me a warm welcome. It seemed that they were
genuinely pleased to see me.

The Colonel wearing his Sam Brown belt, neat
well-cut moustache and ruddy cheeks was first to step
forward.

'Mrs Campbell, I am Colonel Myers intelligence
Corps. I'm very pleased to meet you.'

I smiled as I shook his hand. I was equally pleased that the designation of Mrs Campbell had been revived.

'Hilda, take a seat,' Thornton said.

Thornton seemed purpose driven. No handshake, perhaps not warranted as we had seen each other not so long ago. It must have implied to the Colonel that we were a team.

'Hilda, Colonel Myers will now share some confidential news. News which I feel will please you,' said Dynes like a proud parent at a school function.

'Working in the field of counter espionage is fraught with danger, I need not tell you that... er... Hilda, if you don't mind me addressing you so.'

I shook my head warming to his developing information.

'We have been sharing your intelligence with the American security services. They have made several arrests. Krause, Jaeger, Becker, Koch, Lange, Hinks and Simmons, they are all in custody,' said the Colonel.

'Hinks and Simmons, I've never met them,' I said in surprise.

'No an octopus has many tentacles,' said Dynes.

I looked at him and he lowered his head in shame at his intervention, a better analogy could have been easily found.

'The fact is we've broken a ring, the Duquesne Spy Ring. It has led to thirty three arrests in total, I believe. They are all German sympathisers feeding the Reich with information to harm the Allies. They will face the American Judicial process. This work was started by you Hilda. It is a tremendous achievement.'

An achievement? I had hardly done this single handed. The colonel seemed to be gilding the lily. 'Thank you. I had no idea that it was such a well established and large spy ring,' I said.

The colonel explained that the agents who formed the Duquesne Ring were placed in key jobs in the United States to get information that could be used in the event of war and to carry out acts of sabotage if the war reached American shores. One opened a restaurant and used his position to get information from his customers; another worked in a travel office so that she could report on Allied ships that were crossing the Atlantic Ocean. Others worked as delivery people so they could deliver secret messages alongside mundane letters and packages through the postal services. America was not at war, he reminded us. There was no need to intercept mail. Yet another spy was a hairdresser prising information out of seated customers with every cut of the hair. They were all controlled in America by Frederick "Fritz" Joubert Duquesne, an agent of the Reich. The Colonel adjusted his tie and turned towards Thornton who spoke briefly.

'Now here's someone in a different role. Someone more like you Hilda.'

'He's certainly one of the more interesting characters,' began the Colonel once more. He spoke of a native of Germany, William Sebold, who served in the German army during World War I. After leaving Germany in 1921, he worked in industrial and aircraft plants throughout the United States and South America. On February 10, 1936, he became a naturalized citizen of the United States.

'They all seem to be naturalised Americans. Their accents very much so,' I said.

'Indeed they are. Sebold returned to Germany in February 1939 to visit his ailing mother in Mülheim. You see a similarity?'

'Indeed, back to front but yes, the same maternal pull'.

'On arrival in Hamburg, he was approached by a member of the Gestapo, Herr Gerhardt Eicke, who said that Sebold would be contacted in the near future. Sebold proceeded to Mülheim where he obtained employment,' the Colonel informed me.

'Hamburg; Eicke; contacted in the near future... the exact words Eicke spoke, so familiar to me.' I recalled in greater detail.

'Indeed.'

I learned that William G. Sebold was an interesting and valuable individual. He had been blackmailed into becoming a spy for Germany, became a double agent like myself and helped the FBI gather evidence, but only after they had started to work on the information I had apparently given. I heard that when the war started in Europe, the FBI gave Sebold a shortwave radio for his flat in New York. He learned what information Germany was sending its spies in the United States and controlled what he sent to Germany.

I listened with great interest but wondered whether our work overlapped. 'I thought my position in Portugal was designed to do this. Wasn't I to get the messages from the States?'

'This was a different set-up, Hilda. The messages

from Germany came from U-boats lurking in the mid Atlantic. You in Portugal received the best intelligence by static radio,' said the Colonel.

'I see,' I said.

'Incidentally, Sebold's success as a counterespionage agent was demonstrated by the successful prosecution of several German agents last week,' said the Colonel.

'I think this calls for some sort of celebration,' said Dynes ringing a bell he had lifted from the table.

The door opened and an apron wearing lady came in with a silver tray on which four glasses of sherry were presented. She lay them down on a side table and smartly left us to serve ourselves. Dynes was quick to play host and passed round the glasses.

'To more success and victory,' toasted the Colonel.

'Success and Victory,' we said in unison.

I tasted the dry Spanish sherry. It was good but not a Portuguese glass of port. That symbol of total success was premature.

Coffee followed and then Colonel Myers left with further handshakes all around.

MI6 was the heart of counter espionage and the surroundings fitted that austere yet functional department. A bookcase surrounded the room I was in. I strained my eyes to read book titles. Some spines were faded. Others too high to identify. Dynes caught my browsing attention.

'By all means, do browse the library. Borrow any of the books at any time if you wish, as long as you return them, of course.'

'I've never paid a library fine in my life I assure you,' I said.

Dynes laughed. 'I'm sure you haven't. Then when you are ready, you can leave your bag here. We will meet again at 2pm, prompt.'

'So I have the freedom of London for a couple of hours, to find accommodation?'

'No, not accommodation. Just find some lunch and... here's a gas mask in its box. I don't suppose you have one?'

'Not yet,' I replied.

'As for your accommodation, that will depend on our meeting this afternoon.' Thornton gave one of his penetrating looks which defied any further question. I knew I had to wait till he was ready to share his thoughts. It seemed lunch took precedence at that moment for us both. They set off almost together, I suspect to lunch at an old boys club. I knew I'd find a less salubrious eating establishment.

21

A Gruelling Interview and a New Assignment

Heads were downcast. It was not really raining. It was one of those drizzly days. It seemed a great burden was borne on the backs of the multitude of pedestrians. All had their gas masks round their necks or strung over their shoulders. The war had in no way deterred the stoic Londoners.

I walked along the embankment seeing two small naval ships in their grey and black camouflage await instructions. The view was not dissimilar to that of Hamburg, still so fresh in my mind.

I found the Lyons Corner Tearooms and entered. Most of the tables were already occupied as the waitresses weaved their way with fodder around the seated customers like matadors. I was placed at a single table at the back of the restaurant. There was no view. I didn't need one. My thoughts turned to what I might expect at the immanent meeting in an hour or so.

The soup was thick nutritious broth which I had with two slices of buttered brown bread. It was filling but it was my nerves that made me order a cup of tea to follow. I saw the disappointment in the waitress's eyes that I had not asked for a main course, let alone a sweet, but my mind was four streets away from my body. Another single person would soon be seated where I was and that would be acceptable to the waitresses. I felt safe in this tearoom. Its reputation was well earned and the British cup of tea is not only always sought but seen as the elixir to life in all its trials.

Where could I be sent? I could not imagine. Perhaps a desk job with them in London was on their minds. What could I offer them? Fluent German, some radio experience, maybe even some nerves of steel perhaps? That offering might lead me into an army uniform on the coast to hold back the Hun. I am too old for uniformed service, surely? I am sure of that... suppose.

I returned to the MI6 office, eager to hear their plans for me. I was now hoping they would materialise that afternoon because I had burnt my bridges. Elgin was no longer available to me nor Portugal or Hamburg for that matter but I had banked that parental cheque so I could buy some time to settle somewhere.

'Come in Hilda, have a seat,' said Dynes.

'Thank you.'

'I'll wait for Mr Thornton. He's got some interesting news from Portugal.'

'Portugal,' I repeated in a shout more than a voice. 'You mean I might be returning to Portugal?' Concern etched all over my face.

Dynes laughed and was still laughing when Thornton came in.

'Did I miss a joke, because I could certainly appreciate one right now?' he asked.

'Hilda wondered if she could return to Portugal,' Thornton said still laughing. Dynes began to smile. I remained relaxed and totally unaware why my response should have attracted this mirth.

'You can't return to Portugal Hilda. You see, you are officially dead.'

'What, you mean they found a body?'

'Not exactly, we received news from Lisbon today that you made the front page locally. English woman missing; clothes found on the beach. The chief of police had concluded that Miss Hilda Campbell must have drowned and stood down a coastal search to find her body.'

'I wonder if they sealed off my cottage before the German Ambassador's staff reached the house. If so the radio and probably Inka would still be there.'

'I'm sure the German Embassy sent someone to the cottage as soon as they heard you were missing. They would have found the radio and seized it. Hard to believe otherwise. That is not our problem. I think you have been very clever. Eicke will soon learn of your demise, if he has not already been informed. On his behalf, I must tell you he cannot attend your funeral. I'm a bit busy too, for that matter.'

You could have heard our laughing all the way to Nelson's Column. I even saw Lord Nelson smile in my mind.

'We cannot let you surface again or he will know you are a counterspy,' said Thornton.

I now realised the mirth confirmed I would not be going back to Portugal or head off to any other espionage venue. I felt a weight lift from my shoulders.

'So do you have a future for me now that Portugal is out of the question?'

'I think we have, Hilda. It is highly secret. I cannot stress this too much. I am not prepared to talk about it yet.'

'I see. Can you tell me where will this be, I mean in Britain or elsewhere?'

'You are pushing me Hilda. I'll tell you where. You would be based near London. We have to share your background with higher authorities first. The fact is that you are a fluent German speaker and your experience of the Nazi machine is invaluable. They feel you could be very useful indeed. They of course understood your earlier exploits for the Germans and of course Otto. We had to confirm your days of counter espionage were over. They'd like to meet you this afternoon for themselves and before that; you will have to sit an examination paper, a mathematical paper.'

'Really? I can't imagine why. Sounds like school all over again.'

'Precisely,' said Dynes, nodding his head a dozen times. Clearly he did have plans for me, perhaps a desk job. I'd be content with that as long as it seemed worthwhile. This spying was certainly not for me.

Dynes opened his case and produced an unfolded paper.

'Here, read this Hilda.'

As I read this official document, I could now see

why he thought my future work was crucial and that my commitment had to be total. It took a few minutes to read the document and I did so in total silence. I reached the end where it invited me to sign to verify I had accepted the rules. Dynes gave me a pen and I duly signed.

'That's the Official Secrets document signed. Forget any similar document Eicke got you to sign. Your colours are tied to our masts fairly and squarely now,' said Thornton.

'I thought they always had been,' I replied.

That afternoon I was sent to room eight, on the second floor of the Admiralty office. Two others sat outside the room. They were younger women, Wrens, in naval uniform.

'Good afternoon. All doing the maths test?' I asked to break the ice.

Strangely their collective reply was only in smiles. None of them ventured any information. I smiled too. The poster above their heads declared in bold large letters that *Careless Talk Costs Lives*. They sat beneath the message unable to see it, unless they saw it when entering. I rather suspected it was the last order they received from their superiors as well, before arriving in this corridor. Keep 'mum' and they did.

High ceilings and wooden panels bearing royalty and political figures hung from picture hooks. They looked down on us as if to urge us to do what we could for our country. A maths test seemed to be the last thing to contribute to the war. Perhaps I had not questioned

Thornton enough about its relevance. He seemed to be proposing a new direction but as a maths teacher? I somehow doubted it.

We were led into a room with a dominating dark oak table. We were positioned at top, middle and end where the examination paper lay downturned beside a pencil, a sharpener and a rubber.

'Ladies, you have an hour and a half to complete as many of the questions as you can. There will be no talking, consulting or enquiring of one another. Do I make myself clear?' asked the duty staff sergeant.

We glanced at each other.

'Yes, quite clear,' we said one after the other.

He thrust forward his watch arm in an ostentations manner. His other arm was then raised. It awaited its signal. Then he smartly lowered his arm to his side and gave the instruction to '*UP PENS, BEGIN*.' I turned the paper over to see the questions first. Part one were some very easy fractions, divisions, multiplications and subtractions, an easy starter. Part two was a geometry paper and page three trigonometry. Page four was based on algebraic equations. They used to be my class bread and butter sums so many years ago. I was quietly confident I would remember how to solve them as I lifted my pencil.

I decided to do the more advanced questions first. I thought if I ran out of time it would be better to have done so on returning to page one. I sharpened my pencil without thinking whether it needed to be sharper. My mind wandered in the trigonometry question where the time was sought for a cruiser sailing at 35 nautical miles per hour to come to the aid a sinking ship at point B, while evading U-boats at position C. The problem fell to my advantage as the co-ordinates of the convoys came rushing back to my memory of my time in Portugal.

I began to enjoy this task. I remembered sitting with Otto guiding him through mathematical hoops and rings as he progressed through his school years. The questions were as fresh a subject as it was then. I looked up at the wall clock. I had forty three minutes left. I turned to the Geometry paper. I relished the angles and tackled the questions presented. On completion, I had a little more than ten minutes to complete paper one. Somehow I took great care over this part. A slip here might dissuade an examiner to delve further into my other answers. Yet these final questions were embarrassingly easy. I supposed it was designed to rate and separate the three of us. For what, I still wondered?

I read through my answers checking the logic I had applied to each question. I felt both satisfied that my efforts had been diligent and I was confident that my answers were correct; at least I had done my very best. I put my pencil down and gazed at the second hand of the large clock at the end of the room as it counted down the last couple of minutes. Still I had no idea why this mathematical test had come my way.

'Time ladies, pencils down,' the non commissioned officer said approaching to gather up the papers and making sure our names were on the top of the front page.

'Please take a seat outside. You will each be called to interview with Sir William Raeburn, in alphabetical order. Baker, Campbell then Wheeler.

'Always last, the problem with being a Wheeler,' one of the Wrens said.

'Madam, if the first may be last then surely the last maybe first? This time perhaps? Then I shall reverse the order. Miss Wheeler, you will be first,' said the staff sergeant with an air of superiority.

Just what were they testing us for? I was not sure of his logic either but the one thing made evidently clear was that I would be in the middle. My instinct was to win; I'd prefer to have come first.

Miss Wheeler's interview lasted almost twenty minutes. Now it was my turn to be interviewed by a man with a distinctively Scottish surname. Perhaps a lucky omen was on the cards. That augured well in my mind as I entered his room.

Sir William sat at the end of the room. His head bowed, his hand writing at a fast pace and his broad shoulders dominating his presence. He had white hair, a neat coiffure. He wore a dark if not a black suit, a gold coloured waistcoat with splattered black spots; a white shirt and a dark blue tie. His handkerchief sat peaked in his top pocket, perhaps placed this morning by a dotting wife. Maybe the war had forced him out of retirement. He may have been a professional soldier or a top civil service manger but now he had the task of interviewing three confused ladies.

The pen was in his right hand; his spectacle leg was held in the other. The silence gave me time to analyse the man who was about to interview me, for what, again remaining a mystery.

Without raising his head, he addressed me.

'Frau Richter, sit down.'

I was taken aback with his abruptness. I sat down on the hard backed chair placed before him. This man knew my background. Was he showing me he did or was his motive more sinister than that?

'You are German. We are at war with your country. Why should I not lock you up for the duration of the war?'

My knees were tense, my pulse rate rose. 'My country is Scotland, my loyalty the King. My name is Hilda Campbell. I have specific qualities which this country needs.'

'Your son is in the German army and you have a home in Hanover. Or is that a fabrication in your deception?'

My breathing was shallow and I felt my cheeks drain in colour. This man knew much about my past but very little of my recent activities.

'Yes, I have a son in the German Army and he has our old home. I am a widow. I do not deny these facts. I have lived in the torque turning terror which is the Third Reich. I was house-bound in the First World War. That fate would not be offered me in the present climate in Germany. Hitler will stop at nothing. He is not just a menace to Great Britain; he is a menace to the world. I will play my part in defeating this terror, even if you insist, from a British prison. Sir, your assessment of me is misplaced.'

My outburst was controlled. My voice had been steady and unemotional. But my heart rate was higher than normal and I could hear its beat. This interview had hardly begun, I was now prepared to give as good as I was getting. I awaited his response.

'You were directed to Portugal by Herr Eicke, on his instruction. You provided intelligence to the enemy. This is a treasonable offence.'

'I do not deny being a double agent, or a counterspy, call me what you will. The time I spent in Germany after the war started had to continue without me becoming a suspected thorn in their side. I would not have survived. I did send one message to Berlin, to earn my credibility but I was able to identify a German spy ring based in America. Why would I have done that if I was a German spy? Why I ask you, why?"

I had given him something to think about.

'Why would you possess an Eagle Civilian Cross?'

Only Dynes and Thornton knew about this medal. He must have spoken to them. Surely they were not in on this gruelling interrogation? God, I was being turned over like a pig on a spit. Now I was a viper with a tongue ready to strike.

'That, I can explain. It was given, not awarded, to retain my loyalty to the Reich. It was not for any action I had achieved for the glorification of the Reich. I have been open with MI6 with that information as with all the evidence I have given.'

There was no way I was making him see my point of view; my loyalty. My eyes welled up. I sought a handkerchief to dab them dry.

'Crocodile tears?' he said as a further provocation.

I ignored this jibe. His rudeness was cutting and heartless. I began to hate this man. This was no interview; it was a nasty interrogation, on par with Gestapo questioning.

'How else can I convince you of my loyalty to this country?'

'Through a period of detention?' he suggested.

I had heard enough. Without my backers, I was slipping into a British jail for the duration of the war.

'I demand to see Dynes and Thornton. They have faith in me even if you don't.' I stood up. 'Good day.'

'Please Miss Campbell, please return to your seat.'

I stopped with my back still facing him. A 'please', was he softening? It seemed his voice was less harsh. I had nothing to lose. I turned and stared at his forehead with my penetrating eyes. I could not stare below at his intense gaze. My lips were tense and dry. I kept from him any feminine charm. I was livid. I felt my knees tremble beneath my skirt.

'Do you like crosswords?' he asked.

I wondered for a moment whether he said cross words or crosswords for he had certainly provided the former.

'Crosswords?' I clarified.

'Yes, crosswords.'

'I've not done a crossword for some time, as you could imagine. I have always done them when I came across them, yes in German as well as English. I usually completed them.'

'Cryptic or not cryptic?' he asked.

'Cryptic are certainly more satisfying but all crosswords when I encounter them and when I have the time to complete them.' I wondered if I should sit down once more in front of him. I decided I would not. By standing I was inviting him to terminate the interview sooner, not later.

'You enjoy them?'

'Very much so, why?' I asked forcing him to reply for a change.

He did not respond, of course. It was not in his nature. Instead he made a note of what I had said. A knock on the door diverted our attention.

'Come in.'

The door opened. She closed it behind her.

A women in her mid years approached Sir William's desk with a brown folder. She handed it to him then departed without saying a word or looking my way. Sir William opened the folder and studied the papers, turning them over frequently. I waited and watched. Was this a directive requiring his signature and my detention? That was in the forefront of my mind before he spoke.

'Please,' he said extending his hand to the empty chair. I hesitated. The papers seemed to have distracted him. His venom seemed less poisonous now. I sat down once more clasping my hands over my crossed legs' knees.

'98% Miss Campbell, admirable,' he said.

At last, a positive statement. It was still too little to change my mind about him.

'98%? How did I lose two marks?' I inquired.

He turned the page and smiled. It made him more humane and I would even reluctantly admit he was quite a handsome elderly individual.

'The trigonometry shows your mind must have

wandered momentarily. The working was not all there, the answer was correct, like all the other answers you submitted. The marker chose to fault you on the missing line necessary to explain your working towards the answer. Your mind must have been racing against your hand. But that is a minor detail. It was by far the best result of the three candidates.'

'So you have me now as a qualified maths teacher in a detention camp.'

I detected a smile on his ruddy face.

'I believe you Hilda. I think you will do well in the position now available to you. I cannot emphasis how secret this operation is. Have you signed the Official Secrets Act declaration?'

'Yes, I have,' I said robustly avoiding telling him exactly when I had signed the certificate.

'I will of course have that verified. Any deviation from that and I will advocate the death penalty for treason. You understand? I'd have no hesitation to see you hang if you turn against this country,' he said with the most inappropriate smile as he spoke.

I shook my head at the thought of betrayal. It was difficult to understand the volte-face of this senior administrative official. Yet he seemed satisfied that his gruelling questions had not cracked my resolve. He was seeing my true colours. I slowly accepted that he had met his match in my determination to state my case.

He stood up, drew back his chair and offered his hand as a peace offering. He held it out and I approached to shake his.

'I had to be hard on you Hilda. I believe you, I assure

you I do. Your loyalty had to be tested hadn't it? German son etc etc... I know it must be hard for you not to know where your son is. But your loyalty to our defence of the Realm is not in question. I trust that one day you will be with your son Otto, again.'

'Thank you. You did have me worried,' I said warming to him at last.

'What we have in mind for you is top secret. I cannot stress that enough. Listen carefully. I'd like you to go to Bletchley Station this afternoon. You will be met by a car.'

'And where will I spend the night?' I asked out of curiosity and necessity.

'That will be taken care of, I assure you. Regard this as a crucial assignment. You bring to the task, some much-valued qualities.'

'Wait outside please; you may have a colleague to join you.'

'Just one colleague?' I asked in clarification.

'98%, 92% and 74%. Yes, there will be just one other to accompany you.'

22

A Chance Meeting at Bletchley

The train chugged its way through Buckinghamshire until it arrived at Bletchley station. It struck me as a small rural station that would see few trains in the course of a day. It was after all a quintessential English rural station. However, there turned out to be many more trains crossing through Bletchley from Oxford to Cambridge and vice versa. The air was still and fresh. Birds chattered and lightened our spirits after the noisy starlings of central London, as we left the train. The country seemed much safer than the capital. There was a slower pace to life. Yet we were not far from the city. A stray German bomb might find its way to Buckinghamshire. Nowhere was safe and that had to be our outlook.

'Looks like we have arrived at Bletchley Park,' said Sally Baker my traveling companion.

A driver approached having overheard the remark.

'You won't hear anyone call it that. It's BP from now on, BP,' said the driver. 'Are you the two ladies from London?'

'Yes and we were told we would be met by a driver,' I said.

'That's me. Step in.'

A few passengers set off from the station on foot. Sally Baker and I entered the black Austin Seven Swallow Saloon. I could see its make, written on its front grill. A rather swanky car for the journey, I thought. It was a very short ride indeed to the entrance of Bletchley Park.

The car proceeded past the main stone building through the park to a long wooden hut. Trees surrounded the view from behind. In front was a neatly manicured lawn with only a handful of fallen leaves to mar the perfection of the mown pattern.

'This is HMS Pembroke V. This is where the Wrens are. Wren Barker, this is where you are housed.'

'HMS Pembroke indeed, it must be a dry dock.' Sally laughed as she left the car with her bag weighing her down. She turned back for a last look at me fearing there would be so many new faces; it would be good to recognise at least one known face in the weeks and months ahead.

I was dropped off at the London Signals Intelligence Centre, Hut 4. This was to be my workstation. It was positioned to the rear of the main building. It faced north and I was sure it saw little if any sunshine being in the shadow of the main house. My residential quarters were a stone's throw away in Hut 19. Damp walls and poor internal heating was my first and lasting impression. One perk I soon realised was that we were accommodated on site. Most Wrens seemed to be bussed in from somewhere nearby. It meant however I would be likely to work and be available at any part of the day or night.

There were five other women in the residential quarters. Most were civilian and that made me inconspicuous. I was pleased about that. The others all came from naval detachments. When working, our shoulders bowed over scripts, we saw very little of each other for most of the day.

After our initial training in the so-called 'Spy School' at BP run by John Saltman, I was acutely aware of the secrecy of the work being done. We were told we were all cogs attending to our own specialist wheels. We must never ask or seek out the route the work came to us, or the route it took after each of our part in its journey had been completed. I began to work at Hut 4 six days a week. We rotated through three shifts; 4pm to midnight, midnight to 8am (by far the least liked shift) and the bearable 8am to 4pm. At the end of the third week I was expected to take time off from 8am and come back at 4am. Much of that time was spent in exhaustion cured only by sound sleep

Such a strict working practice caused stress for many of the Wrens. I was not nearly under such pressure. When a text required translation, I concentrated hard to provide it promptly before dispatching it into a wire tray. Then I waited until the next piece of work arrived. However some of the German text was written in a complicated code and I had to make sense of the message. I used a rather noisy adding machine to find a pattern of words to complete the text. I enjoyed this part of the work immensely. It presented a challenge. I could now see why the cryptic crossword question arose in my interview. The excitement made time fly and the satisfaction when the message was interpreted to make sound sense was wonderful. The only outsiders we heard were the motorbikes which arrived and left regularly. I never knew where they came from or where they went when they left BP. Not even a milkman was seen. Goodness knows how they fed us apart from the battery of egg-producing hens pecking around the rear of the huts. Eggs were our staple diet until some American Boffs arrived at BP and we discovered Baloney sausage, Lucky Strike cigarettes, and seamed nylon stockings which we were more than happy to spend from our meagre wages. There were however fewer opportunities to flaunt our silky legs on the village dancehall floor. Indeed no socialising occurred. Many of us now chewed gum as we worked. Some saw it enhance their work concentration but most, like myself, chewed it for its novelty. I gave up chewing gum after a month or so. I could not see how this endless chewing would ever interest the British taste. By now of course America had joined the war and they gave us tremendous hope as well as an insight to a new and exciting lifestyle.

One day, after more than a year at work, a colonel came into my room with a message for translation. He prided himself in his ability to read in somewhat hesitant German. I encouraged him. Then I stopped. I looked up at him.

'Hamburg 1932...' I said.

He stepped back to see my face in profile. He could not make anything of my statement.

'British Consul Hamburg 1927-1932?' I clarified further.

'Yes, yes, that's right. And... are you not... Dr Richter's

wife?' he said cautiously.

'Dr Willy Richter's widow, Colonel Simpson.'

He contemplated what he heard and I thought I could see him wondering how on earth I could have arrived in BP.

'You are working here?' he asked with some degree of disbelief, although it was more than obvious that I was fully employed at BP.

'You doubt my loyalty to the King?'

'I suppose not. I know you are Scottish. I'm just very surprised you are here.'

'Our meeting is a surprise for us both.' The words lingered and we took out of what was said and played with the words in our heads. 'Secrecy is paramount but perhaps we could talk more sometime about our time in Germany. In privacy I hasten to add,' I said.

'Then we shall. May I also hear your oboe again?'

What a surprise. He had indeed remembered me after all.

'You have not forgotten I have an oboe?' I said in delight but regretted I was reiterating his words.

'You played at the British Consul in the late 20's or perhaps, was it the early 30's?'

I recalled those happier times with affection.

'And was it not you Colonel, who sang at one of the Consul gatherings?'

He smiled. 'Yes, I had the baritone voice.'

'You speak in the past tense. Surely you still sing?'

I thought I saw his bottom lip quiver, ever so slightly.

'Not so much in recent years, after my wife died.'

There was a moment's hesitation as we realised we

were two lonely souls in a place of secrecy and hard work. It was then it hit me, hit me hard. A brief thought I allowed myself was that our meeting based on years of happiness elsewhere which we had in common, could lead to a future life of happiness, opened my heart to him.

'Perhaps when I have some time off, we could play music together?' he said.

I focussed on his crown and two pips insignia of a colonel. Any musical gathering would be approved if he said so.

'To enjoy some semblance of normality, I'd be delighted,' I said.

We gave each other a contented smile as footsteps were heard approaching. Formality resumed.

'This document er... Hilda isn't it?' He handed over the piece for translation.

'Yes, Hilda Campbell at your service.'

'And me, Francis Simpson at yours.' Our smiles remained as our eyes and ears sought eager eavesdroppers. The footsteps had passed but other footsteps could be heard to approach. The conversation was over and he left, glancing back at me before he was out of sight.

Before I had time to consider this remarkable chance meeting, he was gone. I turned to the work he had given me, another message apparently from the German High Command. It took several moments for me to compose myself before turning my attention to the work in hand. I could not detect nor ask how we had come into possession of these German messages. This existence seemed to thrive on information. It required each to do their job and mine was translation not espionage. Mine was not to question why, as it was for all, engaged at desks at BP.

That conversation I had had with Francis, had a particular cognisance given everywhere were notices of talking forbiddance. "Do not talk at meals. Do not talk in transport. Do not talk travelling. Do not talk in the billet. Do not talk by your own fireside", posters stated.

That night when I was in my bed I recalled the only conversation I had heard that day. It melted into the time I last saw him almost a decade ago. Francis had a brilliant brain and fine singing voice. He perhaps could have been an academic, not a military man. I was convinced that his status as a colonel reflected his professional past not gained as a professional soldier.

As the weeks progressed I occasionally saw Francis. We shared unspoken smiles as we passed each other with a slight hesitation in our steps. The constant reminders of 'not talking' were an order. They could not be broken.

A few days later a folded sheet of paper lay on my desk when I reported on duty. I lifted it and turned it over. My hand shook. My heart was broken. I learned on 5th June 1942 that Francis had taken up his posting as Consul-General at Leopoldville in the Belgian Congo. I was devastated. I had lost a friendship which had great potential in my mind. I did not suppose Francis wished to leave BP but he had now done so in the most dramatic of ways. Central Africa with its heat, disease, poverty and Belgian colonial overtures was no respite from a world war. He had gone and so too his baritone voice. My memory was left with three concerts we gave in the mess. One for each of the three shifts with some other musicians making up a sizable orchestra of twelve people. It seemed music and song was allowed but no chatter in the audience. Now I no longer felt able to perform a concert again without his baritone voice singing to great applause. He had made an impact on all my senses. I admit that night I shed a tear. Possibly it was because his departure was so sudden and I had no time to see him before he left.

Translation continued at a very steady pace. The work at times seemed tedious but its importance grew in my mind when on two occasions Winston Churchill, the Prime minister, appeared. I did not see him the first time but on the second occasion he came to the desk I was working at, placed his hand on my shoulder and patted it. 'Fine work young lady. Keep it up and we'll win this war.'

I wanted to reply but found no words appropriate to tell the prime minister. Did he really say *young lady?* No Talking signs on the wall seemed to compromise any forming sentences in my head. His presence lightened my load and of course The United States of America was now an important contributing ally. It seemed by the end of 1942, we were beginning to turn the tide. With the no talking rule in force, the newspapers which arrived regularly, were devoured over and over again. Never did they refer to BP or its activities. To all and asunder we did not exist.

One day we heard the noise of night bombers drone louder and louder overhead. I read later that PB had been hit by one stray bomb in 1940 probably intended for Bletchley Station. But we had no direct hit. Nor would the enemy know the significance of the line. I listened as I lay in bed. The noise faded and I knew we had not been the target that night. Perhaps there was no target. Maybe they were the large American planes returning after a bombing on mainland Europe.

The bombing of what and of where? Could Hamburg have been their target? Would Renate be safe? Was Otto on home leave? Oh, how I wished American and British bombers hit Berlin, the centre of the terror, not my beloved Hamburg.

More significant and reassuring I felt the tide was turning. Others sensed that too.

23

Preparing a Return to Hamburg

The new year of 1945 was gilded with expectation, fraught by doubt. Hitler's plans were crumbling but no one seemed able to tell him. The spirit had gone out of the ordinary German soldier, conscious of an advancing Russian army to the east but the die-hards, the unquestioning servants of Nazism hung on tenaciously. If desertion was an option for the soldiers I hoped they could take that risk without repercussions. Perhaps Otto had already returned to Hamburg and home to hide until the last days of conflict.

I had to undergo double shifts and one week I was on call all night before starting my day shift. By the spring there were signs that the war in Europe would end very soon. The Battle of the Bulge may have been the last stand-to engagement. Germany might be cut up by the forces of both East and West, the papers suggested. How much retribution would the victors take? Surely not nearly as much as they took after the First World War? That undoubtedly contributed to this Second World War. Surely there would never be a third world war? These questions I had to ask myself because I needed to find Otto, Karl and Renate. I wanted to get back to Hamburg as soon as I could.

When in May, the war ended I contacted Thornton by telephone knowing all calls were monitored. I simply told him my days at BP were coming to an end and I wanted to return to see my family, especially my son. Of course no one could suspect that meant a return to Hamburg. The intercepted call had no repercussions.

The following week several Wrens and civilian staff were summoned to Hut 13 where we received a stern lecture from a Brigadier. His message was simple. We may be leaving Bletchley but what we did during the war and the fact that we did work at BP must never ever be discussed anywhere or at any time. If asked what we had done during the war, we had to state it was routine secretarial work but the work must remain confidential. In fact the work and the venue must remain top secret, we were told, and the full force of the law would come down on anyone divulging BP's existence. After we all agreed to this commitment, one by one, we were free to leave. Many stayed. Those, like me who wished to leave, were permitted to do so subject to the needs of the slowing down operation. The work being done at BP was far from over as a re-alignment of Europe was now on the political agenda. But the German translations had trickled down to quieter days. There was sufficient cover for me to return to London.

I left BP during the first week of June and made for the capital to see Dynes and Thornton. Everywhere were flags in the centre of the city. People went around with smiles of relief on their faces now that the war was over. Some American naval ratings were having the time of their lives with English girls hooked on their arms. Many different nationalities in the uniform of all the services, the home guard, policemen and special constables were congregating in the centre of the city. The bars were full as were the cafés doing a roaring trade.

A twelve piece Salvation Army band was at full volume belting out Onward Christian Soldiers while bonneted ladies handed out paper cups of hot tea. It seemed that the country was enjoying an extended victory but cautious that the war in the East was not yet concluded.

I made my way to the MI6 offices which had retained its front entrance sandbags and climbed the stairs. I informed the young lady at the desk that I had arrived. I did not recognise her nor did she recognise me, so forgave her when she asked for my name.

'Tell Mr Thornton that Frau Hilda Richter has arrived.'

I saw her take an inward breath with her mouth slightly agape. So soon after the end of hostilities, a German woman had arrived at her desk at MI6. Unquestioningly, she kept her thoughts to herself as she knocked on Thornton's door to announce my arrival.

'My dear Hilda, do come in,' he said.

'Thank you I trust you are well.'

'Yes very well thank you and relieved that the war is over.'

'I certainly am, and Mr Dynes, is he about?'

'No he's gone to Birmingham today. Anyway, it's been a while since we met. So, you survived the war in one piece.'

'Survived? I felt nowhere near the conflict. We were in huts all the time. Except for a couple of concerts I managed to organise.'

'Hmm they would have enjoyed that even although they would have been a captive audience, as it were.' We laughed to relieve the stress which was still bound tight in our muscles.

'Yes, captive and sworn to secrecy. I'm sorry I can't tell you what the work entailed.'

'I know. Remember, I sent you there.'

'Yes but even I don't know the full picture; how we received messages at such a rate, and all had to be translated; but there I go again, in breach of the Official Secrets act already.'

We laughed knowing it was necessary to offload all tensions and pressures of recent months and the past few years as well. My thoughts then turned to my immediate pressing needs.

'I am sure I can be of no use to you now,' I said slowly giving him time to find another vacancy for I had no inkling what work lay ahead for me in Britain. But my thoughts of work had to be placed on the back burner. I had more pressing needs.

'We will have to part indeed, that's in no doubt at all,' he said.

'There is just one favour I ask of you.'

'And that is?'

I could hold back no longer in making use of his contacts. 'I need to get to Hamburg,' I said.

'I see, to trace Otto and your brother-in-law and his wife?'

'Exactly.'

Thornton opened his desk diary and turned a few pages. I wondered if he could pull this rabbit out of his hat. I was sure it was no more than a thin chance. I was not optimistic.

'You know Hamburg will not be as you know it?'

'You mean the bombing?'

'Yes, but do you know the extent of the bombing?'

'No, I can't really imagine.'

'The docks were our target. Any device that did not hit the quays, hit the city. No pilot wanted to waste a bomb over the sea.'

'I don't care it's a need I can't ignore. I need to get to Hamburg,' I pleaded.

He continued to leaf through his diary. Then he lifted his telephone.

'Hello, Transport?... yes, Thornton here. Anyone going to Hamburg? Then let me know when one is leaving. I have a live package.' He replaced the telephone.

'If they can't do it no one will. I suggest you stock up on provisions. It will be very rough over there. No shops, provisions will be scarce. Nothing will be functioning yet. You will have to work quickly and get back promptly. It's not a place ready for you.'

I should have been depressed by what I was being told but I was optimistic that some semblance of life was around Hamburg and I needed to see it for myself.

'Perhaps you can leave notes and follow-up addresses. Perhaps Otto will be heading home too. Bring him home perhaps.'

'That would be a pleasant thought,' I said.

'Come back at three this afternoon and see if we have made any progress.'

'Thank you Mr Thornton. You have been very kind to me.'

I purchased some packets of dried American soup; some dried fruit and a loaf of bread. I purchased a bag which I could carry on my back. Some slices of ham and cheese were not heavy. The fruit tins I bought weighed me down somewhat but the packet of water biscuits filled my bag. I returned to Thornton's office five minutes early.

'Come in Hilda. We've got you a flight to an airport just outside Hamburg.'

'Oh thank you, that's wonderful news. Thank you so much.'

'Don't thank me, thank the Yanks. They'll be over here shortly to pick you up and take you to their base. You'll be heading for Hamburg early, tomorrow morning.'

I smiled a broad smile my face had not stretched for many months. This was indeed the quickest way to my homecoming family. There was just one issue I could see, now that I was heavily laden.

'I wonder. When I return, if you could keep my oboe with you? I won't need it this time in Hamburg and it has quite a heavy case. Anyway, I really have no home to go to yet. And what's more, I'm not sure where I'll settle down.'

Thornton smiled at my request.

'I'd be delighted to help. Regard this office as your base. I fully understand. Mind you, I thought you two were inseparable.'

'We are. But I am sure you won't sell it,' I laughed.

He walked over to a high walled cupboard and climbed a stack of four wooden steps.

'Here, this cupboard has a high shelf. It's locked every night. That seems the most secure place to store it,' he said.

'Yes, that's if we both can remember where it is.' We laughed thinking such a thought impossible.

I did not have to wait too long. The door knocked and in came an American soldier in smartly creased trousers and a flying jacket.

'Sir, Colonel Zak Withers reporting for duty. A damsel in distress I'm seekin'. I'm sure lookin' for one stunning dame,' he said.

'You can't possibly mean me colonel, but I do wish to go to Hamburg. I detect a southern accent there,' I said.

The colonel looked at me.

'Louisiana man I am, Ma'am. Got to the dance late but saw some action in the Battle of the Bulge.'

'Creditable flying skills required for that engagement I imagine sir,' I said.

'Thank you Ma'am, sure was a tricky op. Hear you're headin' for Hamburg. You sure got guts.'

'Guts? I'm not flying the machine,' I joked.

'No, your boys hit Hamburg real bad. Not easy to get around.'

'I know where I am going,' I informed him.

'Sure thing Ma'am. Glad to take you on board. But we leave early tomorrow. I'm taking you back to base at Northolt, not too far from here, a bit north of the city. We leave early tomorrow. 'Yawl ready to go?'

'I sure am ready to return to Northolt,' I said in my best American accent. He slapped my back in a paternal manner even although he could have been my other son.

My bunk bed was in a row of rooms with a shower at the end. A plastic shower curtain drooped down in the centre with a few hooks missing. It informed any passerby that someone was engaged in the shower. The opaque shower curtain hardly hid any modesty.

'Excuse the art work. We're all randy around here,' laughed a young flying sergeant with his haunch on the table, his left leg swinging above the floor. He held a Lucky Strike between his fingers and tapped the ash into an empty beer can.

I chose not to remark on the nude women in various poses which decorated the hut common room. I understood their frustration.

'Don't really get women here. We chose the best room for you. The others are less tasteful,' he said.

I did not doubt him.

'Meal in main the hut across there,' said the sergeant pointing out of the window. '6 pm sharp or you get the scraps. Breakfast from 6 am till 8 am but you'll be away by then, I guess.'

I risked a shower later that afternoon and sang songs to deter any visitors. They respected my privacy. I returned to my room to dress, excited that I'd be returning to Hamburg, to a defeated Germany, to my home and family. I hoped above all I'd not be disappointed even though the bomb damage seemed to have been considerable. A niggle persisted. Was it realistic to find my son? So many young men had died. I decided to assume he was dead to absorb that truth if it came to be. If he was alive, I would have a low base to shoot up in ecstatic delight. Only time would tell. I would sleep with these positive thoughts active on my mind that night.

I ate my first Cobb Salad that evening with a purloined white Alsace wine. It seemed the American chef had been productive and the Cobb salad edible but unusual with sour bread to accompany this meal. It was more than a substantial filler even before the banana split arrived. I had attracted a full table of service men. They were young men and I guessed they were all longing for home, to loved ones and their mother's home cooking. That night I was their substitute mother.

'Say, Ma'm you got any kids in the war?'

I wondered if a white lie would be required but the politics had changed; there was no longer war.

'Yes, one son.'

'In the Navy?' he asked.

'No,' I replied.

'Britain's got a good number on the high seas. Okay he's a pilot like some of us? Did he fight in the Battle of Britain?'

'No, he's in the Army. Light armour infantry.'

'Wow, I bet he's seen some action.'

'I am sure he has.'

'Is he back home safely now?'

'That's what I'm flying out to discover.'

The answer must have confused the airman. He

stood up to leave the table. He pulled his hand from his pocket and flung a packet on the table.

'Chewing gum. Helps the ears from popping in the plane.' I smiled my thanks. Perhaps I could find a use for this small pill requiring constant mastication after all.

The following morning I arrived at the table at a few minutes past 6am. My pilot Zak Withers was already at his bowl.

'Hi, Good morning Hilda. Southern grits on the hob, staple Louisiana diet, fills you up. Have some.'

'Sounds just what I need,' I said helping myself to the gritty porridge.

'Just corn with hull and germ removed. That's our Southern grits. Those in the north make fun of us needing our grits.'

'So it's a southern recipe?'

'Well yes, native Indians gave us it. You like it?'

I swallowed a mouthful. 'An acquired taste perhaps, but I'm hungry.'

'Okay, I hear you,' he said then shouted through to the kitchen staff. 'Two eggs sunny side up, you got that?' The chef raised his arm with his thumb up.

I contemplated a full English breakfast as it would be the last full meal I'd have for a while.

'Hilda, so what you goin' for?'

'Something quite filling. Not sure where my next meal might be.'

'Hey, stack of pancakes with maple syrup for the lady with some bacon and eggs on the side,' he shouted through. 'Sunny side up or down Hilda?'

'Err, sunny side up please.' That seemed to be the accepted condition of the eggs.

'You got that cook?'

Zak gave me enough time to get ready and pack. Then I was driven to the aircraft. It was a RB-1 Conestoga cargo transport aircraft. It was bulky. Large enough for a row of tenement houses to be inside, I thought. It was being loaded when I arrived. Pallets of sugar, flour and milk powder were being delivered to Hamburg and the surrounding district. Each pallet's bags bore the stars and stripes. This propaganda was hardly necessary. The German people would have by now rejected Hitler's dream and swastika emblazoned material. They would now welcome this aid, or any other aid, just to stay alive.

I was positioned in the cockpit where six airmen attended to their fine-honed skills making sure the aircraft was fully prepared to lift off the ground.

24

Hilda Returns to Hamburg

The plane's brakes were let loose. It groaned along the runway, pointing north. The engines got louder and louder. The ambling monster dragged its heavy load along most of the runway and I feared it might run out of land. Then I felt the force of lift. Treetops seemed touchable for half a minute. Then I breathed a sigh of relief. Another thought gave me unease. I hoped that the cargo behind me would remain restrained.

The sun was up early and we followed the river Thames out to the North Sea. The water was deep blue and peaceful with flecks of sunshine reflecting on the ripples of waves beneath us. No angry ships or threatening air flak again. It was a pleasant flight over the water made even more pleasant by the cup of strong coffee I was given with a doughnut. It even had jam inside. Ahh this American life might be ours before too long. Yet I did have mixed feelings about that.

'You say you are flying to Hamburg Airport? Won't it be demolished too?' I asked.

'What? You'll have to shout louder.'

'Is Hamburg airport... bomb free?' I shouted as loud as I could.

'Hamburg Airport Hilda has been going since 1910 when the Airships were in vogue. Between 1937 – 45 it was the Luftwaffe base but very cleverly disguised with trees and bushes to make it look less like an airport. So by the end of May we got it working, just fine. There might have been gross starvation without us getting the food though. These people are starving.'

'I see,' I replied to Zak who was relaxed at the controls.

The British coast slipped behind us and the summer's sunshine seemed to warm the aluminium fuselage. My seat rested against the structure which was in constant tickling vibration. It was not an uncomfortable feeling. Rather it was a comfort to the thoughts I was having about what I might encounter in Hamburg. I finished the coffee, draining every drop of this black strong aromatic drink. I dusted off the icing sugar of my doughnut from my knees. Sure enough, chewing gum was always at hand, so very quintessentially American and so useful in flight. Perhaps I could never be a Yank.

'You know where you'll be staying?'

'Zak, I'll get into the city and work my way along to my home. I'll take it from there. In fact, I'm not sure what I'll find or how long I'll be.'

'Then keep your eyes peeled. Look out for scraps of paper pinned to doors, railings, anywhere, that sort of thing. I've seen that in Nicaragua when we flattened some towns.'

'Flattened?'

'Well not exactly flattened but many of the homes were set alight, burnt to the ground.'

'When was that?'

'Part of the Banana Wars in Central America. It ended in 1933 after many years of troubles.'

A different country I thought, and a story not well known in Britain. The same human suffering at the hands of might; not necessarily right but the brutal strength of military prowess having the final say. When will they ever learn? I shook my head at that thought. I had heard the United Nations in New York was about to be born replacing the League of Nations. I pinned my hopes on being a more successful organisation. If it could intervene in conflict in time, it might lead to a more settled world. I had high hopes for its future.

The moments ticked by in the skies so recently holding pilots driven by fear of flak and being shot down or shot at. How quickly the difference it seemed. The descent was direct from the North Sea. Light cloud hid the city revived from the great fire of 1842 and the pestilence and cholera, fifty years later, to become the second city of the Republic. A home to millions of northern German people; home to me for thirty five years. We taxied along a debris-free runway and came to a halt near the airport terminal.

'Guess we drop you off here.'

'Yes, into the unknown.'

Zak nodded. 'Make your way back here when you're done. There will be a rota of flights back to Northolt, sure thing.'

'That's a good safety net for me.'

'Sure is honey,' he said winking at me as though he had just been in the company of a southern belle.

The airport was not far from the city. To get my thoughts together I declined a lift. After all, I might find someone I knew on my walk, someone with information. Once I was underway, I also realised any lift would be slowed down by the damage of homes blitzed and left sprawling across roads. The stench of rotten dead dogs made me hold my nose. They lay unloved unsure of why they suffered after years of loving care. Cats were not seen. These agile comrades must have lost some lives. Goodness knew how many lives they would have left. They were more likely to survive as rats were seen every few steps ahead scurrying under the debris, escaping cats' attention. Some elderly women passed by pushing prams but there were no children inside. They were gathering anything they could find whether food or wood to light a make-do stove. I could not address them. No words came to me in their distress or mine. They must have looked at me with my recent soap-showered face, my clean clothes, and my well-fed waist.

A few telegraph lines stood undamaged, but they were lifeless. The next was a broken pole and the wires lay on the ground in a puddle. The plaintive meowing of a cat provoked others to join in and brought back memories of Inka who came into my life in Portugal. Their wail reflected the despair of the people. Where was Inka now I wondered? Surely in a better place than this?

Sitting on the doorstep of a home that once was, a woman raised her eyes as I passed by. Still, I could not find words to speak. Her face lowered as I passed. I felt guilty for having avoided communication amid all this destruction.

To the east of the Alster, the oldest part of the city lay in more dishevelled ruins. The oldest part is the new town as the great fire consumed the old town in 1842. It retained its archaic name. I walked by seeing little semblance of life. The Carl Hagenbeek's Tier Park had a British jeep at its edge which its mine-clearing occupants were making safe the unexploded allied bombs. The park showed some uncut green grass, but it was devoid of borders and flower beds. No natural colour at all for dust had settled on the ground like a winter cape in this early summer of devastation. Everywhere was a desolate sight; the cries of children and the despair of their parents unable to provide any food or meaningful comfort. Few men were in sight and those who were seen were elderly, dishevelled, depressed and looking lost with only a make-do walking cane and the heavy winter coats they possessed for a different season.

I was within a half mile of home and knew I was more than likely to find damage there. Miraculously some dwellings did stand untouched. How the bombs could miss a home seemed remarkable and gave me hope that I still had a home.

Hamburg prided itself in its wildlife in its waterways. I had been used to seeing in the great pond hundreds of web footed birds and waders. They were nowhere to be seen. Had they migrated in 1940? Would they ever come back?

I was now in the administrative centre of the city. Standing before me was Gestapo headquarters, Eicke's citadel where he ordered the Jewish cleansing of the city and its environment. Perhaps he had died in the devastation? I would lose no sleep over him. A Nazi flag lay on the ground partly hidden by the rubble of grey stone. Even the London blitz seemed insignificant in damage compared with Hamburg that morning. But deaths both German and British were the consequences of a brutal war. Bomber Harris had certainly been seeking revenge in Hamburg.

I was within two hundred yards of home. The nearer I got the more anxious I became. I passed former neighbour's homes. Some had a wall standing, even two or three but all the windows had been blown out. Glass lay in sharp scatterings. Only sturdy footwear which I wore made progress possible. Ankles took the strain. Then I looked up. Where our house, our home, had been was blue sky with a pile of rubble some thirty feet high as a reminder of our blissful family life only five years ago. Tears came to my eyes. I struggled to climb over the debris, my foot slipped. I steadied myself anxious to seek more familiarity while risking injury. I looked around for anything to save but all I saw was a spilt open tin of white paint. I remembered Willy painting the ceilings with it. I sat down on a level stone and cried my eyes out. My thoughts were everywhere and nowhere, overcome by the devastation and desolation. I had no home and nowhere for Otto to return to. I found no energy trying to trace any more artefacts of my loved ones. Where would I start? How could I start without an army of help? We all needed that. I was no different.

Approximately an hour and a half later, still seated like Guy Fawkes on a stack of rubble, I saw a soldier, a dishevelled German soldier approach. He carried no gun and wore no helmet or cap. His hair seemed matted, in need of a soapy wash. A camouflaged shoulder bag seemed to be his worldly possession. Even one of his boots was lace less and both were muddy. His matted blond hair and grit splattered face epitomised what Germany had become fighting too long to the call of a mad dictator who had now taken his own life.

The soldier stopped. He looked at me without speaking. It was a gaze as if to say, how could you have possibly survived? He took another tentative step forward.

'Frau Richter?' he said quietly and hesitantly.

I looked up and stared at his face. I smiled.

'Yes, Otto's mother,' I said.

He looked down for a moment as if to gather his thoughts. Slowly his head lifted.

'Then you know about Otto?' he asked.

My heart fell. Did I know about Otto, my only son? 'No, I came looking for him. You know where he is? Is he in Hamburg? Do you know?' I asked with growing anticipation.

The soldier's face dropped once more. He sat down near me. At that point I feared the worse, that I'd never see my son again. Surely not?

'Otto was with me in 1941 when Operation Barbarossa began.'

'You mean Otto is dead?' I had to ask before he continued.

The soldier nodded and I felt my heart thud at an irregular pace. I bit my lip as the reality of his death hit home. I stifled a cry as I was anxious to know what had happened. My eyes focused on his. My hands trembled. His expression fought to inform me as best he could.

'Otto and I, that's me Marcus, Marcus Baumann had been with each other through the invasion of Poland. It was far easier than we expected in those days. We thought the Russians would be as easy to overcome. The Blitzkrieg was so effective. But summer of 1941 ended and winter approached as we set in, outside Moscow. We were making no progress. Then the Russians re-armed and we had a set battle. It was... it was then in November, mid November, Otto was hit by a Russian shell. He died instantly. Honest, I was near him, it was that instant. It was horrible.'

I dried my eyes and felt a bond with all German mothers on learning of the sacrifice they had made in losing a son. The five year war inevitably killed so many. I should not have expected Otto to have survived yet finding him was my first aim, in returning to Hamburg.

'His body, I mean was he buried? If so where?'

'I wish I could tell you. I don't know. Our strategy was not successful. Our positions were overrun by the Russians. His body must be in Russian land. I think it best not to think where his remains are but value the time you had with him over his years.'

I smiled through my tears. Such fine words from such a young man. We shook hands. He left walking lonely, away from me. I failed to ask where he was going or what he was looking for. He turned out of sight so soon. Then I let the tears and howls of anguish flow down my face and my voice shattered the eerie peace of the dead city.

25

Death, Devastation and Sorrow

I looked at my wristwatch. It was my normal lunch hour. I was not hungry. The anger of Otto's death somehow prioritised my responses. Grief fed me.

There was nothing worth saving that I could see. Everything lay damaged once I poked around the rubble. I noticed some crockery broken and surfacing like an archaeological Roman find. Treasures of the home now had no worth. Broken chair legs, a buckled bed. Even if the mantelpiece clock could be found and undamaged, nobody could buy it. Money was worthless. Roof slates covered much of the debris and I had no energy or incentive to lift each one up in the hope of I knew not what.

'Hey lady, get off the site. You'll fall and break your leg or something worse.'

I turned round to see a man probably in his eighties. He had said his piece and turned to go. His good deed of the day had been delivered. He noticed my response was like a naughty child caught doing wrong, but I accepted his wisdom. I turned and made for the street below.

I stood still for a moment, unsure what to do next. No pinned notice was required. Otto was no more. I tried to place him in my mind in a convenient place. I could not go around in a daze like so many others grieving. Otto had to occupy a place of easy access storage. Somewhere I could always enter and recall the memories of his short life. He was born at the wrong time in the wrong place. If only Willy had been Scottish, then Otto, or whatever he would have been called, would have possibly been alive today.

Now I must seek out the family I still had. I had to see if I could find Karl and Renate. I turned my steps towards their house.

I passed a man stoking a brazier which restrained dancing yellow flames. He hardly noticed me passing as he gazed into the glow of his mesmerising fire. I saw a swallow dart undulating over the uneven ground seeking a roof eave which was no longer there. Then I heard a low grating sound. It came into sight as I turned right towards Karl's house. It was an American army machine clearing the road of its spilled damage and carnage. The driver's face was masked to avoid the rising dust. I watched it perform its duties and waited until it passed. I was grateful to see a cleared road appear ahead, resulting from this motorised activity. It seemed the start of Hamburg reclaiming its veins. Life was in its infancy. I knew then that Germany's second largest city and main seaport would survive, in time. Eventually it would flourish as it had done so before the madness of the Second World War. In time, some time far away from now, it would stand proudly once more.

In days gone by, it would have taken me about fifteen minutes to reach Karl's home. It had already taken me twenty five minutes and I was at least still three hundred yards away. I recalled the Pied Piper of Hamelin who played to drive the rats out of town. How Otto loved Willy telling him that story. If I had my oboe with me I may not have had the same effect but it would have given the city a moment of musical magic to take away the sadness which I saw on everyone's face.

Many of the buildings in this part of the city seemed less damaged. I even saw a couple of untouched homes with uncared for gardens. Such was the indiscriminate destruction of each bomb hurtling towards the ground.

I saw Karl and Renate's house. The windows had blown in but the building seemed relatively lightly damaged. I approached it hoping I might a catch a glimpse of either of them. My heart grew more hopeful.

'Renate,' I called out three times.

A voice heard me but it was not hers.

'You are looking for Renate Richter?'

I glanced to my left to see a woman holding a young boy's hand. She walked towards me. I vaguely recognised her as one of Karl's neighbours.

'Hilda Richter isn't it?' she asked.

'Yes, I am the sister-in-law of the Richters.'

'Yes, I know. Where have you been? Where have you come from?'

I wondered if my truth might worry her and prevent her divulge what I need to know. I chose my words carefully.

'I was visiting my parents in Scotland when the war

broke out. I was away for the duration of the hostility,' I lied.

'You remember me? I am Martha Roth.'

I nodded. 'I remember your face but I had forgotten your name. Your son, of course, is very young. I don't remember him.'

'No, he's only three. He will grow up in peace. I had him at the right time, although he will have no father. He was killed in Italy.'

A moment's silence was required. 'I am sorry for you. My condolences.'

'That's all we are saying to each other, condolences, condolences... condolences.'

She beckoned me into her home. I followed. I opened my bag and gave the young boy a water biscuit. His mother smiled and placed a kettle on her temporary kitchen stove.

'This part of the city got off lightly. I am pleased for you,' I said.

'Lightly perhaps, but not without pain, much pain.'

The pain was everywhere, seen in all I passed by, but I heard it said for the first time.

The family dog lost its reservations and came to my side. I stroked the affectionate Hygenhund. Its eyes seemed to linger on me as if to say bad news was forthcoming and I have a duty to stay with you to comfort you. I stroked it gently. It did not flinch. It came even closer.

The ersatz coffee was poured into a mug.

'I am sorry there is no sugar or milk, of course.'

'I am sure things will slowly get back together again. It will take time,' I said.

Martha joined me at the table.

'You know about Gerhardt Eicke?'

I wondered why she mentioned my handler. 'Yes, I know who you mean. He was my son's Hitler Youth leader and a Gestapo man of course.'

'Yes, that's true but he was also the man who cleared Hamburg of its Jewish population.'

I looked at Martha. She was clearly not Jewish. I wondered where her narrative would take her.

'The early years of the war saw the Jewish community being rounded up and taken away in trucks. Now we know where they went, where they were killed in great numbers in gas chambers. It will live on our national conscious forever.'

'What could stop it? No-one could. That is the shame of it,' I said.

'I did not know that Renate was Jewish.'

'Renate, she isn't Jewish. Her grandfather was but two generations later and two Lutheran generations at that. Renate married Karl in the Lutheran Church here in Hamburg,' I replied.

'That's not how Eicke's men saw it. Renate was accused of not wearing the yellow star.'

'Of course not,' I said. 'She was not Jewish!'

'But her grandfather was and that to Eicke meant a direct line. She was taken out of the house one afternoon in plain sight. Many saw her being taken away. I've never seen her since. That was about three years ago. But I now know what will have been her fate.'

I replaced my cup on the table. The dog nuzzled between my knees. I gently massaged his ears.

'Muggi, come here,' Martha said.

'No, I need Muggi right now. My world is crashing down. My son dead, my sister-in-law gassed. Her husband... you wouldn't know about Karl would you?'

'Do you really want to know? Can you take all this grief in one day?'

My heart sunk low. 'I must know. Now I suspect the worst. Tell me.'

She nodded and came towards me and rested her hand on my shoulder.

'Of course it's hearsay. Everything is hearsay.'

'There is a saying no smoke without fire. If it's hearsay in the present situation, it will be the truth.'

'You know Karl was with the medical corps, a dentist of course.'

'Yes, that's true.'

'He was with Field Marshall Rommel in Africa. From Libya in 1941 they made great strides through to Tobruk. But the following year they ran out of supplies and fuel. They dug themselves in and laid mines to thwart General Montgomery's advance, while Rommel's orders from Hitler were to stand firm to the end.'

'To the end? Karl was not a fighting man. Maybe he's a prisoner?' I interjected.

She smiled as if it may have been a possibility then looked at her dog and continued.

'The Field Marshall knew the war in North Africa was lost. The British broke through and secured the territory along the north Mediterranean coast. Karl was killed not taking out teeth... but... was taken out by a mine.'

My mouth was open but I was not breathing. 'A mine?'

'Yes, some said he could have avoided it. Others said he had heard his wife had been taken into custody being a Jewess and his brother was already dead. He may have been depressed. Maybe he saw a brighter future in death. All we know is that he was killed by an exploding mine in the desert. I have no reason to doubt the story. I know it to be true, Hilda. I am sorry.'

I had never felt so alone. I now had no close worldly relative in Germany. 'What a day. I feared this would be a possible outcome. It could not have been worse.' Muggi's eyes looked up at me expressively. He raised his paw and placed it on my lap. He seemed to know my tears were about to fall.

It was late in the afternoon, after we had exhausted our memories, I made my decision. I left Martha giving her some tinned meat and the remainder of my biscuits and tinned fruit.

Germany offered me no comfort. Hamburg was not the city I had known and loved. The culture was gone, all the people I knew too, the city had a long way to go to resurrect itself and I saw no part in that process. I made my way back to the airport.

A passing jeep stopped and gave me a lift when I stopped to look at it. The driver took pity on what he presumed to be a German wife.

'So you're not German after all,' he said when I thanked him for the lift and told him where I was going.

'No, no longer German, I have no home. I'm Scottish with no home either.'

I got a plane later that night heading to Northolt. The pilot was Polish and he asked no questions. His mind must have been as full of grief as mine as Russia made its presence felt in his homeland. The view got darker by the minute. The North Sea was as dark as the inky sky. Somehow it seemed a longer flight back. Time moved slowly that night and I had much to contemplate.

I was recognised by the American contingent at the hut where I'd spent another night but I chose not to socialise with them. I went straight to bed and cried until I slept. I cried till my pillow was saturated by my tears.

'Where to this morning, Ma'am? A flight to the United States can be arranged. We're taking a platoon of boys home today. Fancy joining them?' asked one of the airmen.

I smiled at the unexpected offer. One that seemed to please me but it had come at the wrong time. 'A lift to the nearest bus stop will do. I'll be heading back to the city once more,' I replied still contemplating the tempting offer. A new life in America was being gifted on a plate and in truth, it was appealing but it did not matter where I was, I had to find my purpose in life once again.

When I got back to the MI6 offices Dynes was at work. Thornton this time was not around and I wasn't told where he might have been. Perhaps Dynes did not know.

'It's a pity Thornton is not here,' said Dynes. 'If he knew you'd be here, he'd want to discuss things with you. But I am privy to these matters anyway.'

'You mean my oboe?'

'Your oboe? No I don't know anything about that.'

'Well I do. If you open that high cabinet, you will find it.'

Dynes did as he had been told and found the steps to mount. He opened the top half of the cupboard. 'Ahh that black case I presume.'

'I'm pleased to see it is just as it was placed a few hours ago.'

Dynes handed me over the instrument. I tapped the box with a loving touch.

'My true comfort box,' I said.

'In the circumstances, I must decline a recital this morning. I have some news to break to you.'

'Really?' I could not think what he had in mind.

'Indeed, first I have some good news. One Gerhardt Eicke, your old friend. I think you know him, has been arrested and been charged with crimes against humanity.'

'Good news? That's great news. That's the best news I've had for some time.'

'You realise you will be seeing him again?'

'What? Are you joking? There's no way I'd want to encounter that man again. Heaven forbid.'

'Hilda, I'm afraid you may well have to.'

'Why?'

'You will be cited as one of the main witnesses in his prosecution.'

My mind fought to make sense of the situation. A couple of thoughts fought for my attention. Could I face him again and would my evidence be enough to convict him?

'So back to Germany sometime?'

'Yes, Nuremburg. The trials will start there in August.'

'The sooner the better,' I heard myself say with a bitter tongue.

A smile came over Dynes face. 'Some more pleasant news, I hope.' His mischievous eyes glanced at mine.

'The Foreign and Commonwealth office has close ties with MI6 as you can imagine.'

'Yes, I can indeed.'

'We have heard from one man who seems keen to meet you.'

'Meet me? Keen? Are you sure?'

'Yes, by the name of one Sir Francis Simpson. Does the name ring a bell?'

'Sir Francis? Wonderful,' I exploded in a louder than anticipated voice of excitement in reply. Is he not in Central Africa then?'

'Yes he was. He's heading for Finland, now.'

'You mean Ambassador to Finland? What a contrast.'

'Indeed it is. They move them quickly in that department. I'm sure he's missing the heat of the Dark Continent. But he's not there just now, nor is he in Helsinki. He's on leave, he's in London.'

'Really?' I asked in delight.

'Yes. Now I have a meeting to attend to. But before I go,' he said rising from his seat behind the desk, 'I have a piece of paper for you.'

'I see,' I said not really understanding what he meant.

He took a pad from his drawer and produced a pen. 'Here Hilda, have my seat. This is Sir Francis's number.

He handed the pad and the pen to me. He is awaiting your call. I'll send through a coffee for you,' he said as he made his way out of the room.

'If you don't mind, a glass of cold water might be better.'

26

Romance

I gazed at the telephone on its receiver for a full minute wondering how and why Sir Francis had tracked me so successfully. I had not seen him for almost three years. How could he know MI6 was my base? The feelings I had for him then, was cloaked in a fear of speaking too much. It would have detracted from BP's function if a romance interfered with work. Maybe I should not think this way. My feelings for him had diminished over the time since we met. He was gone from my life and in truth from my mind too. That would put an end to any blossoming relationship. He was probably even married by now. This contact might only lead to an 'old time' chat. Perhaps it would just be a conclusion of hostilities and a celebration of success, but no more.

I tore a piece of paper from the faded brown pad Dynes had provided. I lay it by the phone. I dipped the pen nib into a bottle of Quink ink and blotted the tip to prevent an unwelcome blotch on the sheet. Then I looked at the piece of paper which had a number and the name Sir Francis beside it. I took a deep breath then exhaled contemplating a hesitant call.

I dialled Whitehall 2370. I placed the earpiece close to my ear.

'Good afternoon. Foreign Office. How can I help you?'

'Er... could you put me through to Sir Francis?'

'Sir Francis. Ummm... which Sir Francis do you mean? We have a few with that nomenclature. Sir Francis Tomlinson? Sir Francis Ormond-Bryce? Sir Francis Simpson? Sir Francis...'

'Sir Francis Simpson, that's to whom I am wishing to speak.'

'And you are?'

'I am Hilda Campbell, er... no perhaps you should tell him it's Frau Hilda Richter.'

A hesitation followed. It was not surprising. There were times I played with my names. She must be wondering if I had given her a coded name. She would have certainly known I did not speak English with a German accent. I supposed the receptionist must have been used to such deception in this government department.

'Please hold the line while I put you through,' she said a moment later.

I held on tightly eyeing the door hoping there would be no interruption as much as wondering if the expected conversation would be sticky. I heard footsteps approach the receiver.

'Hello, Frau Richter?'

'Sir Francis I presume?'

'Speaking, how are you Hilda?'

'Very well and you? Back from Central Africa?'

'Indeed I came back almost a month ago. My post is now in Finland.'

'Out of the fire into the snow, as it were. The change could not have been more dramatic,' I said with a quiet laugh.

'That's the Foreign Office for you. They keep you on your toes. But I am well and now experiencing the fresh air of Helsinki, and right now, in a recovering London town.'

My heart was beating out of control. 'So...when will you return?'

'I was recalled for a couple of meetings but I've some leave to take. Ten days in total actually. It took a couple of days to track you down.'

My heartbeat seemed to be too close to the receiver. I held my chest to muffle the beat. Then the door opened and a glass of water arrived. Dynes beat a hasty retreat having placed the glass by the phone.

'Am I led to believe I have lost you two days' leave? If so I do apologise,' I said then took a sip of the cold water.

'Not to worry. I was wondering if you would like to go to the theatre this evening. I can get two tickets for The Mikado. Would you be interested in accompanying me?'

I recalled how it was a concert that brought me romance in Hamburg in 1910. Thirty-five years later and the same number of years wiser, was acceptance this evening the first step to finding a new contentment in life?

'I'd be delighted. Entertainment has not featured in my life for many a year now. I'd be absolutely thrilled to join you.'

'I'll call for you at 5pm. We could dine before the performance. Where can I find you?'

'The truth is I'm stateless, homeless and MI6 recognise this. So I have just recently been given an attic room at the top of the building here. I'll be at the reception at 5pm.'

Sir Francis gave a huge guffaw. 'That makes two of us. I'm almost homeless too. Well, my home is in the Cotswolds but I'm rarely there. So I've been put up at the Savoy on this occasion. We can dine here.'

The Savoy! Gosh I'd heard of it and felt it was only affordable to the wealthy and famous. 'I look forward to the evening very much indeed.'

'5pm it is. Bye.'

I replaced the receiver back on its cradle. Now I knew why he wished to see me. Company for him over his extended week and then he'd be off to Finland. It would be enjoyable but really had no prospects in that short window of opportunity. If I wished to see him again after this week, I'd better up the stakes. I needed to make an impression.

Oxford Street was busy once more. There were several ladies outfitters' shops to browse. I did so from the outside before entering. I felt the material, placed dresses against me to test if they clashed with my hair or complexion. Such shopping I had not imagined. I was not rushing to purchase a cardigan or nylons, this was something to dine out in and be entertained. I must have spent three hours shopping. As the shops closed, I had purchased a coat; two dresses both comfortable and fashionable to my eye, brown leather shoes with a slight heel and a pair of gloves. My hands were full when I returned to MI6.

I walked up the stairs slowly, catching a brief glimpse of each step as I made my way towards the front door. I was aware of a hand that passed over my shoulder to open the door.

'Not done much shopping for some time I suppose?' asked Thornton.

'So true. I needed some new clothes anyway. I've been wearing the same things for too long, as you know.'

Thornton smiled a paternal gesture. 'We men wouldn't have noticed. It's our Achilles heel, second guessing a woman's desires.'

'Then I leave you to guess,' I said giving him a teasing smile.

'Did Dynes have a word with you this afternoon?'

'About...?'

'I think you had a call to make.'

'Indeed, how perceptive and, you are right. That's why I needed some new clothes.'

Thornton laughed satisfied he's got to the right conclusion.

'May I ask, how long will I be staying here, at MI6?'

'You want to leave us?'

'I'll have to one day. I need to decide where I want to be. Then find a house and a purpose in life again.'

'I imagine you will stay until you are cited to Nuremburg. You can return here afterwards and stay until you find somewhere to live. You could teach German, I presume at University level. Or you could be a translator in the private sector. There will be many business opportunities for you.'

'You have confirmed one thing for me and I'm grateful.'

'That you'd be a good linguist?' he suggested.

'No, that I'm too old to be a spy again.'

'Now the war is over and you have survived, has it not been a good profession for you as a double agent?'

'I'm glad to have served my native country but I've been a very reluctant spy.'

Precisely as the hour struck 5pm in the vestibule of MI6, a car came to a halt outside. I looked through the window. It was Sir Francis. I opened the door and stood outside as Sir Francis arrived to take my hand down the steps. He paused. He turned towards me and looked at me with a smile.

'Hilda, your eyes...' he said.

'My eyes?' I replied in amazement.

'Yes, your eyes. Your eyes are like holly-blue butterflies.'

I felt weak at my knees. How charming I thought. His remark completely overwhelmed me as it came so unexpectedly. It was a greeting I could have never imagined. It was one I could never forget.

'A butterfly, umm... whatever made you say that?'

'Are you offended?'

'No, not at all. I recognise a compliment when I hear one. It has been some time since the last one, you can appreciate.'

The meal started on a high note and continued through each course. It was a meal prepared with exactitude. It was of such a high standard. One I had not experienced before or in such a splendid setting.

We talked about how our lives had intermingled by chance in Hamburg and at Bletchley. I learned that his wife had died of breast cancer. His response to her early death was to engaged in study and career development he told me but he had come to realise part of him was missing, especially after the heat and strain in central Africa and now in the climate of the Laps. Long dark winter nights could not be satisfied with reading or crossword puzzles alone. Colleagues had turned to glasses of Bacchus, causing some liver complications and for others early retirement and early deaths. He did not wish to entertain that. Even endless summer light left him tired. He had staff of course but ranks beneath him frustrated any close relationship. I found him honest and charming. He was anxious to learn my position in life having given his.

The coffee arrived and we retired to a snug cove at the direction of the waiter. I stirred my coffee then opened the wrapper of a chocolate which lay beside the saucer.

'The future for me is very unclear,' I said.

Sir Francis lifted his cup to his mouth. He let me continue.

'I'm told I am a witness against my German handler, Gerhardt Eicke. That means some time in Nuremberg. Goodness knows how long.'

'And then?' he asked.

'I don't really know. I have no magic glass ball to consult.'

'What are your options?'

His questioning seemed very exact. Was he enticing

me into his web? A web of contentment or perhaps capture?

'All I can offer is fluent German, a teacher perhaps?'

'And where would you teach?'

That was at the heart of my dilemma. I told him so. My loyalty to a Hitler-free Germany remained a possibility. I loved the people, its culture and the land. It brought back so many happy family memories. My immediate family had all died however and it would not be the same. That thought brought me home. But was home Scotland where I had no locus anymore? I had also spent so many years in the Home Counties during the war. Finding home was elusive.

'You see why I am so confused?'

'Confused, yes I see. That has made you the remarkable woman you are. Your life experiences have shaped your thinking, your determination to survive and your charm.'

'How kind of you to say so.' He certainly had the graces and politeness of an Ambassador. 'And you, where to next?'

Sir Francis crossed his legs and returned his coffee cup to its saucer. 'Next week I return to Helsinki. For how long you might ask. I wish I could tell you. The Foreign Office plays games with us. The world is its oyster. The face must fit in the right place it seems.'

I looked down on the red diamond patterned carpet regretting Sir Francis was a career ambassador whose loyalty to the Court of St James was his first priority and perhaps his only loyalty.

'You seem down hearted.'

I looked up at him with soulful eyes. His lifestyle

was in constant change. I was not sure if that suited me or if I was too old to make concessions.

'My butterflies are wondering if they should fly away or not.'

Sir Francis drew nearer and took hold of my hand. It took me by surprise but caused excitement too.

'Hilda, I have a few days left in London. I want to spend them with you.'

Our relationship was being tested. I was ready for this latest test and longed for it to get underway. He caught my smile. It gave him the permission he sought and which I gladly accepted. It was not a long kiss but one which said so much. It was a kiss which brought two lonely people together reeling from the devastation of the war years. For me it gave that chink of light which gave me a new focus for my future.

'Hilda tomorrow, I have tickets for King Lear. Do you wish to come with me?'

I stroked his arm. 'Of course I do,' I said laughing at his entertainment arrangements.

'Then I collect you at 2.30pm from your official dwelling.'

'2.30 pm? It is a matinee I presume?'

'No, it starts at 7.30pm. I thought a walk around the Serpentine and a bite to eat before the performance. You agree?'

'Wonderful, Sir Francis, wonderful.'

'To you, Hilda, I'm just Francis from now on.'

We had taken our relationship to a new level. It had far to go but the journey had begun and I was eager to set out on the path that lay ahead.

'Hey, time is moving on. We'd better get going to the Mikado.'

It was a short walk from the Savoy to the Aldwych theatre. Sir Francis took my hand as we walked in step. To all and sundry, we were a happy couple. To the rhythm of his heel-capped steps, my feet seemed to float on air. I could not have been more content.

The Mikado was wonderful. The tunes stayed in my head all week. I saw myself as one of the Three Little Maids; indeed also a Wandering Minstrel, with my oboe to hand and of course Alone, and Yet Alive. Gilbert's crafted words were sung as if solely written for me that night and Sullivan's tunes were foot tapping and unforgettable.

We walked back to my residence arm in arm humming some of the songs.

'I haven't enjoyed myself as much for a very long time, I assure you,' I said.

'I think we both needed some light entertainment. More taxing tomorrow, King Lear challenges human suffering. God knows how much we have experience of that in recent days.'

Sir Francis brought me home and on the doorstep of MI6 he took hold of me close, we hugged each other and we kissed, longer than I had anticipated. I felt no longer alone.

27

Engaged

How quickly the days passed. I worried what would happen when Sir Francis returned to Finland. I would lose that closeness, that warmth to share our lives. Nevertheless I enjoyed what each day had brought. London Zoo was spared many of the animals during the blitz but many suffered fright from the bombs. They were more timid than I thought they should be. The green nosed monkey, so much a table food snatcher in the Congo I was reliably informed, clung to its soul mate looking over its shoulder to see if the human species had made any advance.

We enjoyed the sunshine, even the showers which were few and the bus trip to Epping Forest. Normality was springing up all around the city. Mobile hot drink bicycles had a good trade going and the shop windows were restocking to make use of the high spirited forces in the city centre seeking presents to take home to a loved mother, sister or wife from dress shops. From the myriad of other outlets, gifts were heading home for the fathers and brothers of the Canadian, New Zealand, Australian and American Allied forces. Back pay and savings made during military engagements meant servicemen had some money to flaunt. The generous Americans certainly knew how to spend money in London and entice young girls to their arms.

On the Saturday morning of our penultimate time together I received a letter. I was required to sign for it. I did so knowing what it was likely to be. I was not wrong. The citation read that Frau Hilda Richter was cited to attend the International Court of Justice at Nuremberg as a witness in the case against Herr Gerhardt Eicke for war crimes. Specifically mentioned in the letter was his charge of having been in active command leading to the deportation and death of thousands of Jews from Hamburg and its environs at the gas chambers of Treblinka and Bergen-Belsen. I was to report to the office of the chief prosecutor on my arrival where I would be reimbursed travel expenses. I would be accommodated in the Hotel Agneshof at 10 Nurenberg-Mitte. My stay would be paid for and I would be there as long as it was necessary.

It was with a heavy heart I informed Sir Francis of my news. Perhaps the thought of seeing Eicke again depressed me or the fact that my hours with Sir Francis were dwindling. Either way I was not at ease and he could see my altered condition.

That afternoon we walked along the Victoria Embankment. Old Father Thames ebbed and flowed as though nothing had ever happened over the past five years. Out of sight lay hidden in its bed were unexploded bombs and the debris of others which had brought the river bed to the surface momentarily. It was the vein of the city and it flowed impeccably to the city's heart beat. As normality returned around me, I realised our relationship was coming to a crossroads. I saw no clear route ahead. My options seemed many and few at the same time.

'The trial will come to an end,' said Francis seeing some clarity for me. I clung on to his arm.

'And then?' I looked up at him. His eyes met mine. He said nothing.

We made our way to the Serpentine later that afternoon and fed the ducks. They had regained their trust in the human fodder providers. They would have been scarce during the war.

'You see that white swan, Hilda?'

'Yes, beautiful isn't it,' I replied.

'It's as beautiful as you.'

'What do you mean?' I said defensively to his exaggerated comment.

'It has survived the war. It hides its feet which motor like a paddle steamer below the water but maintains an elegance and control above water.'

'Yes, but why like me? I am not a river swimmer; I don't have a long neck... I...'

'No, but not many spies get through the war unscathed, especially a counterspy. It makes you a very special creature indeed, like a swan I suggest.'

'Oh Francis, you are teasing me.'

He did not defend his statements but gave me a hug of contentment instead. I was satisfied.

That night as we ate at La Dame Parisienne, the wine gave me a warm glow and an easy contentment. I was relaxed with a feeling of satisfaction. I somehow knew I had crossed the Rubicon in our relationship and hoped that was what Sir Francis was feeling too.

We gathered our coats and set off in the cool evening to the box in the theatre which Francis had booked. I had not seen a Shakespearian play since my school days but here in London the magic of the stage was about to unfold. I was excited to be seeing it.

King Lear seemed to be one of Shakespeare's longer plays. I'll never know. I took that view as Hypnos visited me that night with Morpheus and brought contented dreams as I sat in the box fighting sleep. I tried hard to keep my eyes open. The wine and the heat of the theatre conspired to make me drowsy. Francis was aware of my condition and placed his arm around my shoulders. He understood what must have been going through my mind. The court case of course, but also the realisation of this growing relationship about to be severed within two days.

During the third act, I regained my dignity. I looked at the programme's notes and caught up with the plot. By the time the curtain dropped for the last applause I could say I had enjoyed the evening's atmosphere and of course, being with Francis. King Lear? He had left the stage. I failed to see him go.

Sir Francis walked me back home. He seemed to be in a dreamy mood.

'A penny for your thoughts,' I asked him.

'I think we should attend St Paul's Cathedral for our last day. What do you think?'

'Inspirational thinking,' I said.

'Matins or Eucharist?'

'Steady Francis, I'm a Presbyterian cum Lutheran. Not used to high Anglicanism. Not sure when to stand, kneel, or pray.'

'I'll be with you to show you the ropes. And the Church of England won't turn anyone away, especially at this time of so many troops in town. It never has in the past. Possibly something to do with its established status.'

'I'm warming to the idea.'

We lingered under the gas lamppost outside my accommodation for a few minutes. Francis seemed deep in thought once more, formulating a question he was anxious to ask. I knew it was about to be asked. I had that insight of a Scottish Highlander.

'After Nuremberg, will you come to Helsinki to visit?'

'I'd love to. In fact, that might give me time to sort myself out. In the clear air of Helsinki perhaps after the trial, all will be resolved for me, I hope.'

'I hope so too,' he said.

On our last morning together we entered the Church which stood tall undamaged by Axis bombs, a symbol of defiance, a centre of hope and place of prayer. The incumbent offered prayers and the Bishop brought us to our feet with hymns both stirring and reflective. They were all known to me. I enjoyed singing and hearing Sir Francis' fine voice sing the tenor line as he stood next to me. When the Eucharist was called, the bread broken and the wine transfigured, I followed Sir Francis to the oak barred rail and knelt with my hands in a cupped fashion. The Bishop's curate came along the line and laid a wafer in the hands of those wishing to consume at their moment in time while others opened their mouths to receive the bread. Mine stuck to the roof of my mouth. Fortunately I managed to dislodge it before the wine came in a silver chalice offered to my lips to sup before being wiped and taken to the next recipient. A slight nudge and I was up and walking in a line back to our pew.

'Now that wasn't so difficult was it?' he whispered.

I shook my head.

After the benediction we stood to let the celebrants retire and then to the heart lifting melody of Jeremiah Clark's Trumpet Voluntary, we made our way out through the central aisle. We stopped at the door shaking hands with the Bishop and gazed over the quiet Sunday morning London. The city was at rest while the strains of the organ and now Purcell's music remained in our ears.

Half way down the stairs, Sir Francis took a couple of steps in his stride ahead, he turned and stood before me, blocking my way. He fumbled in his pocket and then bent down on one knee.

He took my hand. I gasped in quiet astonishment. What was happening I never could have imagined not so long ago. It was such a public place too.

'Hilda, will you do me the honour and become my wife? Will you marry me?'

What washed over me was a thrill of excitement, of acceptance, of wonder and of delight. I had been proposed to on the steps of St Paul and those departing the church stopped in their tracks, expecting the response which was called for.

'Sir Francis, of course I do. I will marry you, my darling.'

Francis rose and from his pocket, he produced an engagement ring. It shone in the light of the day. He placed it on my finger and it gave little resistance. It was the right size and I drew him near. There and then we clinched the new relationship with a hugging kiss oblivious to all the applause filtering in our ears from those leaving the church.

I was engaged to be married. I was so very happy. I wore my ring for all to see. My only disappointment was that I had no family with which to share this special moment of joy. Sir Francis noticed my sudden sad reflection and knew why.

'It is a new life you have, Hilda. One I want to share with you forever. You will never be alone again.'

28

The Nurenberg Trial

Monday morning dawned far too early and our last moments together for some time approached till we knew not when. Recently opened Heathrow airport was host to a few European flights and several to America. A Scandinavian airliner was parked on the runway.

We had time to say our good-byes with a lingering cuddle and a shorter kiss. I had not taken my engagement ring off since the moment it was placed on my finger. It was there for all to see and ward off any suitors, I told myself. A silly thought really, as none had approached me since I was widowed, apart from Sir Francis.

I saw his plane lift off safely then enter flecks of cloud. I watched it until it seemed to be a fly in the sky, then it was gone. I looked at my ring again. A symbol of love and a symbol of my future, it would see me through the trial that I now focused upon. I returned to my MI6 flat to pack. I'd be leaving in twenty-two hours.

'Many congratulations, Hilda. Have you named the wedding day?' asked a very contented Thornton.

'What? I have not even decided on the venue. I will be leaving here though, as soon as the trial is over.'

Thornton looked over his hornbill glasses. 'Returning to live where, now the war is over?'

'I suppose until Sir Francis retires, we might be anywhere and everywhere till retirement to the Cotswolds.'

'Ahh God's country,' said a dreamy eyed Thornton.

'That's where you are from?' I asked.

'No, I have a sister there as well an old friend and so know it well. It's peaceful. Quiet rural lanes and many thatched cottages,' recalled Thornton with eyes fixed on the ceiling.

I looked through the window unfocussed into the distance. 'It must be wonderful to have a family.'

Thornton recalled Hilda's loss. 'Will you ever return to Hamburg?'

He touched a raw nerve but I was not upset. I owed much to Thornton. 'Germany has little to offer me now except grief. My future will be where Sir Francis is.'

'Have you no regrets at all about leaving Germany, after all those years?' he asked.

'Regrets? No. I have memories though, wonderful memories which no one can take away.'

My worldly treasures were with me when I reported to Northolt air station the next day. My suitcase was packed till the seams stretched and my hand luggage was bulky too. Strapped onto the bag through the leather handle was my oboe case. I would need its comforting notes after each stressful court day.

It was a three and a half hour flight to Nuremberg. Throughout the journey I concentrated on the evidence

I might be giving. Would there be a QC for Eicke's defence making sure I was more of a Nazi spy that a British agent? Could I end up in the dock? Every possible angle I thought through. It would not be a plain sailing experience, I concluded. Indeed of that, I was certain. Then a bolt of fear travelled right through me. My best defence would be BP. But I was unable, at point of death, to make any mention of it. That I found hard to cope with and harder to avoid mention. I must be highly disciplined during this trial.

I was driven in an army jeep to my hotel in Nuremberg and booked in. The driver told me he would let the prosecutor's office know I had arrived safely. He told me that was what he was doing with the witnesses. It was a welcomed gesture.

That night to make me relax, I played my oboe. I placed a glove into the end of the oboe to quieten the instrument's volume, so as not to disturb any guests. The first piece I played was Beethoven's Pastoral symphony, the Shepherd's song. I played from heart and imagined the wanderings of Beethoven in the countryside as he composed the symphony. Then I played from Carl Maria von Webber's opera *Der Freischütz* from Act II Agathe's chamber. I closed my eyes as I played and walked around the bedroom slowly as if a huntsman after game. This German music played in Germany seemed so right. As I contemplated what to play next, there was a knock on the door. I placed the oboe on my bed and answered to find the hotel manageress standing before me.

'You played that music?' she asked.

'Yes, I hope I did not disturb or annoy you,' I said looking concerned.

Her smile foretold her response. 'No, no, you play beautifully,' she said with what seemed to be an emotional tug in her facial expression.

'Do come in,' I beckoned. Then I saw a tear well up in both of her eyes.

'German music is so beautiful,' she said.

'Yes, I know, I have played with tears in my eyes too,' I empathised with her seeing she was still in pain.

'All I have heard for many years now is military marshal music. In the square, on the radio, always marching music. It has been years since I heard a single wind instrument play the music I first learned as a child.' Her last sentence faded. Her last word was a mere whisper.

I sensed what caused her pain. 'My son, Otto, was killed in the war,' I said giving her the confidence to tell of her grief.

She approached me and we gave each other a hug.

'My son too. Herman. I am lost without him.'

'How old was he?' I asked to comfort her feelings.

'He was twenty-two. He was the man of the house since his father died.'

She was telling my story. 'My son too was the man of the house. That is why we feel the loss so keenly.'

'Yes,' she said. 'But Herman played the piano so well. Your music was the first to be played in this hotel since his last visit to me.'

Germany was grieving in many homes, it was the national condition. I wondered if revenge would be the dominant feeling in the galleries at court tomorrow.

The following morning as I was having breakfast, I listened to the radio. I heard a follow-up report of the August atomic bombs dropped on Nagasaki and Hiroshima. The announcer spoke of the dreadful fires still causing deaths in great numbers. His conclusion was that there must never be another atomic war. Surely the future of the world would be uncertain if these bombs were used from now on, in conflicts.

My feelings were mixed. The report mentioned the burning and deaths of so many innocent people but a bomb as large as an atomic bomb may have brought to a halt the Knights of Bushido's barbaric treatment of prisoners and bring an end to the war in the east. Strangely I had thought little about the war in the Far East. It was just that; far-east. I had been preoccupied with my own war. Now that the war was over in Europe, I prayed that the Japanese would in time forgive our deployment of that terrible bomb. Dramatic though it was, surely the world was now coming to the end of its global conflict? Surely it was beginning to be a more peaceful place?

I reported to the prosecutor's office in person as requested. I was told I would be witness number four in Gerhardt Eicke's case. We would have to stay in the witness room until we were called.

I read the paper which had been brought into the room. The Nurenberg trials were given prominence but there were no photos of the proceedings.

I was neither pleased nor unpleased that I did not recognise any of the other witnesses. If I had known any then I'd be able to speak about Eicke perhaps. With no-one there, I had no idea what would be their evidence. Would mine support their memories? That was one of my worries. The other more pressing anxiety was to be discovered as a German spy myself.

I watched the clock tick slowly round. Each minute gave a hesitant click. It amplified the tension building up throughout the day in that room, for everyone.

At last I heard my name called. I stood up and left the witness room hardly acknowledging the men and women witnesses left behind. Such were my heightened senses. I was led along a corridor and into the large arena. It was larger than I anticipated. It was a vast theatre of professionals in close discussion both on the Judges bench and around long tables where evidence was prepared and laid out, labelled for convenience. Surrounding the building both externally and internally were the white helmeted and white splatter-gaited leg protectors of soldiers standing at ease while several in their ranks kept their weapons ready at all times. I was ushered into the witness box. Instinctively I lifted the bible.

'Not yet, Frau. The accused has not been brought into the court. His counsel is still with him,' the court usher whispered to me.

I replaced the bible. I remained standing in the witness box to take in the enormous significance of the court proceedings. Defendants were seated at right angles to the Judges' bench and scribbling furiously, like late arriving exam students, were the world's press. The eyes of the globe were upon this court and on me in particular, in just a moment. It gave me little time to relax and see the organised machinery of justice in action. My evidence alone would not perhaps convict Eicke but it would be a brick in his wall.

I was aware of the three previous witnesses, when they returned to the waiting room before I was called. They broke their silence as if to purge for the last time their pent up evidence. All were mothers from Hamburg who knew what he was doing. Some who had witnessed Jewish neighbours being taken away, others had seen his brutality and spoke passionately about his demeanour as he shot dissenters. Their recollections relived through tears and sobs.

At last I caught sight of Gerhardt Eicke as he returned to the dock. He looked haggard, much older than the years apart should have spared him. He now wore dark glasses, possibly to disguise himself as he seemed to peer towards my direction lacking focus. Gone was this visitor to my house who strode from hall to living room making his presence and importance felt. He seemed a timid mouse now. Defiance had not been chosen as his defence this day.

I took the oath. The International lawyer prosecuting stood beside me. Only the microphone stood between us.

'Tell the trial your full name.'

'Frau Hilda Richter.'

'You are a citizen of Hamburg?'

'I was, not now.'

There was a disturbance from the defendant. He leant forward and was agitated. The huddle attracted the prosecutor's attention. The inevitable rebuff came.

'Objection, this witness is an imposter,' said his counsel.

The judges looked at each other. They shook their heads. They called over the prosecutor and spoke with the microphones turned off. He returned to question me again.

'You told the court you are Frau Hilda Richter. Remember you are under oath. Tell the court your real name.'

There must have been at least two hundred people in that courtroom. All ears focused on my voice. Not one moved an inch as I explained the discrepancy. 'I was born in Scotland and grew up as Hilda Campbell. I married Dr Willy Richter in Hamburg in 1913. If there is any confusion it is because of that. I am Hilda Richter.'

The court awaited the defence council to acknowledge the response.

'My Lords, the objection remains. My client maintains this is not Frau Richter. Frau Richter was drowned in Portugal. Her body was washed into the Atlantic sea off the rugged Portuguese coast. She could not have survived. This woman is an imposter, a very clever imposter. We detect a well conceived deception.'

The prosecutor raised his eyebrows at me as if to question his own case. I smiled and whispered I would explain the further discrepancy.

'During the war, my work was that of a double agent.' I head a few gasps at that revelation.

'And whose loyalty were you serving? Germany or the Allies?' I was asked just as I had got into my stride.

'I was acting on behalf of the Allies. That did involve

training in Germany and some espionage in Portugal on behalf of the Reich but when I learned I was sending messages which would put convoys at risk I feigned my death by apparently drowning. Herr Eicke is right. I seemed to have drowned off the Portuguese coast. However they never found my body, my body was never in danger and appears before you today. My training in espionage was very thorough, you might say.'

'What did you actually achieve when under the direction of your German handlers?' asked the tall, lean spectacled prosecutor.

'To my regret and this will remain my biggest mistake in my life, I provided one set of co-ordinates to Berlin from an agent in America. That led to the sinking of an allied cargo ship. That was when I realised I had to revert to my British handlers. That was why, when the time was right, I feigned my death.'

'And your work for the British?'

I looked towards Eicke but his eyes were hooded by his right hand. His ears remained glued to his translator's ear-phoned voice.

'This radio work in Portugal led to the capture and imprisonment of the Fritz Duquesne Ring. Thirty three spies acting against the allies from American shores, even before America joined in the World War. In a way it was like a pincer movement because a German double spy named Sebold who took the pseudonym Harry Sawyer, confirmed the names. I was able to provide evidence of their training in Germany as well as his own list.'

'Did it lead to convictions?'

'Six days after the tragedy of Pearl Harbour, every

member had either pled guilty or was found guilty in a court of law in America and was imprisoned.'

'And who informed you of this?'

'My British handlers.'

There was a brief silence. 'Who were...?'

I hesitated, thought, and then repeated:

'My British Handlers.'

The Prosecutor realised his question was not germane.

There was no time to think of the consequences that might arise from this question and my stubborn response. Had I already broken an official secret in admitting I had British handlers?

Revealing that I did have British handlers must have been a bitter pill for Eicke to swallow too. I could see he had lost this battle by his open mouth biting the back of his hand. It remained open much of the time as the court heard how I first met Herr Eicke at the funeral of my husband. How Otto had Eicke as his Hitler Youth leader and how when in 1938 I set off home to see my ailing parents, he saw a role for me as a Nazi spy. I gave the best part of thirty five minutes evidence but I was not finished.

I informed the court further that on my return to Germany, I was acting for the Allies. The war began and I learned Herr Eicke's main purpose was to cleanse Hamburg of its Jewish population. 'He relished in his work but kept a close eye on me.'

Counsel approached Eicke once more. There was a hesitation in proceedings.

'Objection. How could Herr Eicke keep a close eye on Frau Richter and why would he want to?'

I rephrased my response. 'Herr Eicke found my dual nationality useful. He sent me on a spy training course. There I learnt radio transmission skills, cover working arrangements, and even received a death pill, all the aspects of a covert war environment. All this training was arranged by Herr Eicke. He was my handler at the time.'

The prosecutor wished to hear no more evidence from me. He had got from my evidence that Eicke was indeed the main Gestapo man in Hamburg and responsible for mass deportation of the Jewish community. Similar evidence came from the previous witnesses I was to learn later.

Sandwich lunches appeared for the witnesses in the waiting room but I was not hungry. I sipped some lukewarm water. I could hardly wait to return to the court. The prosecution had been gentle despite being put ill at ease by Eicke's allegations and outbursts. I knew his defence counsel would be less compassionate with me. Eicke's life was at risk. I anticipated some hard questioning. I returned to the witness box at five past two.

The Defence council was an imposing man. He stood well over six feet tall and beneath his black gown a dark suit with a bright red tie. It looked like he was after my blood.

'You say, Frau Richter that Herr Eicke was your son's youth leader, a responsible position, not so?'

'That is true. He was the Hitler Youth leader. My son did speak highly of him,' I said showing I had a soft and honest response for him.

'And the man who you trusted to care for your son, also awarded you, is that not so?'

'Awarded?' I questioned what he was delving at.

'Yes, did your association with my client not lead to an award?' he reiterated.

I hesitated. Was I being forced to declare a hidden fact, an uncomfortable one at that?

'Your answer, Frau Richter, I am waiting.'

'Indeed I must be the only British spy to have been awarded the Eagle Civilian Cross. Not for a piece of Axis espionage, but because I overheard that it was to retain me as their German spy, an incentive as it were. It was also my late husband Dr. Willy Richter's treatment of Heydrich's mother who had tended to her singing voice, that met his approval.

'Overheard, you said?'

'Yes, when I left the room, I bent down to tie my shoe lace by the door. The only people in the room behind me at that time were Gerhardt Eicke and Reinhardt Heydrich who had presented me with the medal.'

There was a gasp of astonishment when I identified the men involved. It also brought into place the fact that Gerhardt Eicke was in personal touch with Heydrich, the Butcher of Prague, the practitioner of the final solution. The lawyer pondered his next question. It failed to arrive. He then went over to Eicke and spoke to him for a minute or so. I felt the palm of my hands sweat as I fiddled with the last button on my cardigan, out of sight from all. I waited for his next round of difficult questioning. It never came. It seemed whatever he might ask, I would reply defeating his client's case. It was a high risk strategy this tall defence lawyer was taking. He returned to his position on the floor.

'I have no more questions of this witness' he said.

On hearing his words, that button broke loose and fell to the floor of the witness box. I bent down to gather it and found a court usher running to my aid. He apparently thought I had fainted. I stood up again and as if to explain my sudden jack in the box act, I raised my hand showing the orange button which had been my comforter throughout my evidence. I felt pangs of relief as I stood down from the witness box. My evidence must have added to the prosecutor's case. Perhaps Eicke was so amazed at my appearance he failed to feed his defence with damming facts. My apparent enthusiasm noted in my training had slipped by and they had not made the most of the first set of Portuguese co-ordinates I had supplied to Berlin. It was a lucky button I held in my fingers that afternoon.

The last session that day lasted till after half past four. I was drained. Both the questioning and the atmosphere of the court exhausted me. Yet it was a sight to remember, this was the concluding act of the Second World War and I had played my part in it. Now I was able to observe it at close range. It was a privileged position.

That evening after eating in a local restaurant, I felt free. My evidence would either imprison Eicke for life or worse and I knew my departure from Germany was approaching. From 8pm for an hour I played my oboe with the host of the hotel in my room. We played some German children's tunes to remind ourselves of our sons when they were young and finally I played, not on the oboe, but in the lounge on the piano her son last played, Mahler's Piano quartet in A minor. Its soulful minor key began the music but soon Mahler's rich melody filled the room bringing more guests to the lounge. As I played I wondered how Austria could have produced within such a short span such a joyous composer and such an evil dictator.

When the final chord was played, I felt a seminal break from Germany. Tomorrow I would start my journey to Finland and prepare for a happy future. But first there was a pressing engagement.

I returned the following day to hear the conclusion of Gerhardt Eicke's case.

29

Death and a New Life

I sat in the gallery of the vast arena as the prosecution began the closing statements. Everyone both professional and attendee wore sombre attire. Their facial expressions were in keeping with their dress code.

I could tell from the prosecution summary, many of my responses had been included. They seemed to dovetail with those of other witnesses before and afterwards. The defence summary was less welcome. Much was made of my work for the Reich and little of my work with the Allies. Inevitably my covert training at Bautzen was highlighted as me being a German spy in training. I could not deny that.

Oh how I wished to break the silence of my translation duties at Bletchley Park but that information was strictly out of bounds and off the cards. It did not seem fair. Eicke still believed I was an imposter but his counsel did not and I don't think anyone else in that hall did either.

The closing statements took until mid-day. I cannot say I hung on to every word. My mind wandered into darkened alleys as I imagined first the fear in Renate's eyes when she was taken from her home. Then I saw the shell being loaded by some young Russian soldier doing what was asked of him to defend his country. I saw in my mind's eye the shell's trajectory and its explosion where Otto stood. And Karl, I'd never know the truth. Did he invite death in the desert or was he obeying orders and stood in the path of a mine which in all probability was laid by his own troops earlier in the conflict? I'd never know. Nor did I wish to pursue the unfathomable.

I was not expecting the court to break for lunch when it did. Then I realised the defence had concluded its closing statements and the jury of Judges retired to consider the evidence before them.

I took a walk at lunchtime to get some fresh air and found others did too. No-one spoke. The gravity of all the Nuremberg trial cases was such that for the victims a sense of decorum was required. No, it was demanded. That was the least we could do.

The atmosphere in the city was equally sombre. This was once the city of military showmanship; great outdoor marching rallies and political statements. No wonder it was selected to be the venue where Germany would purge itself of a regime which had brought its people no favours.

We walked smartly back to the gallery in good time to ensure we had a clear view of the proceedings. All the seats open to the public were occupied. There were many more men than women in attendance. I could not tell what nationalities were there. The men possibly came from many different countries. Some were obviously court appointed journalists. They eagerly took shorthand notes of every utterance for their readership. During the lunch recess, photographers descended to take photos of the courthouse from all angles. Their photos would be on the front pages of the papers on breakfast tables at home the following morning. Gosh, my evidence would be read over marmalade and toast.

The women observers were German. They all had that gaunt look of the dispossessed. They wore faces which asked the question why? Why did the war end this way? Why were all the atrocities done in their name? It was a heavy burden to bear but something brought them to court that day. Perhaps it was the necessary bleeding to prepare for a new era of peace in the land.

It was almost five minutes after 3 pm when the Judges returned. The chairman of the Judges asked Eicke to stand. The court fell silent.

The President of the Court cleared his throat. 'This International Court of Justice finds you, Herr Gerhardt Eicke, guilty of crimes against humanity. Guilty in respect of murder and complicity in the mass murder of Jews in Hamburg and elsewhere in the State of Holstein. The Court sentences you to death by hanging. The court is adjourned.'

I could not bring myself to smile at the verdict. It was not appropriate. Eicke did look up to me and with a smirk, shook his head. At that moment I wondered if I should go to his cell and make my peace with him. Then I thought of Renate, Karl and Otto, and the millions of Jews who died at his hand. What would they think of that? It would have been most inappropriate. If

Eicke returned in tears to his cell, he would deserve no compassion. It was a word he did not know himself.

I went to the Prosecutor's office to make arrangement to leave Nuremberg that afternoon. I asked to be flown to Helsinki and awaited their permission. I did not have to wait long. There were no planes going to Finland at present from Germany. They would fly me back to England.

I arrived back in London after dark. It was already 9pm. I found a telephone box at the airport. I decided to ring Francis to announce the satisfactory end to the trial. The line was both cracking and out of sequence. I seemed to be answering his last question as he asked the next.

'Darling this line is no good. I will get to Finland as soon as I can. Do take care my dear.'

'Let me know the date you will fly from London. That's important for me to know,' he said.

'Why?' I asked.

'What?'

'I said why? Why is it important?'

'Because some things are important. That's all. I send my love to you. Goodbye darling.'

I replaced the handset. What an enigmatic phone call. Not an easy one to make but it was good to hear his voice again and it lifted my spirits. I still had a purpose in life though and I needed to make progress. I was missing him so badly.

When I returned to MI6, Dynes was eager to hear how the trial had gone and was delighted with the outcome.

'All in all a just verdict but I have one bitter regret.'

'Should you, Hilda?'

'That set of co-ordinates I sent to Berlin will always be on my conscience.'

Dynes listened with a solemn face not offering a response. He paced the room tapping his pen on his forehead.

'You must be realistic Hilda. Had you shown your card too soon, you would not have trapped the Americans. They would have gone on to down many more ships. Of that, I and the Americans, are certain.'

I nodded. 'I suppose so, yet lives were lost at sea, a terrible way to die.'

'War is terrible.'

I looked up at Dynes and saw him move to the fireplace.

'Your work at Bletchley Park made up for that incident hundreds of times over. You must remember that also Hilda.'

I nodded, accepting he had made a valid point. A few silent seconds elapsed. I set a curious expression on my face.

'Bletchley Park?' I asked. 'I've never heard of it. Where is it?'

We both laughed. We needed that outbreak of nonsense after the horrors of war that we were always talking, re-experiencing and blethering about.

The plane left two days later. Fortunately although my bags were in excess of the stipulated weight restrictions, the plane was not full so a blind eye was turned on my excessive load. I was expecting Sir Francis to meet me at Helsinki airport. Last night that had been confirmed with a rather long and clear telephone line. Our conversations were that of lovers saying things to each other which comforted us till we met again.

To fly freely over what had been a war zone gave hope to the world. The plane did not show much of the land or sea. We were flying so high. When the cloud broke each time I looked out, I saw only mountains and fields. It seemed the land was unscathed. No fractured town or tortured city came into focus.

Four hours later the plane touched down and my heart fluttered as if in its youth once again. I saw birds on the grassy runway pecking at the stubble. I saw the fire engine stand down. We had made a safe arrival.

I left the plane and followed the line of twelve passengers to the terminal. We awaited our baggage to arrive on the airport trucks. They were then deposited on the ground for us to reclaim. Then came the customs officials. I had nothing to declare but was asked to show what was in my case.

'It's my oboe. Do you wish me to play it?' I teased

'No Ma'am, but I wish you and your fiancé well.'

I looked at the man with a curious eye.

'You know him?'

'No, I have no idea who he is but I see you are wearing his engagement ring.'

I smiled realising my error.

Going through the door marked with a sign *Welcome To Finland*, I saw Sir Francis for the first time in almost three weeks. He looked immaculate in his dark blue suit.

I dropped my baggage and we hugged each other a welcome greeting. Then I planted a kiss on his cheek. He reciprocated. When I bent down to take my cases they were not there.

'My driver will be packing them in the boot of the car. Come on, time to get you home.'

Outside the airport I noticed the flag first. A Union Jack stood limp on the bonnet of a Daimler car. The car was black but shone in the sunlight and Sir Francis opened the door for me. We sat together on the rear seat. The separating glass partition was closed.

'Are you hungry?'

'Yes, I am as a matter of fact. Shall we go somewhere for lunch?' I asked.

'I have somewhere in mind.'

It was a fifteen-minute drive to the residential part of Helsinki. We drove up the drive and I saw a guard of honour awaiting us.

'Goodness me Francis, what's going on here?'

'Just an official welcome party for my fiancée.'

It was a very fine welcome indeed. I was introduced to British and Finnish staff and then taken to my quarters.

That night Sir Francis and I sat in the front lounge by the flame-licking and sparkling wood fire. The scent of the burning wood was pleasantly intrusive.

'Engaged for a couple of weeks, how does it feel?' Francis asked.

'I must be honest, if not selfish. I did not wear my engagement ring at the trial. I worried about what

I might say or if I said too much. It was a strain. The responsibility on my shoulders to do my part to convict Eicke was immense.'

Francis took from his pocket a pristine white handkerchief and polished his glasses. 'On your shoulders, you say?'

'Yes Francis, Otto, Renate and Karl were on my shoulders giving me courage. It may not make sense to you but I needed them there.'

Sir Francis came forward and sat close to me soothing my arm gently. 'It's all over now Hilda. The war, the trial and the espionage, it's a new era darling. A time too, for new beginnings.'

Francis was right of course. I had reached the end of my war career with all its demands. Leaving it behind would not be as easy. It had left an indelible mark on my life. Its repercussions would not diminish for some considerable time in my mind, if ever.

Sir Francis stroked my hand running his fingers over my engagement ring.

'So we're engaged. The next step is marriage.'

'Have you any thoughts about the subject?' I asked in anticipation of some good news.

'Well, I don't think we should wait for any length of time. Do you?'

'I would agree with that,' I said not wishing to have the woman in the back attic status for too long.

'In a couple of weeks, perhaps?'

'Goodness. That's quick? That doesn't give us much time,' I said realising wedding invitations might prove somewhat difficult.

'How much time do we need? The Lutheran pastor says he will marry us and the staff is beside themselves with the prospect of a reception at the Embassy.'

'And the guest list? A small wedding I assume, a second for us both.'

'Darling we can't fly all our second cousins over, especially as it's a second marriage as you say. There will only be a very few.'

The thought of so few in attendance disappointed me. 'I hope at least a few, Francis.'

I detected a crease in his eyelids, then a broad smile. He had been teasing me.

'There will be enough guests I assure you. Some of the other national Embassy staff will be invited, the pastor and his wife and the staff of our Embassy. I suspect some one hundred and fifty will attend. We will dance to the music from the Finnish Military band and there will be a few smorgasbords for all to enjoy.'

'You have been planning all this since your return to duty?'

'Well yes, the work has been quite quiet; I've had some time on my hands to get things going. I hope you don't mind?'

I smiled and cuddled in to him. Francis was a man who got things done. Frankly I was tired of the war and its responsibilities. I was drained of the spying game. I never wished to spy but it took a hold of my life. Espionage and my part in it were gone forever. My future was with Sir Francis.

I looked up at him and kissed him on the chin. He let his hand slide down my dress and he caressed my left breast. He held me firm and it was pleasurable. Then I tapped his hand.

'Two weeks, you will have to wait, so you can start to count down from today.' We gave each other a good night kiss and I retired to my bedroom at the back of the Embassy and Sir Francis upstairs to his.

30

The Wedding

A blue and white scarf was given to me after I indicated I'd go for a walk in Helsinki. It would seem like a football scarf to those at home but it was the national colours of this proud Scandinavian nation. The scarf tails bounced on my back as I walked down the Ehrenstromsvagen by the sea. A sea at rest but I imagined the low lying islands would almost be submerged under a stormy sea. A multitude of islands surrounded the capital's southern flank. Sea birds darted and soared all around the coast, a bountiful coast richly fished each day by birds and man alike.

I heard a language which was strange to my ear. It had a few Germanic overtones but the Finnish influences were also perhaps Estonian, a country now swallowed up by the Russian advancement. There would be no point learning Finnish as Sir Francis's terms of appointment would lead him elsewhere before long. What I heard people speak seemed such a strange and difficult language. I had no incentive to learn more than a splattering of words and phrases just as I had done in Portugal. Where might we be after Finland I wondered? For a moment I dreamt of Pacific Islands, Caribbean banana crops or Peruvian Andes treks. Only time would tell where and when we would find our next posting. The Helsinki post may have to be short lived but together as a married couple, it would become a very special posting for us both.

I asked for directions to the Helsinki Cathedral. After a lengthy walk I came to its doors. This is where Sir Francis had arranged for us to be married. I went inside. The organ was playing but no service was taking place. I sat down on a pew and reflected on my life.

War was the father of all things, I remembered the quote from Heraclites. It seemed to me that the world had to bleed itself from time to time. The universal soldiers had soldered new borders and fathers would tell sons of their ventures in war, so that their children could tell their children. Twice Germany had been brought to its knees. This time Germany had lost its eastern border. Surely it had learnt a lesson this time? It would not start a third World War. Brakes and checks were needed to anticipate conflict and then defuse the aggression of the nations. There was talk of international bodies making rules. I was optimistic about the new body, the United Nations which was receiving coverage in the papers frequently. They would surely strive to prevent more world wars.

Having lived through two wars I was weary. Glad that I had survived both conflicts, yes, but at what price? A wonderful loving family had been torn from me. The separation had eaten out my heart. Yet I was now on the brink of a new beginning and the music of the cathedral which started as I contemplated life seemed to say to me, peace my child, I will give you peace.

Francis arranged for me to meet ambassadorial staff from different countries on three different nights. That way they would not seem out of place at the reception. Some brought their wives and we retired to get to know each other better as the men struck their matches by the fireside.

Two weeks later as I sat at the Embassy waiting for transport to take me to church, I felt fresh, invigorated and ready to formally take Sir Francis' hand in marriage. Colin Hunter, deputy Ambassador, bachelor and the most handsome of the embassy staff, stood ready to accompany me to the wedding and lead me down the aisle.

'I've never done this before,' he admitted opening up the palm of his hand.

I accepted his hand. 'I've experienced this only once. That was a long time ago. Makes us both inexperienced, I suppose.'

Colin laughed.

'One more than me. I only hope I let go of you at the right moment.'

We laughed again aware of our giggles which would have to cease soon. Marriage was after all, a serious matter.

'That's the car driving up. No turning back now, let's go, Colin.'

He stopped in his tracks and swivelled round to face me. He looked at me with a warm smiling face.

'Miss Campbell or Frau Richter... Sir Francis will make a fine husband. I know he will.'

I patted his arm gently. My smile showed I agreed with him.

As we approached the cathedral I heard the unmistakable groans of the first notes of the highland bagpipes. The car stopped at the foot of the church entrance and Colin took my arm as we proceeded up the steps which had two pipers on either side of us. They played *A Wee Sprig o' Heather*. I realised Sir Francis had a hand it its selection. That sprig of heather I laid on Willy's grave was now welcoming me to a new relationship. Our late night chats about my past must have influenced his choice of music. When I reached the top step I turned to show my appreciation to the pipers and the gathered Finnish crowd cheering from the street below. Then the thunderous tones of the Edvard Friedrich Walckeer organ played Mendelssohn's *Wedding March*, from *A Midsummer Night's Dream*.

I walked down the aisle holding on to Colin's arm. With his other hand, he gave me a reassuring tap to calm my nerves as I saw Sir Francis turn to see me and gauge my progress down the aisle. He looked very smart in his frock tail coat. I would certainly contrast in my recently bought long powder blue dress. I presumed all knew I was a widow, or did they? I saw in the congregation diplomats wearing their regalia and medals. It seemed Helsinki's Diplomatic and Ambassadorial staff had something to celebrate that afternoon too. It was probably their first happy and significant occasion since the war ended. Ladies in their glittering tiaras turned and smiled as I made my way down the aisle. I looked forward to chatting to them at the reception. Women of my age had been few and far between over the past few years and I needed that comradeship once more. A flutter in my heart helped me up to the last step where I stood by the man I was about to marry.

I need not dwell on the details of the church service or signing the marriage certificate for that is a ubiquitous experience. But I happily recall leaving the church to the strains of the organ's Bach inspired *Jesu Joy of Man's Desiring*. When we went through the great arch at the front of the Cathedral the organ stopped. The pipes resumed their elbow squashing melodies as we proceeded down the stairs to an open Landau carriage amid showering of confetti from spectators. The horses led the way back to the Embassy and after a sumptuous Finnish meal with raucous laughing at Sir Francis' groom's humorous speech, we danced till after midnight.

Our short honeymoon touring Sweden and Denmark made me realise just how fortunate I had become.

Sir Francis was a caring and loving husband. He opened my mind to the wonders of the diplomatic world. No longer were my movements compromised by word or action. I had to remember simply that my days of being a reluctant spy were over.

One mid-morning, shortly after our first week of married bliss, I had coffee with a honey-coated waffle on the Embassy lawn. The skies were clear. Not even one cloud could be seen. A silent world lay before me as I looked out beyond the Embassy grounds towards a misty far-off hillside. I should have been happy. I had found my feet and the adventure of Embassy life had just begun. Perhaps in the future, we would be in new countries finding their feet after the war. It would give a renewed purpose to my life. But today I was sad.

Tears began to fall down my cheeks. I had doubts. Was I right to have earned this position? Was I not best employed translating German texts in a new Europe? Or as a teacher of modern languages at a secondary school? The tears increased and a few quiet sobs accompanied my thoughts because in each scenario I saw Otto smiling at me. He was no longer a soldier in uniform but a young man making his way in the world with Gisela on his arm.

And I saw Karl lost in the desert, stretching out a hand but nobody was there for him. I wiped my eyes as the thought of a stripped Renate being thrown into a gas chamber, still maintaining her Aryan status. Or was that recognised. Was she saved? Was she raped and tortured before dying or could she possibly have survived and one day, yes one day, I might see her again? Some questions kept filling my mind yet I knew no answers to those enquiries would ever produce a definitive conclusion.

Francis took a break from his work and joined me on the lawn. He steadied himself as he approached with his cup and saucer

'You've been crying.'

I looked up at him and smiled.

'Yes, I have. Thoughts of how I arrived here in peaceful Finland...'

'Peaceful indeed. But why the tears, my dear?'

I placed my coffee down on the grass. I turned

towards Francis and held his left hand with both of mine.

'I have been remembering all the loved ones I've lost. The ones I'll never see again. And I am determined I am not going to lose you.'

'And Hilda, I'm not wishing to lose you either. I could not have been happier marrying you.'

'Really? With all my nerve-wracking experiences, my dual loyalties, my mistakes and my doubts. I was a bag of nerves.'

'We all have flaws. We can learn from them. We gain experiences and develop by them. Yes, you have had a remarkable life and against all the odds, you have survived. You have survived to be rewarded in this new life, with me at your side.'

I nodded. I stood up and offered Francis both hands. He gulped down the last dregs of his coffee. He joined me as we walked arm in arm down the Embassy lawn towards the boundary flower bed. A ginger cat was disturbed from its sun trap in the flowers. I called to it but it ran away. Not all cats liked me it seemed. That reminded me of my walk to town yesterday.

'Francis, I saw some dachshund puppies for sale.'

I let the moment linger for him to consider my thoughts.

'A dachshund? Hmmmm to complete the family, as it were?'

I looked up at him to gauge his response. He smiled.

'Yes, I think that's a very good idea Hilda. A dachshund, a very good idea indeed.'

Postscript

Fergus Harper of the 10th Highland Light Infantry was mentioned in dispatches in 1943 during the Allied invasion of Sicily. He was killed during the assault on Tilburg, Holland on 28th October 1944.

After five years in Helsinki, Sir Francis was appointed as Ambassador to Iran between the years 1950-52. Their final posting was to Warsaw, Poland, where Sir Francis was British Ambassador from 1952-54. Hilda died in 1956 and Sir Francis in 1961.

I used the name of Gerhardt Eicke as the protagonist throughout the book but was unable to identify the true Gestapo individual's name. In fact there were two particular SS men responsible for clearing Hamburg of the Jewish population. Rudolf Querner was responsible for deportations between May 1941 and June 1943. Between 1943-45 Georg Henning Graf von Bessewitz was the officer in charge of policing Hanover. He died in a 1949 as a prisoner of war at Magadan, in Russia. Rudolf Querner was detained in Magdeburg where he cheated his death sentence by suicide.

Hilda wrote a letter to Dr A. S. Caldwell, my late uncle, in 1951 containing some of her German stamps and news from Iran. Over the years somehow page one of the letter went missing from the three-page letter. She wrote:

We are now up in our summer quarters, and are very happy here. It is cooler certainly, but July & until Aug. 15ᵗʰ (generally) the heat is very great; but of course it is not so dusty up here and it does cool down at night. The mountains are quite near which of course helps. Everyone finds it quite trying. Those living up here, to go up & down every day to the office, but they begin at 8 A.M. and finish at 1³⁰ so they get the afternoon free unless any special work has to be done. I am having a difficult time trying to get our little dachshound to be friends with a little Bitten, it appears to be difficult. Unfortunately Sir Francis is in bed again. When stooping a few days ago his disc suddenly snapped out again, so he is on board for 2 weeks & then see how things are. It is not pleasant being in bed when it is so hot, and when there is so much to do.

Please remember me to your Mother and to Quin & family when you see them.

All the best to yourself

Aunty Cecily xx

*The Jim and family referred to was my father, Rev Jim Caldwell 1916-1995, the author's father. 'And family' referred to myself and my sister Joan. My brother Bruce was yet to be born.

This is the British Embassy envelope from Tehran which contained several German stamps and the letter from Mrs Campbell-S, Dineira, British Embassy, Tehran, Iran.

A selection of her German stamps are also displayed.

The German Eagle Silver Civilian Medal with crossed swords established in 1937 for German nationals and foreigners.

Hitler's Plans to Invade Northern Scotland 1940

Previously classified files which have been unseen for 75 years were released on 1st January 2016. They reveal that the war cabinet became convinced that a Nazi invasion of northern Scotland was imminent. (The Reluctant Spy was completed in November the previous year when the author was unaware of this classified document. The need for information about the north of Scotland's air bases and troop movements by the enemy was crucial and Hilda was at the centre of this espionage.)

The threat of invasion only receded after the Royal Air Force regained air superiority following the battle of Britain between June and October of that year. In August British commanders were still uncertain how Hitler's armies were planning to hit the UK from occupied continental Europe. One document brought to the attention of General Alan Brooke the commander-in-chief of Home Forces was entitled "German airborne landings in northern Scotland with a view to the neutralisation of fleet bases as a preliminary to the invasion of England."

The document from August 6th 1940 claimed that

there was every chance that the Germans "could land in Scotland 20,500 airborne troops during the first three days for the purpose of capturing and holding all aerodromes north of the river Tay." It further stated "they could reinforce these troops by approximately 900 men per day, bringing the total number of airborne troops landed during the first week of the operation to 24,000."

This file which was recently opened and placed in the National Archives at Kew, London, warned "enemy forces could capture RAF airfields at Dyce, Inverness, Perth, Lossiemouth, Leuchars, Kinloss, Montrose, Evanton as well as a further six bases on Orkney and Shetland. It was further thought that 440 parachutists could be landed round the outskirts of each of the aerodromes in some cases after a preliminary bombardment. Losses before landing would not exceed 20 %. After releasing their parachutists, transport aircraft would return to bases in Norway, Denmark and Holland to refuel and reload."

One entry which demonstrates how serious a prospect of invasion was being taken, states "An attack may come at any moment. The most dangerous time is from now until the end of September."

The briefings were drawn up at a time when Britain was isolated and vulnerable. The Germans had just completed the occupation of Norway and the Channel Islands. Nazi troops had reached Paris and the battle of Britain was being fought.

General Alan Brooke adopted a pessimistic view on whether an invasion of Scotland and the northern Isles could and should be repelled, writing: "It is not possible

Hitler congratulates German paratroopers after the capture of a key Belgian fort in 1940. Fears that Scottish air bases were next on the Nazi list were taken seriously. General Alan Brooke said that he did not have troops to defend them.

Photo by courtesy of Marc Horne of The Times.

to send and maintain in the Shetlands a garrison which would be proof against a large-scale air and sea-borne operation and I have told the Commander-in-chief, Scottish Command, that he is to make it a primary objective to secure and hold the port of Lerwick, without which the enemy would also find it difficult to maintain himself. The moral and psychological effect of a German occupation of the islands which are separated by so short a distance from our main fleet anchorage would be most unfortunate."

General Brook concluded: "As regards the rest of

Scotland, I have only a certain number of troops and I consider it preferable to maintain preponderance in East Anglia and the Home Counties for the defence of London."*

Hitler's plans to invade Scotland in 1940 would involve 1,000 Junkers 52; 100 Junkers 86; 15 Junkers 90 and 15 Condor planes all flying from air bases in occupied countries and particularly from nearby occupied Norway.

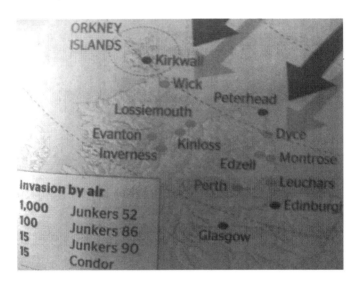

---

*   Had General Brook maintained this conclusion, Germany could have invaded Scotland successfully and in time occupied the whole of Britain.

Bunchrew House Hotel near Inverness where Hilda met with Mr and Mrs Brown, the German High Commission staff, from London in 1938

This is the gazebo in the hotel's grounds where Hilda received instructions as the Delphin short-wave radio

Hilda's oboe

Nuremberg Trial Court where Hilda gave her evidence.

Acknowledgements

Firstly my thanks go my god-mother Vera Wild (nee Caldwell) 1900-1994 who told me Hilda's story when she was 93 years old. Then to my late uncle, Dr A. Stanley Caldwell, former Medical officer of Health for the kingdom of Fife who provided me with the letter and stamps belonging to Aunty Campbell. I am indebted to my mother-in-law G Shirley France who served in the Wrens at Bletchley Park during the final two years of the Second World War. It was in her 90th year that the Government at last gave her and the surviving workers at Bletchley Park, a medal in recognition of their valued and most secret work. Many never ever divulged what they did at Bletchley during World War 2. She died aged 98. Ron Hull looked over the text to correct errors which authors never spot and much gratitude goes to Marc Horne, the Times journalist, who permitted me to reprint Hitler's plans for invading Scotland in 1940.

BY THE SAME AUTHOR

The Novels
Operation Oboe
A tale of espionage in West Africa.

The Last Shepherd
An arrogant city banker clashes with the rural ways of
the Last Shepherd, in south-west Scotland.

Restless Waves
A writer in residence aboard a cruise ship faces daemons
on board and onshore.

Miss Martha Douglas
A nurse and seamstress, Martha obtains a Royal position
but becomes a suffragette. When released from prison
she serves in the trenches where she finds true love.

The Parrot's Tale
The comic tale of an escaped parrot in the Scottish
countryside sits alongside the tragedy of a missing girl.

The Crazy Psychologist
Set on Rousay in the Orkney Islands, the childhood
difficulties of Dr Angie Lawrence come to light to

explain her bizarre treatment programmes while her fragmented family come to terms with their past, placing her marriage in jeopardy.

The Clown Prosecutor
This is a story about a prosecutor from a circus background who brings his antics to court. He gets fired and finds himself constantly in trouble of one kind or another till he finds romance.

THE ARRAN TRILOGY
Murders at Blackwaterfoot
Seaweed in her Hair/ Dementia Adventure
Ruffled Feathers at Blackwaterfoot
Missing from Blackwaterfoot

CHARITY BOOKS
Penned Poetry for Parkinson's Research
A Dream Net for Dementia Research.

BIOGRAPHIES
Untied Laces
The author's autobiography

Jim's Retiring Collection
The illustrated cartoons and musings of a city and then rural Church of Scotland minister gathered and set in biblical context.

Poet's Progeny
The story of a line of descent of the national bard.

Robert Burns maintains his influence over succeeding generations.

7 point 7 on the Richter Scale
The diary of the Camp Manger in the NWFP of the Islamic Republic of Pakistan following the 2005 earthquake. (Profits have gone to Muslim Hands for earthquake relief.)

Take The Lead
The quirks of dogs experienced by the author over his life in Scotland, Pakistan and Ghana, together with canine poetry and recording medical advances in their training.

CHILDREN'S BOOKS
Chaz the Friendly Crocodile
Chaz the Nigerian Crocodile visits a Scottish river to help people keep their towns tidy. Set as a poem, this is a book all parents require to train their growing children with manners.

Lawrence the Lion Seeks Work
No more animals are in the circuses. So what happened when Lawrence the Lion went in search of a new job?

Danny the Spotless Dalmatian
All Dalmatian puppies have no spots at birth. They appear after three weeks. But Danny's spots never appeared. Follow him as he searches for spots to make him a real Dalmatian.

SELF HELP
Have you seen my Ummm...Memory?
A valuable booklet for all whose memories are declining. Student memory tips as well as advice for those more senior moments to get through life.

Ponderings
IN LARGE PRINT
Poems and short stories, as it says, in large print.

It's Me Honest It Is
This is a short book commissioned by the School of Nursing to record the decades of the elderly and offer them a page for their last requests. It is a valuable aid for family members as well as medical attendants.

I have also Ghost written the book, **Never Give Up**, about a Cockney, who grew up in an orphanage not knowing his parents or his date of birth. He became a central London plumber and his clients were celebrities.